MW01283338

Dead Texas: The Initial Outbreak Series

Book 1: Day Zero
Book 2: No Comfort
Book 3: Lonesome Road
Book 4: The Journey West
©2018 (individual books)
©2020 (collection)

This four book series serves as a lead-in to the ongoing Dead America series. This series has more than 30 books currently in print and new releases monthly. Follow along at

www.DeadAmericaBooks.com

DEAD TEXAS: DAY ZERO
BOOK ONE
BY DEREK SLATON
© 2018

CHAPTER ONE

Tuesday, 9:47 A.M.

On a normal weekday morning, the newly renovated Austin police station would have been a bustle of officers and personnel. But on that day, it was sparsely populated, and half of the people who had managed to show up to their post were coughing up a storm.

Homeland Security Agent Harris was no exception.

"What do you mean you aren't coming in today? Do you..." he coughed into the phone, lungs rasping like hell. "You hear how I sound? And *I'm* here! I expect more out of my team. You can expect a reprimand in your file." He slammed the phone down in frustration before giving in to another coughing fit.

Captain Schultz stopped short as he walked by the office, taking in the sight of the middle aged agent trying to steady himself on his desk. He'd never seen the fit and sharp man look so sickly and broken.

"Are… are you okay, Sir?" the Captain asked, raising an eyebrow. "I can hear you from my office next door." He rested a hand on his considerable belly, figuring that if everyone was home sick, there'd be lots of extra donuts in the break room.

"Yeah, I'll live," Harris replied once he caught his breath. "It's my fucking team. They're dropping like flies to whatever plague is going around this office."

"Is there anything I can get you?" Schultz scratched the back of his head at the sound of his coworker's hoarse voice. "Coffee? Tea?"

"I need warm bodies, preferably from your SWAT team," Harris replied, sitting up straight. He abhorred looking weak, and the way that Schultz was looking at him made him want to mop the floor with the doughy Captain. "Short-handed or not, we have to act on this intelligence."

"I'm sorry sir, but SWAT left twenty minutes ago," Schultz swallowed hard. "Apparently there is some major disturbance going on at the UT Campus."

"I don't care where you find them… just…" Harris wheezed and hacked, desperately trying to catch his breath and his words. "Goddammit. Our mission takes priority. I don't care where you pull them from, just find me some people capable of participating in a raid. Bring them to the briefing room in ten minutes."

"Yes sir, I'll see who I can round up." Schultz nodded and left.

Harris leaned back in his chair, closing his eyes and rubbing his temples in firm circles. Congestion in his chest, pressure in his head—regardless of being angry at his team, this sickness was definitely unpleasant, to say the least.

His cell phone vibrated on the table and he picked it up without even looking at the caller ID. "This is Harris."

"We need a status update," an aged male voice demanded through the line. "Is your team ready to go?"

"Most of us," the Agent replied. "There is a nasty flu running through the PD here and nearly half my guys are down and out. I have the locals digging up people to fill out our ranks."

"I'm disappointed in the way you are managing your team, Special Agent Harris," the man on the other end said with a click of his tongue. "Don't make us regret giving you the promotion."

"We'll get the job done," Harris replied, injecting as much authority into his voice as possible. "I'll give you a status update after the raid."

"Very well then," the voice conceded. "Go get it done."

Harris ended the call and threw his phone on the desk in frustration, scrubbing his hands down his face. "I

swear I'm making these assholes walk back
to DC after this is over."

CHAPTER TWO

Tuesday, 10:02 A.M.

Agent Harris made his way to the briefing room, the lurch of his equilibrium reminding him with every step that he was unwell. It was getting worse; he felt like he was being eaten alive from the lungs out.

"Agent Harris!" Schultz called from down the hall, and the Special Agent turned towards the Captain with two people in tow. "Here are the officers you requested."

Harris set his tired gaze on the thirty-something Latino man with the hard eyes and the young looking redheaded woman with the small but athletic frame.

"Two people?" He squeezed the bridge of his nose momentarily, scrunching his eyes shut. When he released them, he ignored the officers, leveling his attention on Schultz. "That's all you could find me was two people?"

"I'm sorry Agent," Schultz said quickly, holding up a hand, "but the situation at UT still isn't under control, and half my officers are out sick today. So unless you want old overweight slowpokes like myself, this is what you're going to have to work with. I honestly

11

wish I could do more." The determination in his face made Harris sigh.

"Okay, I appreciate it Captain," he said, and turned to the two officers. "You two, sit in the back, pay attention, and see me as soon as the briefing is over for your orders, you got it?"

"Yes, Sir," they both answered in unison.

"All right, let's go," Harris entered the room and immediately the six strike team members dissolved their milling about and took their seats. The two officers took the available back seats, feeling tiny in comparison to the burly strike team members.

Harris stepped up to the podium and picked up a remote control, dimming the lights and starting a slide presentation on the overhead projector.

"Okay men." He stifled a cough. "Here is what we have." He clicked to the first slide which showed a middle-aged white man in a lab coat. "This is Dr. Alexi Sokolov, AKA the Russian Plague. Russian national, worked in bio-research for the government since his recruitment right out of college, and an all around despicable human being. In 2012 he-" Harris broke off into a coughing fit, and one of the strike team members leaned forward with a bottle of water outstretched.

The Agent took it and nodded gratefully, taking a deep draught and setting it down on the podium. "Thank you," he replied gruffly. "Goddamn. Sorry, as I was saying. In 2012 he was assigned to the Assad regime to help them with their chemical weapons program. We were unsure of his specific task, but we heard varying stories about compact bio-weapons that individuals could release while on the ground. Kind of like a plague suicide bomber.

"It's unknown exactly how successful he was since in 2014 his lab was struck in an airstrike, killing his wife and lab partner Irina. It was assumed that Dr. Sokolov was also killed in the blast, but his body was never recovered. It wasn't until 2015 that one of our sister agencies picked up his trail in some of the less desirable parts of Africa." He clicked to the next slide, showing the same man with severe burns to the side of his face.

The look in Sokolov's eyes was haunted and severe, as if he'd come out of the picture and tear them all apart with his bare hands. He had clearly been unstable, especially after all he'd been through.

"As you can see, the good doctor here was alive, but did come away from the airstrike with a souvenir," Harris

13

continued, pausing on a wheeze and taking another quick sip of water. "Over the next eighteen months he was tied to half a dozen chemical based attacks around the globe. These rarely got news coverage in this country because they were in places very few people here give a shit about. But those of us paying attention were growing more concerned as his attacks were becoming more sophisticated.

"Then, in the spring of 2017, he vanished. We didn't know if some third world dictator killed him, imprisoned him, or if he was on his own cooking up something large scale. We knew he was upset over the death of his wife, so we couldn't rule out a strike on our homeland. Which is why we were activated." He clicked through to the next slide.

The image showed a crowd of people in the stands of a football game, everyone wearing Texas Longhorn gear. In the center of the photo was a man in jeans and a plaid shirt with a severely burned face.

"Is that *here*?" the red-haired officer blurted, startling most of the room. A blush crept up her cheeks as the strike team turned to look at her, more than one gaze of annoyance at her outburst.

"Anyway…" Harris cleared his throat, sounding like someone was juggling wet marbles in his chest. "Three days ago at the University of Texas Longhorns football game, an eagle eyes security guard spotted him walking around the crowd. The cameras outside of the stadium found him buying a ticket from a scalper and then walking the outer rim for the entire first half.

"About halfway through the second quarter a security guard noticed he had passed his post five times already, always walking in the same direction, so he called it in. Cameras picked him up and followed him from there. At halftime he stood in line for a giant pretzel and walked around the crowded concourse one more time before exiting the building a couple of minutes after the third quarter started.

"The security team captured him getting into an Uber and driving off. Thankfully, someone had the good sense to run his face through the system. Three hours later we were notified and dispatched-" Harris doubled over, this time with his coughing, taking a few minutes to catch his breath and stand back up. "Again, my apologies," he wheezed, taking a drink and waving off the concerned faces of his team. "This shit is the worst.

"Once we had a positive ID, we had the locals monitor the address where the

Uber driver dropped him off. It's an old warehouse about ten miles outside of town. The building has been under constant watch since Saturday afternoon, and according to the records half a dozen men have entered in that time, with nobody leaving."

One of the strike team members raised his hand, the deep scar running down the back of his hand to his elbow glaring in the white glow of the projector.

"Yes, Jackson," Harris wheezed, motioning to the Agent.

"How confident are we that Dr. Sokolov is in there?" he asked, lowering his hand and sitting up straight. "And more importantly, why haven't we already gone in?"

"The Uber driver said he didn't see any vehicles when he dropped him off, and the stakeout team got there within a few hours to keep watch," Harris explained. "We are confident that he's still in there. As for the second part, after reviewing the footage it didn't appear as though anything was planted or released, so the working theory was that it was a dry run.

"Homecoming is next weekend, so it's going to be the largest crowd of the year. With that in mind, we wanted to hold off for as long as possible to get as much of this cell as we could. Any other questions?" He brought a fist to his mouth to stifle another cough.

The redhead raised her hand in the back. "Yes, I have one," she piped up.

"Okay," Harris said, surprised that she had the courage to speak after her last embarrassing outburst. "Everyone say hello to the two locals that will be helping out with the raid," he encouraged, but the strike team ignored her, looking unimpressed. "What is your question, ma'am?"

"Why is he here in Austin?" she inquired, voice level and firm. "And how did he even get into the country if he's on the most wanted list?"

"Good questions," Harris replied with a nod and a cough. "Our best guess is that he snuck into the country with the help of a coyote, and this is pretty much the largest congregation of people that is close to the border. I don't think he has any personal vendetta against the city of Austin, but this may be the only large target he can risk getting to." He looked around the room as he attempted to clear his throat again. "Okay, anything else?"

The redhead raised her hand again, prompting a glare from her partner. She shrugged her shoulders at him flippantly. "What? He asked."

"Okay mystery local officer, I'll give you one more," Harris motioned to her.

"If this really was a dry run, then why take an Uber back to the hideout?" she asked. "He's avoided capture for so many years, snuck into this country without detection, and he gets sloppy now? Just before an attack? It doesn't make sense."

Jackson spun around in his chair with a sneer. "Listen sweetheart." His voice dripped with condescension and she narrowed her eyes. "We know you're excited to be up here with the big boys, but you need to learn your place. And right now that's for you to shut the fuck up and let the grownups talk."

"That's enough, Jackson!" Harris barked, and then immediately regretted the strain on his throat. He hacked and then took another drink of water as the scarred man faced front again. "Officer, it's a great question but ultimately a moot point, because we are going in now. I want everyone geared up and ready to go in fifteen. Let's get it done."

He turned off the projector and the lights came back up. The strike team stood and bustled out of the room, the two officers standing off to the side and out of the way to await Harris ambling over to them. He leaned on the backs of one of the chairs, taking a deep, shaky breath.

"What's your name, Officer?" Harris addressed the man, who stood at attention.

"Officer Antonio Cruz, Sir."

"Cruz, fantastic, what's your story?" Harris asked.

"Ex-marine, two years in Iraq, spent the last five years on Dallas SWAT before coming here," Cruz listed off his history.

"Why aren't you on the SWAT team here, Cruz?" Harris raised an eyebrow.

"I transferred in about three weeks ago and they felt I needed to go through some exercises with the team before being put into the field," he replied stiffly. "Supposed to be wrapped up next week."

"So you are highly trained and professional," Harris mused and cleared his throat, taking a sip of his water, emptying the bottle. "I like it. Report to Agent Jackson, he's the big asshole who doesn't take kindly to questions from rookies."

"Yes, Sir!" Cruz nodded in approval and turned on his heel, leaving the room like a bird taking flight.

"And that brings us to you, my inquisitive officer," Harris continued, turning to the redhead, who was standing casually with her arms crossed. "What's your name?"

"Lacy Sparks, Sir," she replied.

"Nice to meet you, Sparks," he said with a nod. "So tell me, what's your story? Why out of everyone in the building were you brought to me?"

"I spend three years on the prison Use of Force team," she began, but Harris put a hand up, clearing his throat.

"I'm sorry, I don't mean to interrupt, but *Use* of Force team?" he asked.

"Yeah, whenever an inmate was being a pouty little bitch and didn't want to come out of his cell for an inspection, I was on the team that would go in and remove him." Sparks shrugged as if it wasn't any big deal, but Harris raised an eyebrow.

"Impressive," he mused, and crossed over to the water cooler in the corner. "I can't imagine too many women have that job."

"I was the third woman in the history of the prison to have it," Sparks replied.

"Very good," Harris said as he refilled his water bottle. "Please continue."

"I decided I wanted more than the prison life, so I went to the academy, graduated third in my class before I became a hand to hand combat instructor there," she said. "Been at this precinct for a year and a half trying to get on the

SWAT team, but it's a good ole boys club and breaking trough is tough to do. So to take out my frustrations, I'm a wrestler and current middleweight title holder with the South Texas Wrestling promotion."

"Wrestler, huh?" Harris wheezed but smiled. "Okay, pop quiz. Who is the greatest of all time?"

"The correct answer is Ric Flair," Sparks replied without hesitation. "Unless of course you find yourself in the company of some old timers in Dallas, in which case the correct answer better include a Von Erich."

"That…" Harris stowed the bottle in his armpit and politely clapped his hands. "That is the correct answer. Intelligence plus self preservation. I think you are going to do well on my team, I mean how can I go wrong with the women's champion of South Texas Wrestling?"

Sparks straightened a bit and quietly added, "Just champion, Sir."

He blinked at her in confusion.

"I won a three way Texas Death Match against the Dudek Brothers," she explained, and pulled up her sleeve to reveal a three-inch scar on her upper arm. "It's how I got this."

"Ouch." Harris winced.

"Yeah, that cowbell is a bitch," she agreed. "But I won the match and claimed the belt for the third time."

"My apologies, Sparks." He put up his hands in surrender. "You are way more hardcore than I initially gave you credit for. Welcome to the team."

CHAPTER THREE

Tuesday, 11:02 A.M.

The strike team assembled a few hundred yards away from the warehouse, taking cover behind a line of trees to remain out of sight. Harris crouched and waved everyone around him, so they were in a loose squatting circle.

He wavered for a moment, face flushed with probable fever, but his gaze was still stern. "Okay," he began, "here's what we got. Two entrances, one at the north end and the other south. Jackson, your team is going to circle around and take the south entrance."

"Yes, Sir." Jackson cocked his assault rifle with a firm nod. "I'll make sure we clear them out."

"Calm down, cowboy," Harris said quickly, putting up a hand. "WE need intel, because if Sparks was right and Saturday wasn't a dry run, then we need to know what we're up against. Shoot only if necessary, and aim to wound. I know you got thrust into this position because Murdoch is MIA today, but I need to know you can be level headed and do what needs to be done."

Jackson scowled, but reluctantly nodded his acceptance.

"Good." Harris coughed. "Okay, let's saddle up and get this done. Jackson, signal when you are in position." He waved the strike leader off, and Jackson moved with haste around the building, four of the other team members in tow, Cruz included. "Okay, I'm leading this charge. Harper, you are behind me, Taylor is up next and Sparks is covering our six." Nods all around, and Harris turned to the redhead. "I know this is your first raid, but we're going to make it was easy on you as possible. Leave it to us to take the terrorists down. As we move forward it will be on you to secure them, provided they are alive. Can you handle that?"

"Yes Sir, whatever you need," Sparks nodded.

"Good enough for me," he replied, and three clicks sounded in his earpiece. "Okay, that's the signal from Jackson. We're a go."

He led his team across the open ground, encountering no resistance. They moved quickly and silently, and reached the door, pressed against the wall on either side. Harris gave a silent countdown before turning and flinging open the door.

He swallowed the thick mucus in his throat and ignored his gag reflex entirely, work mode taking over and bringing him to attention. He led them into a mid-sized storage area, with floor to ceiling shelving and wooden boxes strewn about. They moved forward slowly, about four feet apart at most, training their attention on the hidden areas of the shelves to make sure nobody was hiding.

The group froze at the sound of automatic gunfire muffled through the building.

"Contact! Contact!" Jackson cried through the earpiece, and Harris immediately motioned to Harper. Before they could move, the crackle of nearer gunfire echoed in the space and Taylor's head tore in half.

Harris grabbed Harper's arm, pulling him behind a crate as a bullet caught the strike member's shoulder. Sparks dove behind a stack of boxes across the room, peeking back out to make sure that Taylor was well and fully dead and didn't need assistance.

She spotted the gunman on the far end, continuing to unload a flurry of bullets through the air to keep the group pinned down. She ducked back behind the crates, looking to her superior who was doubled over in a violent coughing fit. Harper was trying desperately to stop the bleeding in his shoulder, but it didn't look good.

Harris finally took in a breath and caught Sparks' eye. She motioned for him to lay down covering fire and he nodded, fighting the wheezing in his chest as he thrust his arm over the top of the crate to shoot.

She immediately darted out from behind the crate, sliding underneath one of the bottom shelves. As she came out the other side she fired, catching the terrorist in the kneecap, forcing him to the ground. Before he could get back up, she sprung to her feet and launched a flying knee strike to his face, rendering him unconscious.

She stood over him for a second to make sure he was fully out and kicked his gun away. "Clear!" She called and strode back over to her superior as Jackson gave the all clear over the earpiece.

"10-4, Jackson, we're clear too," Harris touched the earpiece and then switched frequencies. "Locals, we have the building secure. I need a couple medics at the north breach point and some uniforms to detain a suspect."

"You doing okay, Sir?" Sparks asked as she approached, brow furrowed in concern. **

"Doing just fine, thanks to you," Harris replied with a coughing groan. "That was one hell of an effort, Sparks.

Once we get everything under control I'm going to have a nice long chat with the SWAT leader about the fact you haven't had a chance with him."

"Thank you, sir," she replied with a firm nod.

"Agent Harris, do you copy?" Jackson's voice came in through the earpiece.

"Harris here," the Agent slowly got to his feet. "What do you have, Jackson? Do you need a medic or backup?"

"We're fine, but we have something you need to see," Jackson replied, and Harris and Sparks shared a look of concern as officers entered the space, descending on Harper's bleeding form.

"Come on, let's go see what he wants," Harris motioned for the redhead to follow him, putting his fist to his lips to stifle another coughing fit. She held her gun at the ready as she tailed him, exiting the warehouse into an office area that had been devastated by a torrent of gunfire.

Harris wheezed a growl at the sight of lifeless bodies strewn in an ocean of blood splatter.

Jackson approached him. "Sir, you need to-"

"What the *fuck* happened in here, Jackson?!" Harris cut him off. "You had orders to use non-lethal force!"

"Well Sir, it's simple." The tall strike leader shrugged. "They had guns, we felt threatened, we removed the threat."

"Guess what?" Harris stepped forward, nose a hair's breadth from Jackson's. His hoarse voice didn't waver an inch. "Taylor got his fucking head blown off, and Harper caught a round to the shoulder, yet that girl right over there was able to follow orders and secure a live suspect. Are you telling me you can't do the job of a local fucking Officer?"

"Sir, you can reprimand me later," Jackson replied, pursing his lips and glaring at Sparks, who didn't give him the satisfaction of a reaction. "Right now you need to see this."

"Fine," Harris stepped down and cleared his throat. "What do you have?"

Jackson turned on his heel with a huff and led them down a row of desks into a large office. Along the far wall was a series of maps, and a lone desk with a laptop. Next to it there was a plexiglass cell with a single person huddled in the corner.

Harris' breath caught in his throat, and he narrowed his eyes. Who was this prisoner? He reached out and tapped the glass, and the man sprung up and dove for him, smashing his face into it. Harris took a step back in shock at the sight of bloodshot, unblinking eyes as the man creature gnawed at the glass as if trying to take a bite out of it.

"Oh my god, it's Sokolov," he said, noting the burns down the side of the creature's face. "What in god's name is wrong with him?"

"I have no idea Sir, but it gets worse," Jackson replied, and motioned to the desk. One of the maps on the wall was of the UT campus, with arrows charting a path through it and around the stadium. The open laptop had some medical jargon on the screen.

"Holy fuck, the attack may have already happened," Harris coughed, "we… we need to get this analyzed."

"I can take it over to our contact at UT," Jackson offered.

"That's no good." Harris shook his head. "SWAT has deployed there this morning for an undisclosed incident. Between that, the zombie doctor over there and this info we have to assume the bio attack has already been launched."

"So where do we take it, then?" Jackson asked.

"I have an idea," Sparks piped up, and both men turned to her.

"Okay Sparks," Harris said with a wave of his hand, "let's hear it."

"Texas State University in San Marcos," she replied. "It's about a forty-five minute drive due south from here, about halfway to San Antonio. There is a lab run by Doctor Alvison. He's not going to be winning any major awards, but he's a solid researcher who has been at the school for the past couple of decades. At the very least he should be able to make sense of what's here so we know what we are up against."

"How in the hell do you know that?" Jackson narrowed his eyes.

"I went to undergrad there before joining the academy," Sparks replied, eyes much harder when she looked at him than at Harris. "I was an English major, but my final two years there I was one of the ambassadors for the school that would show potential freshmen what the school had to offer."

"Good enough for me," Harris wheezed. "We have to assume Austin has been hit and proceed from there. Jackson, take Sparks, Ross and Michaels. Get this info down to her contact. I'm going to stay here and interrogate the lone survivor."

Jackson pursed his lips as he stared down his nose at the redhead. "Yes, Sir," he said reluctantly. "Come on, Sparks, get the stuff and let's go."

"One more thing." Harris put up a hand. "I'm activating the hostile zone protocol, and will let D.C. know where you are going to be. Based on what Sokolov turned into, I don't want to take any chances."

CHAPTER FOUR

Tuesday, 12:16 P.M.

The SUV tore down the I-35, lights flashing as Jackson wove in and out of traffic.

"Before we left, Agent Harris said he was activating the hostile zone protocol," Sparks broke the subdued silence by leaning forward in the backseat. "What is that?"

"Look sweetheart," Jackson replied, voice dripping with disdain, "the only reason you are here is to give me directions to this lab. You aren't here to ask questions."

"Whether you like it or not, I'm on this mission," she snapped. "So you can drop the attitude and give me some basic goddamn information."

"It's used as a failsafe," Agent Ross cut in, turning in his seat beside her to try to diffuse the situation. He was a dark-haired man with kind eyes, and she relaxed a bit at his far more respectful tone. "When we have to go into hostile territory or an unknown situation, we activate this protocol. Once this happens there are several computer geeks back in D.C. that monitor all locally generated non-traditional communication from the area."

"Why, though?" Sparks raised an eyebrow. "What would that accomplish?"

"Traditional communications might be jammed or taken out entirely, so you may have to get creative to get a message out," Ross explained. "You might only have access to a ham radio for example, so if you put out a distress call the boys in D.C. will hear it."

"Gotcha." She nodded. "Good to know."

"Where the hell am I going, Sparks?" Jackson barked.

"Take exit 205, drive about half a mile and turn right," she instructed. "School will be straight ahead."

A tense silence fell over the vehicle as they drove the last leg of the trip. Jackson drove into the quad and parked beside the student union, eyes sweeping the area for any sign of people. There weren't even any other cars. It was a virtual ghost town.

"Where the hell *is* everyone?" Agent Michaels asked absently.

Sparks opened her door. "There was a massive bed bug outbreak at the school last week, so they cancelled classes and sent the resident students away so they could fumigate the dorms," she explained.

"That would have been fan-fucking-tastic information to have an hour ago," Jackson snapped, turning around in his seat to glare at her as she hopped down to the asphalt. "If the school is closed, then how do you know this doctor is even going to be here?"

"He's a hermit who lives for his work," she said. "Even without students, he's going to be hunkered down in his lab doing research." She slammed the door and the strike leader growled, exiting the vehicle with the other agents.

"You'd just better hope he's here," he warned as he fell into step with her. "So where are we going?"

"Through the Student Union, third floor walkway and we're in the science building," Sparks instructed as she walked, short legs managing to keep a brisk pace.

They reached the front doors, but when Michaels reached out to pull it open, they were locked. Jackson pushed him out of the way and rattled the handles in frustration.

"So now what?" His voice raised an octave and Sparks fought the urge to roll her eyes.

"Looks like we're going on a hike," she replied. "Just follow the sidewalk around and it's the building directly behind this one."

The tall agent shook his head in disgust. "Okay, let's go."

Tuesday, 12:38 P.M.

The foursome exited a dimly lit stairwell into a long hallway, the only illuminated lab at the very end. There was no movement, but at least the lights were on.

"You'd better hope he's here," Jackson sneered. "If not, we're all kinds of fucked if an attack has happened."

Sparks ignored him and led them down the hallway, stopping to knock politely on the doorframe to the lab. There were two young college kids standing with their backs to the door, and they jumped at the sound, whipping around.

"You aren't supposed to be in here!" The slight and taller one with glasses said, though his high pitch didn't really give off an air of authority.

"We're here to see Dr. Alvison," Sparks replied gently.

"Yeah?" The other kid, a short and stout fun-house mirror reflection of the first one, crossed his arms. "And who are you exactly?"

Jackson growled and pushed his way through the door. "We're from the motherfucking U S of A government and we don't have time for your bullshit," he fumed. "Now is Dr. Alvison here or not?"

The kids blinked at him in fear and shock, but before anyone moved an older man appeared from the back room. He was wearing a white lab coat and silver-rimmed glasses and he snorted, wiping his nose clean before straightening to look at the agent, seemingly unimpressed.

"I'm Dr. Alvison," he said. "What can I do for you?"

"Doctor, we have a situation and need your help," Sparks spoke up, and walked over to him, taking his arm to help him sit in his desk chair.

"Very well," the old man replied. "What is it?"

Ross approached and set the laptop and documents on his desk, leaning over to motion to one of the folders. "We believe that there has been a bio-terrorist attack in Austin, and we need to know what we are dealing with," he explained.

Dr. Alvison took a moment to look over the first folder and then pursed his lips. "Okay, I'm going to need some time."

Jackson slammed his hand down on the counter behind them, startling the whole room. "We don't *have* time!" he snapped.

"Well," Dr. Alvison coughed. "Ugh, excuse me. Been under the weather for a couple of days now. Ted over there brought me this little gift on Sunday, didn't you Ted?"

"Hey, focus." Jackson snapped his fingers. "Can you decipher this or not?"

"Yes, I can," Dr. Alvison replied in a steely tone, staring the agent down with no sign of being intimidated. "But as I stated before, it's going to take some time. This isn't a football box score, this is complicated material. Could take me hours to figure out what this is."

"Fucking hell," Jackson grunted. "Ross, get on the line back to Agent Harris and give him an update."

Ross nodded and left the room to make his call, while Dr. Alvison swiveled in his chair to fully face Jackson.

"If you can run an errand for me, the process might be sped up considerably," the old man said.

"Great, what do you need?" Jackson rolled his eyes.

"Two of my research assistants, Ben and Ashley, went to Mike's Diner on the quad about half an hour ago for a late lunch," the Doctor replied. "If you can get them back here they can help me figure this out faster."

"Now we're talking," Jackson huffed and turned to the redhead. "Sparks, go collect the young people so we can get this ball rolling."

"Why me?" she asked without thinking.

"Because I gave you a fucking order, that's why," Jackson hissed, stepping right up into her face. "You wanted to be a member of the team, well here you are, on the bottom rung of the ladder. So go get this done."

She bit her tongue, and as much as she wanted to comment about the way his breath on her made her skin crawl, she managed to hold back. "Yes, Sir."

"Jackson, I got nothing," Ross rushed back into the room.

"What the fuck do you mean, you got *nothing*?" Jackson snapped.

"Can't reach Harris." Ross shook his head. "I tried the police station dispatch and the Captain's direct line. Nothing all the way around."

Jackson's gaze turned from fuming to concerned. "Sparks, hurry," he urged. "This could be a real shit show in the making. And for the love of god, don't tell anyone what's going on. Last thing we need is a panic on our hands."

She nodded and practically flew down the hallway.

CHAPTER FIVE

Tuesday, 12:59 P.M.

Sparks jogged across the quad to Mike's Diner, red hair fluttering behind her in the afternoon breeze. She'd frequented the place a lot when she was an undergrad, being a staple of the campus.

She opened the door and almost clocked Mike Venture in the face who was standing right behind it.

"I'm sorry ma'am, but we're closing up for the day," he said in a tired voice. "My staff called in sick so it's just been me today. And frankly it's not worth staying open past lunch since nobody is on campus."

"Don't worry Mike," she said and flashed her badge. "I'm just here to collect a couple of people and we'll be on our way."

"Who are you arresting?" His eyes grew wide. "What did they do?"

"No, no, nothing like that." She put a hand up. "I'm looking for Ben and Ashley. Doctor Alvison sent me down here to collect them."

"Oh, okay, I gotcha," Mike replied with a sigh of relief. "They are the couple in the center booth there." He motioned and she nodded.

"Thanks, Mike," she said, and made her way towards them as he locked the door. The sight of the Mike's military themed decor to honor his Vietnam war days brought back a wave of nostalgia, but she focused on casing the joint. There was a large bald man that looked to be in his late 30s wearing a black leather jacket at a table to the left, and two other inconspicuous looking men sitting by themselves along the far wall.

She stopped in front of the center table with a fit black man sporting a tight afro and a blonde girl that looked like she just walked out of a fashion magazine. They couldn't have been much older than 20.

"Are you Ben and Ashley?" she asked.

"Who wants to know?" Ben narrowed his eyes in suspicion.

"My name is Lacy Sparks and I'm with the Austin police department," the redhead explained and flashed her badge again. "Doctor Alvison sent me down here to retrieve you for a time sensitive project."

"Why in the world would he send a cop down here to get us?" Ben asked. "An Austin cop at that?"

"That… that's classified," Sparks said quietly, squaring her shoulders. "Come on, we really need to get going."

"Is this about all the sick people?" Ashley piped up, eyes curious.

"I… I don't know what you're talking about," Sparks bit her lip.

"Don't treat us like children, Ms. Sparks," the blonde girl straightened in her seat. "We both know what kind of research Dr. Alvison does, any my roommate is an intern at the hospital. She has been sending me updates on what's going on over there. Hundreds of people have checked in just today, all with the same symptoms. That isn't normal."

Her voice was loud enough to alert one of the male patrons from the far wall. "Do you know anything about the sickness going round?" He called.

"I assure you, I don't know anything." Sparks put a hand up.

"I took my wife to the hospital six hours ago and the place was packed," he continued, walking towards them. "They took her to the back and the doctor isn't allowing me to see her. Please, what do you know?"

"Sir, I'm sorry but I can't help you," Sparks replied, shaking her head. "I don't know anything." She was about to go on the defensive as the man continued to move towards her, but a banging on the front door made them all stop.

"We're closed!" Mike yelled from wiping tables, but the banging continued. "Goddammit I said we're closed!" He approached the door with a heavy sigh and unlocked it. "Are you deaf I said we're-"

As the door swung open a man shoved his way in, snarling and attached himself to Mike's throat. The diner owner tumbled backwards in shock, screaming as the rabid looking man tore at his flesh with his teeth.

Sparks drew her gun. "Put your hands up, now!" she screamed, and the grotesque man turned his attention on her like a bird hearing a noise. His whole face covered in blood from his ministrations, he leapt from Mike's lifeless body and darted towards her.

Sparks unloaded three bullets into her attacker, but they didn't slow him down, and she ducked under his grasp and took him around the waist, flinging him up and over her head. He flew into a table and flopped over it like a rag doll, and she spun around to see him bounce right back up onto his feet.

The bald patron intercepted the attacker with a shoulder bash and leapt on top of him once he hit the ground. He held the cannibal by the throat with one hand and an arm with the other, his prisoner's free arm flailing and smacking wetly against the leather jacket.

"Can one of you assholes help me out here?" The bald man grunted, and Ben ran over, skidding to a stop to hold down the free arm.

Sparks rushed over, staring down at the milky dead eyes on the creature's face. It looked like Sokolov. What was happening?

"Don't just stand there, kill this motherfucker!" The bald man barked.

"I put two in his chest and it didn't slow him down, so I'm open to suggestions!" Sparks snapped.

"Take his head off!" Ben cried. She aimed her gun but then thought better of it, holstering the weapon. "What are you doing?!" he wailed, and she turned to grab the heavy based sign next to one of the tables reading *This Section Closed*. She got a good grip on the neck and raised it to bash the creature's head in.

"STOP!" the other patron from the far wall screamed, standing with his hands out. "That's a human being! Don't kill him!"

"You! Shut the fuck up!" the bald guy demanded and then looked up at Sparks. "You! Kill this motherfucker!" She didn't hesitate this time before bringing the sign down onto the creature's face. A few forceful blows and it stopped moving, and the trio relaxed.

The terrified patron ran straight out the door, and Sparks watched in horror as he got halfway across the quad before a pile of zombies took him down. One broke away from the feeding frenzy to tear at the open door.

"Get the door!" She screamed and dove forward, shoving it as hard as she could. The zombie hit the wood, applying just enough pressure that she couldn't get it closed, so Ben and Baldy threw their weight against it as well.

"Ben, look out!" Ashley shrieked as Mike's hand closed around Ben's foot. He stared down in frozen horror at the dead, gunked face of the man that had served him lunch so many long school days.

There was a sick squelch as Baldy brought his combat booted foot down on top of Mike's skull, twice in quick succession.

Ben swallowed hard as the hand let go. "Thanks, man." He rushed over to Ashley quickly, folding her into a tight hug.

"You." Sparks pointed at the man who'd been worried about his wife. "Go make sure the back door is secured and there isn't another way in here." She instructed, and he darted off before she turned to Baldy. "You okay?"

"Just fine, thank you," he drawled, but then clucked his tongue as she started to walk away. "So, are you ready to drop the act and tell us what the fuck these things are?"

Sparks sighed. "I don't know what they are, but I will tell you what I do know."

"Fair enough," he replied, crossing his arms expectantly.

"Earlier today, we raided a terrorist compound outside of Austin," Sparks began. "We took out what we thought was a cell that was prepping a bio-terror attack, but as we're finding out may have already launched it. We found one of these things at the hideout along with a lot of data, so we came here to see Dr. Alvison in the hopes he could decipher it and let us know what we're facing."

The banging on the windows and doors continued to escalate, and they looked around at each other.

"We should probably lay low, get away from their view," Baldy suggested.

"Not a bad idea," Sparks agreed, and led him back towards Ben, Ashley, and the patron that had secured the door. They hunkered down behind the food counter, out of sight. The bald man took off his leather jacket with a whoosh of breath, revealing some crudely drawn World War II era German military tattoos.

"What the hell, man?!" Ben's mouth fell open. "You're a fucking Nazi?"

"Relax kid," Baldy replied calmly. "They were necessary for me to survive some youthful transgressions, that's all."

"What does that even mean?" Ben snapped.

"It means he got ink in prison so he wouldn't get shanked in the meal line," Sparks piped up.

"Bullshit!" the dark-skinned boy countered. "Man, what do you have against minorities?"

"Really?" Baldy threw his hands up. "We just saw two people get eaten alive and we're currently surrounding by half a dozen zombies, and you want to know my thoughts on race relations?"

Ben crossed his arms. "Call it self preservation."

"All you need to do is ask yourself one question," the older man replied. "Given our current situation, would you rather have me standing here, or some pansy ass liberal that would want to go hug it out with them?"

"Um, I…" Ben stammered.

"He…" Sparks looked at the bald guy expectantly.

"Jeff," he offered.

"Jeff has a point," she continued. "Let's try to focus on the problem at hand and not create new ones."

"Ms. Sparks?" Ashley cut in, wringing her hands.

"Please, just call me Sparks."

"Okay, Sparks." The blonde nodded. "What's the plan?"

"We're going to lay low for a few minutes and hope they lose interest and move on," Sparks replied.

"And what's the plan when they *do* move on?" Jeff asked.

"We need to get to the science building," she told him. "My team is there with Dr. Alvison so we'll have some protection and can find out what we're dealing with. Unfortunately it's a long ass haul to the science building since the student union is locked."

"I have a key that can get us in," Ashley put in. "Dr. Alvison lent me his faculty key when we came out for lunch."

"That makes me feel a little better," Sparks admitted. "Running across the quad is a lot easier than trying to get all the way around the union. At least when we're inside we'll have some choke points where we can hold them off."

Jeff nodded. "That's sounds like as good a plan as any." He hopped up into a booth and stretched out his legs, taking up the entire seat in a pose of pure relaxation. The banging and groaning from outside intensified. "Guess we should get comfortable. Sounds like we might be awhile."

CHAPTER SIX

Tuesday, 6:22 P.M.

As the sun started to set, the banging slowly ceased, though upon peering through the windows the inhabitants of Mike's Diner could still see the zombies milling about.

"Fuck, they are up to ten," Sparks murmured as she squinted through the blinds, and turned back to face her impromptu crew. "I don't see our situation improving, so once the sun sets and we have a little bit of cover we need to make a run for it."

"That gives us what, about fifteen minutes to come up with a plan?" Jeff scoffed.

"I'm open to suggestions," Sparks retorted.

"What if we barrel through them?" Ben asked.

"Might work for us, but not some of the slower members of the group," Jeff replied, motioning to the diner patron who'd been worried about his wife. He hadn't said a word the entire time since he checked the back door, and they didn't know if he'd even run with them. "Unless of course you're okay sacrificing our boy over there."

"Man, come on." Ben sighed. "I wasn't suggesting that."

"Relax kid, I know," Jeff insisted. "The reality is though that most of us wouldn't make it if we tried your plan."

"Okay, so what's your big idea?" Ben crossed his arms.

The bald man smiled. "Let's give em the ole okey doke."

There was an awkward silence until Ben raised a hand. "Umm… what the hell is that?"

"You know," Jeff prompted, "from Dawn of the Dead?"

"Is that the one with the dad from Modern Family?" Ashley asked.

"Goddamn kids these days," Jeff muttered, scrubbing his hands down his face. "No respect for the classics." He sighed. "What it means is that we're going to create a distraction to clear our path. This place has a back loading door, right?"

"Yeah." Ben nodded. "In the kitchen. Leads directly out behind the building."

"So we pop our heads out there, make some noise and those zombies out there come and see what's up," Jeff said. "At the very least it should thin their numbers out some."

"Seems risky," Ben replied.

"Ben, anything we do at this point is going to be risky," Sparks piped up. "This seems like the best option."

"Okay, it's settled then," Jeff said with finality, rolling his shoulders. "Let's get loaded up." They started pulling some of the memorabilia from the walls, machetes and batons, anything that could be used as a weapon or to make noise.

Sparks took pause as the mute patron didn't move, curled up in the fetal position in a booth. "What's your name?" She asked gently.

"My- my name is Kyle," he whispered.

"Okay Kyle," Sparks said firmly. "I'm sure you heard, but we're going to make a run for it." She motioned to the front door with the baton she'd liberated from the wall.

"Nope." He shook his head violently in protest. "I'm just going to wait right here for the police to come."

"Kyle, I *am* the police," she said, leaning forward. "And I'm all that's coming to help. It isn't going to safe here once we open the front door."

"Nope, nuh-uh," he continued as if she hadn't said anything, "I'm staying here where it's safe."

Jeff walked up and flattened his hands down on the diner table, staring

Kyle down. "Listen motherfucker, it's the end of the world and you got two choices. You can fight or you can lay down and die. If you'll notice wasting my goddamn time and endangering my life because you're a pussy isn't one of the choices. So what's it gonna be?"

Sparks blinked at the bald man's sudden harshness, but Kyle clenched his jaw and stood up from the booth.

"Okay," he said firmly. "I'll come."

Jeff winked at Sparks before leading the way to the back door.

"Okay guys, here we go," the redhead said. "Jeff and I will create a diversion. I want the three of you to wait by the front door. If this goes to plan, we're going to be moving quick."

"We'll be ready," Ben assured her.

Sparks joined Jeff, gun drawn, and he raised his machete and put his hand on the door handle.

"Okay, on three," he said. "One. Two."

"Wait," she said.

"Don't puss out on me now." Jeff raised an eyebrow, and Sparks shot him a death glare that said *motherfucker please*.

"First off, if you ever had to pick up my balls, you'd throw your back out," she huffed, and he cracked a smile. "Secondly, I'm going to grab some pots and pans. Should go a long way towards making noise."

"And here I was thinking you'd just fire off a couple of rounds." He watched her rummage for a few thin pans with a skeptical look on his face.

"I only have twenty-six shots left, and I get the sense I shouldn't be wasting them," she said as she rejoined him at the door.

"That's a valid point," he agreed, and then took the handle again firmly.

Sparks nodded. "Okay, zombie distraction, take two."

"Again, on three," he said. "One. Two. Three!" He flung the door open and they burst outside, scanning the vicinity for enemies. There were two zombies about fifty yards away who were feasting on a victim, and they shot to attention at the noise.

Sparks gave Jeff a nod and dove for the dumpster to the right of them, banging on it with the pots and pans like a death metal drummer. Screeches in the distance alerted them that zombies were headed their way, and she dropped the pans to dart back towards Jeff at the door.

He reeled back and slammed the machete into the top of a wayward zombie's head, stopping it dead in its tracks. Before he could wrench the blade free,

Sparks landed a flying kick to the zombie's chest, dislodging the body from the weapon.

"Let's go!" She exclaimed and tore back inside. Jeff slammed the door and locked it, banging on it a few more times for good measure. They barreled back through the diner to meet up with the rest of the group.

"There are still some out there," Ben said tersely, clutching his baton with white knuckles.

"We're gonna have to chance it," Jeff replied, peering at the three zombies milling about, still relatively close to the door.

Ben swallowed hard. "But…"

"Jeff is right," Sparks cut in. "This is our only chance. Here's the plan. When that door flies open, I want Ashley to run as fast as she can to the Student Union to get that door unlocked. Jeff and I will take the two on the right, Ben, you take the one on the left."

"Wh-what about me?" Kyle stammered, his big eyes watery.

"You can help Ben," Jeff said, and the student scowled at the skinhead, receiving only a smile in return.

"Okay." Sparks nodded. "Go!" She flung the door open, and Ashley sprinted straight ahead, a blur of blonde zipping across the quad. Jeff lunged to the right and in a powerful arc, beheaded his zombie quickly. Sparks bludgeoned hers in the head three times in succession before it stopped moving, just as Ben's zombie grabbed him by the arms.

"Goddammit man, help me!" he cried to Kyle, who was frozen in the doorway of the diner.

"I'm… I'm sorry!" He backed inside slowly, fear frozen on his face, and Ben let out a groan of frustration as he continued to wrestle with his snapping enemy.

"Duck!" Jeff screamed, and the student complied, leaning just out of the way so that the bald man could swing his machete into his opponent's face. "Let's go!" He screamed as the body fell, and he shoved Ben after Sparks.

"They're coming!" the redhead yelled, sprinting in the direction of the Student Union. A few zombies staggered from around the building and ambled after them. "Open the door!" Sparks demanded as they caught up to Ashley, the blonde fumbling with the key.

"The key isn't working!" she shrieked, and Ben looked fearfully behind them to see two zombies overtake the diner door. He swallowed at the thought of

Kyle's demise and shook his head to try to focus on the task at hand.

"Well, you've got about ten seconds before we're overrun," Jeff said, sounding as calm as could be, and Ben shot him a glare before Sparks shoved Ashley into him. He caught her with an *oof* and clutched her close as the officer fired her gun at the corner of a large pane of glass in the door.

"Come on!" Sparks kicked in the shattered glass and then waved the others inside. She hopped in before Jeff and the four barreled down the hallway just as zombies started to squirm into the building.

"Stairs are at the back of the building!" Ben cried as he ran, holding Ashley's hand like their lives depended on it. They burst through a set of double doors and Jeff and Ben slam back against them to hold them shut against the pack of zombies behind them.

"It's the third floor," Ashley huffed.

"Go, make sure that key fucking works this time," Jeff instructed. "We'll hold them off until you give us the signal."

"When you come up, hug the right side of the wall," Sparks countered, and the guys nodded. As the girls took off up the stairs, the skinhead turned to the student.

"Bet you're really glad I'm a big badass motherfucker now, aren't you?" Jeff sneered, and Ben simply shook his head, grunting all of his energy into holding the door shut.

"We're clear up here!" Sparks called down the stairwell.

Jeff met Ben's gaze. "You ready?" he asked.

"After you," Ben replied.

"Alright, on three," Jeff said. "One. Two. Three!"

They both sprang off the door and hit the stairs, running up the right side as quickly as they could. The zombies fell all over each other as they staggered in the door, but quickly regained footing to pursue up to the first landing. They piled up towards the second floor, but Sparks stood there, opening fire on them as they attempted to follow Ben and Jeff.

She struck the first zombie in the chest, the force causing it to slam back into the rest of the zombies, giving them a chance to gain ground. They hurtled up to the third floor and slammed through the double doors, slamming them shut behind them.

The zombies hit the doors, causing both Ben and Jeff to leap away from it.

Ashley quickly ducked under Ben's arm and clicked the deadbolt, securing it.

"Okay, they're locked," the blonde said, chest heaving and heart pounding. "They aren't getting in. At least not through there."

"You okay?" Jeff clapped a hand on Ben's back.

The shorter man scowled. "Peachy."

"Where to?" Sparks asked, and the blonde pointed.

"Walkway is just through those doors. Building should be clear," she said.

Sparks reloaded her gun and cocked it with a *click* of finality. "Forgive me if I don't take your word for it."

CHAPTER SEVEN

Tuesday, 6:45 P.M.

Sparks led the group cautiously towards the lab, holding up a hand to stop the group at the sight of a pair of legs in the doorway. She readied her weapon and raised her chin.

"Jackson?" she called. "Michaels?"

"Sparks?" Jackson's voice from inside. "Is that you?" ·

"Yeah, I got the doc's assistants," she replied as he stepped into the doorway.

His eyes were wide and skin pale, and his gun was drawn but not in that normal arrogant way of his.

"What the fuck happened here?" Sparks demanded.

"My guess is the same thing that caused you to take fie hours to run across the quad," Jackson retorted. "Get in here, we need to talk." He backed up and allowed them access to the room.

Sparks stepped over the body, which was one of the kids that had greeted them when they first arrived. He was missing the entire back of his head, shot clean off. Michaels' body was slumped against the far wall with a giant shard of glass sticking out of his neck, blood pooling beneath him.

The taller skinny kid tended to Agent Ross in the corner, who was missing a substantial chunk of his upper right arm.

"Let me guess, somebody got hungry?" Sparks asked.

"Deke here," Jackson began, kicking the body in the doorway for effect, "went into a serious coughing fit before collapsing to the ground. Michaels went over to check on him and next thing we knew, Deke pounces on him. Michaels lost his balance and went head first into an experiment, which is how he got the glass in his throat. Ross ran over and this asshole-" Jackson kicked the corpse again with a grunt. "-took a fucking chunk out of his arm. Just clamped down like a gator on an unattended child. Once that happened, I opened fire. Put two in his chest, but all that did was piss him off. So I put one right between his eyes, which calmed him down. Didn't see any other option."

"Yeah, headshots were the only thing that worked for us, too." Sparks ran a hand through her hair with a sigh. "And Jackson, you did the right thing. Those things are vicious and there is no reasoning with them."

"Ms. Sparks is correct," Dr. Alvison spoke up as he walked out of the back room. He held a clipboard in his hands.

"Doc, you got anything for us?" Jackson asked.

"I think you all need to sit down," the old man replied, following his own advice as he lowered himself into his desk chair. "This is going to be difficult to hear."

Tuesday, 6:58 P.M.

Jeff and Ben deposited the corpses outside of the lab door and secured it, locking the deadbolt and making sure it wouldn't budge. Ted, the tall kid that had tended to Ross, drummed up chairs for everyone and they all sat in a crude semicircle around the doctor.

"I need to preface this by saying I've just started my research and everything I've found is preliminary," Dr. Alvison wheezed.

"Doc, just get to the fucking point," Jackson demanded.

"With that said," the doctor said with a huff, pointedly ignoring the rude strike leader, "what I'm about to tell you is accurate, although my timeline may be off by ten to twenty percent." He coughed and took a deep breath. "Okay. So,

61

approximately eighty hours ago there was a
bio-terrorist attack on the UT football
game. A man infected with an unknown virus
exposed roughly a hundred thousand people
to it by wandering the grounds. I've
determined that this virus is airborne, so
everyone that attended that game was
exposed.

"To complicate matters, it has a
nearly one hundred percent infection rate,
and once you are infected you become a
carrier as well. I haven't been able to
determine how long of a dormant period it
has once someone is infected before they
are contagious, but it doesn't appear to
be too long. Maybe even as little as a few
minutes."

"So what are you saying, doc?"
Jackson cut in, furrowing his brow. "Are
we all infected? Are we going to become
those fucking flesh eating things?"

"To answer your first question," Dr.
Alvison replied, "yes, we are all
infected. As to your second, it depends
entirely on your blood type."

"Blood type?"

"Yes, Agent Jackson," the doctor
confirmed. "Blood type. Whatever this
virus is, it only becomes deadly if it
infects someone with the A blood type.
Something in the A blood type caused the
virus to mutate, killing the host and

reanimating it into the killing machine we witnessed a little while ago with Deke.

"I have been able to determine that for people with the A blood type, there is roughly a seventy-two hour incubation period before the mutation takes hold. Within twenty-four to forty-eight hours the person will develop flu-like symptoms."

"Like what you have?" Jackson asked.

"Yes, Agent Jackson." Dr. Alvison nodded. "Just like what I have."

A sob tore its way out of Ted's throat and he turned away from the group to hide his tears in fear and embarrassment.

"And I'm guessing Ted over there as well," Jackson mused.

"Yeah," the young man stammered through his tears, "I have A blood type... but I'm not sick."

"You will be, son," Dr. Alvison said gently. "You just came into the office this morning, so it's possible you weren't exposed to it until you met up with Deke."

"So doc, lay it out for us," Jackson cut in. "How bad is it? How do we contain it?"

"The only way this could have been contained is if you'd nuked Austin on Saturday morning," Dr. Alvison replied.

Jackson growled. "Don't give me that bullshit, doc."

"You don't understand." The doctor narrowed his tired eyes. "This virus is airborne, and it infects nearly every single person it comes into contact with. It has a hundred percent kill rate with people who have the A blood type, which is roughly forty percent of the population. As soon as the infected person left the stadium, this became impossible to contain."

Jackson turned and slammed a fist down onto the counter, knocking over a few beakers.

"Jackson, keep cool," Sparks snapped.

"I'm fucking cool, Sparks," he shot back. "I just don't like this defeatist attitude."

"The doc is right, though," she replied with a shrug. "Just stop and think about it for a moment. You have a hundred thousand people leaving the stadium that afternoon. Those people go downtown to 6th street for some music and infect tens of thousands more, including touring bands.

"They then take it on the road and infect more. Some people flew in for the game, including the opposing team. As soon as they hit the airport, this virus goes global, especially if anybody they come into contact with has a connecting flight in a major international hub."

Her diatribe began to sink in, and Jackson's eyes seemed to glaze over with the severity of the situation.

"I've done some preliminary estimates on the spread of the virus." Dr. Alvison flicked through the pages on his clipboard. "Within ten days every major city in the world will have active cases of these creatures. If they are able to spread without the knowledge we possess, I fear upwards of sixty percent of the population will either be those things or killed by those things within a month."

"What if the bites can infect someone who doesn't have A blood type?" Sparks wondered, and Ross stiffened, his free hand absently rising to clutch his wound.

"What do you mean?" the doctor asked.

"At the diner we saw two people who weren't showing signs of illness turn into those things after succumbing to their bites," Sparks explained. "I mean, it's possible that they both were A type and just hadn't been exposed yet, but one of them was the diner owner so it's unlikely."

"Assuming you are correct, the situation becomes much more dire." Dr. Alvison pursed his lips in thought. "Best guess? Seventy-five percent of the world's population will be dead within a month, and potentially as high as ninety percent here in the USA since we are at Ground Zero."

There was a somber silence, save for the sniffling as Ted's sobs started to mellow out.

"So, doc," Sparks finally broke the quiet, voice strained. "Realistically, what can we do?"

"If you can let your higher ups know the situation, they may be able to get the word out and some sort of quarantine effort may save some lives," the doctor replied.

"Well, given our immediate superior was worse than Deke when we left," Jackson cut in, "I'm going to go out on a limb and say that's not an option."

"Well, we're open to suggestions, Jackson," Sparks snapped.

"You know what?" He threw up his hands. "Y'all do what you want, but I'm getting the fuck out of here." He snatched one of the bags of gear and threw it over his shoulder.

"Oh yeah, and where are you going to go?" the redhead asked, crossing her arms. "Seeing as how you aren't familiar with the area, let me lay out your options. If you go North, you'll be in Austin, which is where this shitshow began. South isn't much better since it's San Antonio with one and a half million people. Now, you may be thinking east and trying to hit the coast. Assuming you survive the journey through the various back roads, you'll be dealing with the population of Houston trying to escape this madness. So good luck finding a boa when a million people are all doing the same thing." She raised an eyebrow.

Jackson sneered. "Guess I'm going west, then."

"Great idea," she supplied, "except unfortunately for you it's all back roads. Take the wrong one and you'll be in a major city suburb. Now, I know a way to get us out, but we need to finish our mission first and get the word out about this."

"So, how are we getting out?" he conceded with a scowl.

"Canyon Lake is pretty close to here, and it connects right to the Guadalupe River," Sparks explained, turning to face the group. "One of the most popular spring break destinations is attached to it. You can get rafts to float, or you can get some boats if you want to explore. This thing is happening so quickly that I don't think the people here will be able to take all of them and escape. So if we get there, we'll have a good chance to jack a ride and escape via the river."

"And then what?" Jackson prompted.

"Haven't thought that far ahead," she admitted. "But it's sparsely populated once you get away from the lake. We'll be able to get away from all the major population areas and give us a chance to regroup from there."

"Well, I've heard worse plans," he said. "But what's your grand plan to get the word out? Everyone immediately above us is dead."

Jeff picked up the phone on the desk next to him and then slammed it back down. "And, anyway, the phone is dead."

"Yeah," Jackson confirmed. "So let's have it, Sparks. What's your plan?"

She shrugged. "We use the Hostile Zone Protocol."

"Great." He rolled his eyes. "So all we need is a functioning radio station, which I'm sure are plentiful in small towns this close to major cities."

"Well," Ashley said quietly, and then cleared her throat. "There is the campus radio station. Do you think that would work?" She wrung her hands in front of her. Sparks raised an eyebrow at Jackson to accentuate the question.

He sighed. "Goddammit."

"Ashley, where is the radio station?" Sparks asked gently.

"It's in the building across from this one on the top floor," the blonde replied. "Unfortunately, there isn't a walkway, so you'd have to go in through the ground floor."

"Which, if you've forgotten, isn't that easy of a task," Jeff put in.

"Then we do another distraction, only something a lot louder," Sparks said firmly. "I mean, we're going to need to do one anyway if we want any hope of reaching the SUV."

"What about firing some guns off of the second floor?" Ben suggested.

"No, our ammo is too precious." She shook her head and let out a deep breath in thought. "And besides, we need something sustained."

"What about music?" Ted wiped furiously at his red eyes, finally having overcome his pity party. "I have this battery speaker set, you just put your phone in. The doc is always yelling at me to turn it down, so it's plenty loud."

"Alright," Sparks said with a nod. "Anyone got a phone with some loud music they don't mind parting with?"

"I got some R and B music on mine," Ben said with a shrug. "Not sure how loud that would be, though."

Jeff shook his head. "Lost mine back at the diner."

"I'm not giving up my phone." Jackson crossed his arms. "We may need the maps."

"Pretty sure mine is in the SUV." Sparks sighed.

Ashley put up her hand shyly. "I have some Slayer on mine."

Everyone gaped at her, and a blush crept up her cheeks.

"Goddamn, girl, you are a catch," Jeff said with an impressed grin. "If you ever decide to go back to vanilla."

"Motherfucker," Ben huffed. "Once you go black-"

"Yeah yeah." Jeff laughed, waving him off. "Don't worry, Chocolate Thunder, I'm just bustin' your balls."

Ben smirked, and the skinhead clapped him on the back in appreciation.

"Slayer it is," Sparks said, bringing the topic back on track.

"I'd suggest Raining Blood," Ashley instructed, holding out her phone. "It has a mellow thirty second intro before it kicks in, so you would have time to set it and run."

"Great, let's do it," the redhead agreed, nodding her head.

"Whoa, whoa," Jackson cut in, holding up his hands. "Wait a goddamn minute. I'm not going anywhere with anyone until I

know who has what blood type. I'm not
going to take a nap and wake up to one of
you motherfuckers feasting on me. I'll
start. I'm O positive."

Sparks pursed her lips. "O positive."

"B positive," Ben put in.

"O negative," Ashley added. They all
turned to Jeff, who simply blinked.

"Do I look like the type of man who
knows what kind of blood type he has?" he
asked, raising an incredulous eyebrow.

"Ted, if you would, please test him,"
Dr Alvison motioned, and the student with
the red-rimmed eyes scurried forward.

"Of course, doc," he said, and
motioned for Jeff to hold out his hand. He
pricked the bald man's finger and headed
over to the corner machine.

"Ross, what do you want to do?"
Jackson asked his team member in the
meantime. "I can end it for you right
now."

"Fuck that," Ross snapped. "I want to
go out fighting."

"That's the spirit," Jackson said
with a grin. "You want to kill some of
those motherfuckers for us?"

Ross sneered. "Hell yeah."

"I don't mean to eavesdrop,
gentlemen," Dr. Alvison piped up.

"What do you want, doc?" Jackson
asked.

"Agent Ross." The doctor ignored the team leader and addressed his subordinate directly. "I know you want to exact some sort of revenge as your final act on this planet, but may I suggest another path?"

Ross shrugged. "Sure."

"I have a day left, maybe a little more before this virus overtakes me," Dr. Alvison continued. "In that time I plan on doing as much research as I can. Having you to study and do tests on could potentially help stem the tide of this pandemic."

"How you gonna get the info to them there, doc?" Jackson scoffed. "Carrier pigeon?"

"If Sparks is able to get a message out, I'm going to request she mention my research and where it will be," the doctor replied. "There is roof access to this building, so they can fly in and only have to deal with the three of us to retrieve it."

"Ross, it's up to you." Jackson turned to his comrade. "If you want to go down fighting, I can use you. If you want to be a guinea pig, that's your call."

Ross sighed deeply, lowering his gaze to the floor in thought. His lips twisted and he raised his eyes to the doctor.

"Do you really think I can do some good?" he asked quietly.

"I really do," Dr. Alvison replied with a nod. "And if it will help put your blood lust at ease, you have my permission to take me out when I turn. I'm sure Ted over there will appreciate it since he has an extra day or two before he goes."

Ross nodded. "Okay doc, I'll do it."

Jackson patted his subordinate on the shoulder as the doctor shuffled over to Sparks, who was speaking with Ted.

"I got the big fella's results," the student was saying. "O positive."

"Good to know," the redhead replied. "Thanks."

"Sparks, I have a request," Dr. Alvison cut in.

"Whatever you need, doc," she affirmed, turning to him.

"I'm going to write down some info about this building and my lab," he told her. "I need you to read it over the air so your people hear it. This information could potentially save millions of lives."

Sparks nodded. "Let me know when you got it, doc. Just hurry because we're on a tight schedule." She turned to the group that had gathered behind her, her own post apocalyptic strike team. She took a deep breath. "So, this is our group then, huh? All right." She looked to Ben. "I need a guide to take me to the radio station."

"I got that covered," he assured her.

"Jackson, can you three take care of the decoy and get to the SUV?" she asked, and he held up Ashley's phone.

"Yeah, we're parked just outside the Student Union, so it shouldn't be that bad," he said.

"That's no good," Jeff spoke up with a shake of his head. "We had to open it up in order to get up here. God only knows how many zombies are running around there."

"Great, so how do we get to the car?" Jackson furrowed his brow.

"There's another walkway that goes into a dormitory," Ashley put in. "I have the key to the building and can guide you there."

"Good enough for me," Jackson agreed.

"Okay, here's the plan," Sparks instructed, commanding everyone's attention once again. "In twenty minutes that song needs to be blaring. Hopefully, it will clear the path for me and Ben. You guys get to the SUV and get to a safe spot. When you hear me finish the radio broadcast come pick us up."

"What's the station?" Jackson asked.

"89.9," Ashley replied.

"We'll be there," he affirmed.

"You better be, since I'm the only one who knows where we're going." Sparks smiled, but she was only half-joking.

CHAPTER EIGHT

Tuesday, 7:32 P.M.

"That's a whole lot of motherfuck right there," Jackson said quietly, taking a step back from the dormitory window.

Jeff shook his head. "Man, you ain't kidding," he agreed. He glanced at Ashley, whose face had gone deathly pale at the sight of the sixty or so zombies milling about in the quad. "You got any bright ideas?"

"Yeah, but you ain't gonna like it," Jackson replied.

"Seems to be the way today's going," Jeff huffed with a sigh. "All right, let's hear it."

"Ashley, do you have a key to any of the second-floor rooms?" The strike leader asked, and the blonde pursed her lips, taking in a deep ragged breath.

"No," she said. "They are all individual and only the RA has the master key."

"Don't worry about it," Jeff squeezed her shoulder reassuringly.

"You think you're strong enough to break down the door?" Jackson raised an eyebrow skeptically.

"No, but there's a reason I went to prison," the skinhead replied with a roll of his eyes. "A dorm room deadbolt isn't going to be much of a challenge."

"Fair enough." Jackson looked impressed. "You're a lot more useful than I thought you'd be."

Jeff barked a laugh. "I guess that qualifies as a compliment."

"Closest you are going to get from me," Jackson admitted. "Now look, I need you to go to the corner room and get the music going. Once you hit play you're going to have thirty seconds to haul ass to get out of the building and meet up with us."

"Man, you are out of your goddamn mind!" Jeff gaped. "This building is fucking huge. I mean that's gotta be what, an eighty yard run just for me to get to the stairs, then out the front door and over to the car? Maybe if I was twenty years younger."

"All right, it's your ass." Jackson sneered. "What do you propose?"

"I'll have a good vantage point from up there," Jeff explained. "I'll hit the music and keep up the distraction until I see you get to the SUV. As soon as you start the engine I'll kill the music and they'll start following you."

"Oh, *loving* this so far," Jackson snapped.

Jeff narrowed his eyes. "Yeah, well, unless you want to be the music man, you'd better."

"Fine, so I'm the pied piper, so then what?" the taller man muttered.

"You drive those things around the block," Jeff suggested. "You are going to be faster than they are, so when you make the return trip the entrance should be free and I can just hop in and we're on our way. I'll even restart the music just to keep them occupied."

"Works for me," Jackson sighed. "Ashley?"

"If all he's doing is hitting play and then waiting, wouldn't it make more sense for me to wait here?" the blonde asked, wringing her hands in front of her.

"Jackson and I can both handle ourselves against those things," Jeff said gently. "Unless you have some hidden ninja skills I'm not sure your ninety pound frame is well suited for hand to hand combat."

"Jeff's right," the other man agreed. "Stick with me, we'll be fine."

"All right, let's do it," the skinhead announced.

"Maestro, the floor is yours," Jackson said, and held out the phone.

Jeff collected it along with the speakers and headed upstairs. He took them two at a time and scurried down the hallway, keeping his senses on high alert even though it was unlikely there were any zombies around. He fiddled with the deadbolt for seventeen seconds before it gave, and he swung the door open to a bright pink room.

"Yikes," he muttered as he strode through the kitty cat themed room and opened the window. He positioned the speakers so they were pressed right up against the screen, clicked the phone into place and hit play.

As the intro to Raining Blood permeated the thick air, he sighed. "Well, at least if I'm going to die, I'm going to go out rockin'."

The zombies began to take notice of the noise as the crescendo built, and they sprinted as the song kicked into high gear. As they hit the wall in a vain attempt to get to the skinhead above them, he stood up and flipped them off, banging his head along with the crunchy riffs.

He stopped head banging in time to see Jackson and Ashley cautiously moving away from the door and break into a run for the car.

"Yeah, go get that big beautiful SUV," he said with a grin, but his smile faded as he noticed two zombies take off after them. With their trajectory, they would cross paths with his comrades before they made it to the car.

His breath caught in his throat as Jackson took notice, and then shoved Ashley hard, causing her to face plant into the asphalt.

"No!" he cried, frozen in place, heart pounding in his ears. "You goddamn motherfucker!" His mouth fell open in shock as he watched helplessly while the zombies descended on the poor blonde girl. He cranked the music up higher to drown out her screams, blinking in a daze at the sight of her flailing arms going limp.

Jackson, upon reaching the SUV, clicked the lights a few times to get Jeff's attention, and the skinhead's gaze darkened. He didn't want to give the bastard a reason to leave him behind too, so he cut the music.

The silence was deafening, and Jeff moved back from the window, ears ringing with the sudden quiet. He held his breath as the horde made a beeline for Jackson, who was revving the engine. He watched the SUV lead the zombies away and then crept back to the window.

Jeff swallowed hard as he looked down at Ashley's body, splayed in the quad, half eaten, blood streaming everywhere from bite wounds.

"I don't know if you can hear this, girl, but I hope you can," he whispered. "You deserve at least that much."

As the song began anew, the gathering storm of the intro seemed to bring the blonde zombie back to life. She staggered to her feet, turning slowly with bloodshot eyes and a snapping mouth. And then when the intro led into a loud shredding guitar, she sprinted towards the building and growled, clawing upwards towards Jeff.

He looked around the dorm room frantically and spotted a pair of dumbbells by the bed. He scooped up two twenty pounders and returned to the window.

"I hope this finds you, girl, because nobody deserves to be cursed like this," he wished, and then punched out a screen, holding one of the bells out the window. He dropped it and watched as it plummeted directly onto her forehead.

She crumpled to the ground in a heap, and he nodded, cranking up the music to the maximum and running off to catch his ride.

CHAPTER NINE

Tuesday 7:59 P.M.

Ben and Sparks barreled through the door to the radio building, the student slamming back against it. He locked it with a click and tugged to make sure that it was secured, and then turned to the redhead. She raised her flashlight that rested over her drawn gun, sweeping the lobby cautiously in case the building wasn't clear.

"Don't worry, this building has been locked for a few days now," Ben assured her.

"Better safe than sorry," Sparks replied.

He nodded. "Fair enough."

She motioned for him to lead the way, and he jogged to the stairwell.

"Just a short walk up to the third floor and we're there," he said, trying to sound optimistic. In reality, he was worried to death about Ashley. But he had to focus on the task at hand. He glanced over at the police officer, who was shaking her head in thought. "You okay?" he asked, brow furrowing.

"Yeah, I'm just thinking," Sparks mused. "I wish there was a way to get the information out to the people close to us.

I know this message is for the Feds, but people here need to know what's happening."

Ben pursed his lips. "I might have an idea."

"I'm all ears," she replied, glancing at him expectantly as they hit the second floor landing.

"About six months ago, the radio station made a big push to get new listeners, so they ran some contest that required people to sign up to receive the occasional text message," he explained. "That way when some of the big shows on the station would have an important broadcast, people would get a text."

"I can't imagine there are a whole lot of people who signed up," Sparks said with a sigh. "I went here, and the radio station wasn't that good."

"Some is better than none though, right?" Ben asked.

She chuckled dryly. "Thanks for the optimism." They reached the third floor and entered the broadcast room. Ben secured the door once again and then headed into the booth to check the computer. Sparks grabbed one of the notepads and a pen and jotted down a few bullet points for what she needed to say, as well as uncrumpling the paper Dr. Alvison had given her.

"Hey, Sparks, I found the message app," Ben called from the booth. "What do you want me to say?"

"Just say there is an emergency broadcast in two minutes," she replied, and at the sound of his fingers hitting keys, she took a few deep breaths. She muttered to herself, running over the way she wanted to give her speech.

Ben hit enter and poked his head out of the booth. "Are you ready?"

"Let's do it," Sparks replied with a firm nod. "Just be sure to record it so we can set it to repeat."

He set it up and started the broadcast as she entered the booth and took a seat. The LIVE button flickered on and she straightened her back.

"Hello everyone, this is an emergency broadcast, so if you can, please listen carefully," Sparks began, and cleared her throat. "My name is Lacy Sparks, and I'm an officer with the Austin Police Department. I have been working with Homeland Security under the direction of Special Agent Harris, who was assigned to Austin.

"Three days ago, there was a bio-terrorist attack in Austin that sickened a lot of people, and has turned them into the zombies that you have no doubt encountered. We don't know a lot about the virus, but I will share what I know. It is airborne, and it targets everyone with an A blood type. If you or someone you know has A blood type, they need to be quarantined immediately. Do *not* try to get to the hospital or attempt treatment, as there is no cure.

"The virus turns the victim within seventy-two hours of infection, and is preceded by flu-like symptoms. Once someone turns, they will attack everyone in their vicinity by attempting to bite. If you are bitten, regardless of blood type, you will be infected too. If you encounter one of these creatures, do *not* attempt to communicate or reason with them. Either run away or destroy the brain.

"To the feds who are hopefully listening, you need to send someone to the Texas State University Campus and Dr. Alvison's lab. It's on the third floor of the science building. There is a treasure trove of research that will hopefully save lives there. The entry point is on the roof, however, be ready when you enter the lab as Dr. Alvison and two others may be reanimated there and ready to attack.

"To any survivors in the San Marcos area who are listening." Sparks swallowed hard and took another deep breath. "It's now eight o' seven PM on day zero. There are a small group of us who are going to attempt to escape via the Guadalupe River. We are leaving at the end of this broadcast and are headed to Canyon Lake. If anyone does make it out, we will leave a notice of where we stop on the river. It's rural and sparsely populated, which is our only real chance and survival.

"Once this thing fully hits Austin and San Antonio, there will be hundreds of thousands of those things running through the streets. If you are thinking of trying to ride this out, I implore you not to. There is no help coming. This virus will end everything. From this moment forward, for all intents and purposes, we are on our own. I know that's not an easy thing to hear, but it's our reality." Another beat, another deep breath. She looked to Ben, and he gave her a thumbs up and an encouraging smile. "This message will be left on repeat for as long as the station has power. Good luck," she finished, and nodded to him.

Ben switched off the live feed and set the recording to repeat. After a few seconds, her message started again over the airwaves.

"How'd I do?" Sparks asked.

"You did well, Sparks," Ben said with another smile as he stood up. "You did well."

"Come on," she replied, and cocked her gun. "We hopefully have a ride to catch."

CHAPTER TEN

Tuesday, 8:06 P.M.

Jackson backed the SUV into an alley and killed the lights. He and Jeff held their breaths for a beat, straining their ears. There was no sign of any zombies following, having gone after Slayer to trample Ashley's body in an attempt to get to her phone in the window.

"I think we lost them," Jackson breathed, and then his vision exploded in fireworks as Jeff's fist connected with his face.

The skinhead went in for another lunge across the seat, but the strike leader cocked his gun.

"Calm the fuck down there, cowboy," Jackson warned.

"You motherfucker," Jeff growled, "you just murdered that girl."

"That girl was fucking useless," Jackson snapped. "What good is a ninety pound waif going to do in this situation?"

"So, what," his reluctant partner replied, throwing his hands up. "You just going to kill everyone who isn't useful?"

"Well, it's the only reason I haven't pulled this trigger yet." Jackson sneered and leaned forward a touch. "You have skills I can use that will help me survive. That's all I care about. Now, are you going to shut up and keep being useful? Or do I have to end you right here and now?"

Jeff scowled, but lowered his hands. He turned in his seat to face the front of the vehicle and let out a deep sigh.

"That's a good doggy," Jackson cooed. "Now, when we pick them up, you don't say a goddamn thing. You got it?" He slung his hand over the wheel as his passenger nodded in defeat.

"*This message will be left on repeat for as long as the station has power,*" Spark's voice said over the radio. "*Good luck.*"

"Sounds like they're done," Jackson said, starting the engine and putting the SUV in drive. "Let's go get them." He rounded the corner, but a few of the zombie stragglers began following behind. "Shit, they spotted us." He furrowed his brow in thought.

"Remember asshole," Jeff spoke up, breaking into his train of thought. "I don't know the way to the escape point." The strike leader grimaced before punching the accelerator in the direction of the radio building.

Tuesday 8:10 P.M.

Ben had his hand resting on the deadbolt, ready to throw the door open at a moment's notice. There was a *honk-honk* in the distance and he furrowed his brow.

"That can't be good," he muttered.

Sparks cocked her gun. "Get ready to move." He unlocked the deadbolt, and they both dropped to their knees a bit to be ready to spring. As soon as the SUV rounded the corner, he threw open the door and the two darted outside.

Sparks grasped the handle as soon as the vehicle was within range and flung the door open. Zombies hurtled towards them as Ben dove in and she leapt up after him.

"I'm in, go!" she screamed, and Jackson punched the accelerator.

"Where is Ashley?" Ben looked around the SUV maniacally, even looking over the backseat into the trunk. "Where the fuck is Ashley?!"

"She didn't make it, kid, now shut the fuck up and let me drive," Jackson replied, and the student launched himself into the front seat. Sparks lashed out and grabbed his shoulders, wrestling him back with her.

"It's okay," she whispered, and he struggled to steady his breathing, throwing her arms off of him.

"Sparks," Jackson prompted, "where the fuck am I going?"

"We gotta get on highway 308," she replied, keeping an eye on Ben as he leaned his head back, closing his eyes.

"That doesn't help me," Jackson warned.

Sparks turned to face front and her heart skipped a beat. "Turn left now!" She cried, and he skidded over the sidewalk, tires squealing. He slammed on the brakes at the sight of a zombie horde blocking the road.

"Ideas?" he drawled.

"This thing have four-wheel drive?" Sparks pursed her lips.

Jackson raised an eyebrow. "Yeah." The zombies realized there was a meal on wheels in front of them and started to move towards the SUV, groaning and snapping.

"Hit the field, try and stay as close to true south west as you can," Sparks instructed.

"Good enough for me," Jackson agreed and hit the gas, turning to the left and directly into a chain-link fence. The SUV tore through it like butter, but the bumpy field was a lot slower than the vehicle's capabilities on pavement. "Not the swiftest of getaways." He glanced in the rearview mirror where the zombies were keeping pace with them.

"Just keep going straight," Sparks said, pulling up a map on her phone she'd retrieved from the floor. "In a couple of miles we should hit the road. When you do, hang a left." Jackson made a noise of affirmation, and Sparks turned to check on Ben.

"You okay?" she asked quietly.

"No, I'm not," he seethed. "Once we're out of danger, I'm going to find out what the fuck happened to her." He leaned forward. "You hear me?!"

Jeff clenched his fists in the front seat, biting down on the inside of his cheek to keep from saying anything.

CHAPTER ELEVEN

Tuesday 8:37 P.M.

"Clear," Jackson called from the back of the boat shop.

"Clear," Sparks called back, and the bell jingled as Jeff secured the door, standing watch. "Ben, get behind the counter and see if you can find some keys to the boats outside," she instructed. "Having a motor boat is going to get us a lot further than a canoe."

He nodded and headed to the counter, ducking down to check all the shelves and drawers.

"We have survivors," Jeff called, and both the redhead and Jackson ran to the window, watching a young couple sprint to the pier. Two zombies emerged from behind a stack of canoes and made a beeline for them, but they continued trying to get to the boats.

The zombies tackled them and chowed down, the sounds of snapping and gurgling echoing off of the water.

"Motherfucker," Jackson muttered as the couple reanimated, effectively doubling the amount of enemies outside.

"Jackson, what's your ammo looking like?" Sparks asked as she checked her clip.

There was a series of clicks as he checked his own. "Mostly full mag, one in reserve, you?"

"On my last mag," she replied.

"Think we can get four headshots on moving targets in the dark?" Jackson asked wryly.

"Maybe with a scoped AR-15," Sparks scoffed. "Not liking the odds with a handgun."

"Well, whatever we're going to do, we'd better do it before the horde gets here," Jeff pointed out. "Four against four is a lot better than four against four hundred."

"Ben, you got keys?" Sparks asked.

"Yeah, not much else, though." He stood up from behind the counter, a handful of silver in his hand. "Just some knives. No guns."

Sparks nodded. "Grab the knives." She glanced over at a stack of wooden oars, picking up a few to inspect them. She brought one down over her knee, testing the strength.

"What, you want to beat them to death?" Jackson asked, skepticism in his voice.

"We're going to do a little teamwork," Sparks replied, slinging an oar over her shoulder, satisfied. "You guys are going to run ahead of us and use the oars to clothesline them. When they are on the ground, Ben and I will finish them off with the knives."

"You've got to be fucking kidding me." Jackson rolled his eyes.

She put a hand on her hip and shot him a level stare. "Well, we have a matter of minutes before we're overrun, so if you have a better idea, I'm all ears."

He contemplated for a moment before letting out a disgruntled sigh. "Give me the oar." He held out his hand and she plonked the length of wood into it.

Ben handed her a knife and they followed their oar-wielding teammates outside.

"You ready?" Jackson held the impromptu weapon out in front of him.

Jeff grinned. "Whenever you're ready, sunshine.

Jackson let out a yell in response, grabbing the attention of the four zombies meandering around the pier. The living men sprinted towards them, holding their oars up in perfect position as the zombies came at them.

Jeff's oar hit with tremendous force, sending both of his zombies flipping back onto the sandy ground. Jackson wasn't so lucky, his oar snapping in two with the first opponent. He slammed directly into

the last one, tumbling them both to the
ground.

Ben and Sparks darted in behind Jeff
and stabbed his two in the face before
they could scramble back up. Jackson's
first managed to get halfway up before the
skinhead swung and took its feet out,
giving Sparks an opening to stab it in the
temple.

Jackson cried out, on the bottom of a
wrestling match with his opponent. He held
the zombie's throat, twisting his head
just out of reach of snapping teeth, and
then got a grip on his broken oar. He
shoved it directly through his attacker's
head and kicked the body off of him as
blood spewed everywhere.

"Yeah, thanks for the help there,
asshole!" he snapped as he got to his
feet, glaring at Jeff.

The skinhead shrugged."Hey, I carried
my weight."

Before a tussle broke out, the sound
of shuffling feet and groaning wafted in
from the distance, and the quartet glanced
around at each other.

"Finish this later guys, we gotta
go," Sparks barked, and ran towards the
motorboat at the end of the pier. Ben
stayed hot on her heels, and Jackson
simply cocked his gun while staring Jeff
down.

"You'd better watch yourself, boy," he said darkly and walked off towards the others.

Jeff stood motionless for a moment, deliberating.

Ben turned back when he realized he didn't hear the others coming, and his jaw dropped at the sight of Jeff smacking Jackson in the back of the head with his oar.

The strike leader hit the wood with a thud, fumbling his gun. It slid across the pier to the student's feet, and he took in a sharp breath. Sparks whipped around at the sound, drawing her own gun.

Jeff stepped over Jackson's groaning frame and picked up the gun, handing it to Ben.

"Jeff, what the hell are you doing?!" Sparks cried.

"The right thing," he replied, and put his hand on the young man's shoulder. "That motherfucker killed Ashley. Just pushed her into a couple of them so he could escape."

Jackson staggered to his feet, and a ragged breath escaped Ben's throat. He raised the gun with a shaking hand, blinking back tears.

"I did what needed to be done so we could *all* survive," Jackson said, raising his hands as the horde noises grew in volume.

"Kill this asshole and let's go," Jeff prompted, and Ben aimed the gun. He clenched his jaw and then lowered it as the horde emerged from the tree line, closing in on them.

"I'm not going to kill him," Ben said, and the strike leader breathed a sigh of relief. But after the crack of a gunshot he clutched his exploded kneecap and hit the pier again. "But they will," Ben added in satisfaction.

"Goddamn that's cold-blooded," Jeff said with a grin. "I like it."

"Come on, we gotta move!" Sparks screamed, untying the boat. Jeff and Ben raced over and hopped in as she fired up the engine, propelling them out onto the water. The guys watched with pride as the zombies overtook Jackson, his screams quickly muffled by the thick pile of rotting flesh on top of him.

"I'm so sorry man," Jeff said, and patted Ben's shoulder. "I wasn't close enough to her when it happened."

"It's okay, Jeff," the young man replied. "I know you would have saved her if you could." They turned to Sparks, who hit the throttle to speed the boat off into the darkness.

They were out of immediate danger.

For now.

END OF BOOK ONE

DEAD TEXAS
BOOK TWO: NO COMFORT
BY DEREK SLATON
© 2018

CHAPTER ONE

Two hours.

Two long hours since the trio of survivors had escaped the zombie horde at the docks, and they still didn't feel safe. Even though it had barely been a day, they'd gotten to used to the danger, the constant battle for their lives, that it was difficult to relax.

In two hours, it was difficult to have hope.

Two hours since Ben had avenged the murder of his girlfriend by putting a bullet in Agent Jackson's kneecap, leaving him to be food for the enemy. Two hours of slowly bobbing up the Guadalupe River in their attempt to escape the horror and make it out west.

"How's the fuel looking, Sparks?" Jeff asked, running a hand over his bald head.

"Not too good," Officer Lacy Sparks replied. "The current is picking up a bit though, so I think we could cut it and coast. Water is getting a little shallow for my tastes. Last thing we need is to blow out the motor by hitting some rocks." The redhead motioned to the rocks at the bottom of the river.

"Not a bad idea." Jeff nodded. "If some of those things spot us, it would be good to have the ability to make a speedy getaway." He glanced at the kid, pursing his lips. "Yo Ben, how you doing man?" Jeff asked gently, but there was no response.

His dark-skinned companion hadn't said a thing the entire trip. His eyes were glazed over, staring into nothingness, still in shock.

Jeff softly put his hand on Ben's shoulder, and the kid still didn't say anything, but turned a steely glare at the older man. The skinhead immediately removed his hand, nodding and backing off.

"Just give him some time, Jeff," Sparks said quietly, and her companion nodded in agreement.

The only sound between the three of them was the babbling trickle of water, and had it been any other situation, it might have even been soothing.

An explosion racked the stillness of the night, and they all startled, tensing right back up again.

"What the fuck was that?!" Jeff exclaimed.

"Sounds like it's coming from up ahead," Sparks replied, brow furrowing.

"I thought we weren't going to be coming close to civilization?" he responded with a snarky question.

The redhead pulled out her phone and opened up a GPS app.

"The 281 bridge is just up ahead," she said. "If this thing has hit San Antonio it's possible people are already trying to get away."

Jeff grunted as he grasped the two emergency oars, extending one to Ben. "I know you're hurting man, but we might need you to paddle here in a minute."

The kid eyed the oar reluctantly, reaching out to accept it before turning to continue his staring into the darkness. Jeff stood at the bow of the boat, steering it as best he could in the dark around a bend.

A gasp escaped Sparks' lips at the sight of the bridge of flaming wreckage. There was a massive pileup of cars, one at the far end on fire. Without a fire department to deal with the blaze, it made its way from car to car, detonating them as they go.

"You think someone's in there?" Jeff asked, motioning to a trapped car surrounded by zombies.

"If there is, there's nothing we can do for them," Sparks replied, clenching her jaw. They watched helplessly as the fire spread to the car. A zombie managed to get up on top of the car and upon reaching the sunroof, flying backwards with the *pop pop* of gunfire.

"Fucking hell," Jeff snapped. "Someone *is* in there."

"We have to paddle," Sparks instructed. "And do it now. Watch the rocks. It looks like the river is only a few feet deep here."

Jeff tapped Ben a little harder than was maybe necessary. He wasn't happy about having to leave these people to die; but he knew that it was their only play. The kid nodded and dipped his oar into the water.

They propelled themselves silently under the bridge, holding their breaths to try not to attract any attention. Just as they cleared the other side, there was a scream and another pepper of gunfire.

Sparks turned just as a body fell from the bridge, the sickening crack of a spine making them all wince as it hit the water. A few more splashes as half a dozen zombies flopped down.

"Might be a good time for the motor," Jeff piped up as the zombies managed to pick themselves up from the rocks and stagger through the water at them.

"We need about thirty more yards to clear the rocks," Sparks replied with a shake of her head. "And I wouldn't worry, they look far too damaged to keep up with us."

"I think we're good, Sparks," Jeff agreed as they floated into a deeper portion of the river, the zombies struggling to keep their heads above water.

She nodded and fired up the motor, steering them into the darkness once again.

CHAPTER TWO

The engine let out a few rough chugs before shutting off completely.

"Well, that's all she wrote on the motor," Sparks said, and the guys dipped their oars back into the water to continue paddling.

"What the hell time is it, anyway?" Jeff asked after a few strokes.

She checked her phone. "Close to one."

"We really should be thinking of finding some shelter soon," he suggested. "We need to get some rest."

Sparks opened up the GPS again. "Looks like there are some structures about a mile upriver. Could be some houses."

"Here's hoping it's some rich people wanting the river lifestyle, and not the Deliverance kind of river people," Jeff grunted on the upstroke.

She couldn't help but chuckle in reply. "So you prefer champagne over moonshine, I take it?"

"I prefer thousand thread count sheets of the prospect of squealing like a pig," he said.

"No argument there," Sparks agreed.

Before long, they paddled up to a dock that led to a large two-story home.

As they bumped against the wood, Sparks leapt out and tied off the boat.

"Well, there you go, Jeff," she said, wiping her hands on her pants. "Looks like we're sleeping in style this evening."

"After the day we've had it's about time we caught a fucking break," he said with a roll of his eyes. "And look, the power is still on, too. Hopefully that means cold beer."

"First things first," Sparks pulled out her handgun and cocked it. "We have to make sure we're alone."

Ben held out his gun to Jeff, who raised an eyebrow as he took it.

"Why don't you hang onto this, man?" the skinhead asked. "I can handle myself."

Ben pulled out his knife and stuck it between his teeth, cracking his knuckles before taking hold of the blade again. "I'm good."

Jeff shrugged as the kid led the way at a brisk pace, his companions following close behind, guns at the ready. He flung open the door and stalked straight in, Sparks and Jeff flanking him, each taking a side to make sure the main floor of the house was clear.

Ben led them into the living room and clenched his jaw.

"Come and get me, motherfuckers!" he screamed suddenly, causing both Sparks and

Jeff to startle, whipping around to stare at him, wide eyed.

A zombie barreled out of the kitchen, a formerly well dressed soccer mom covered head to toe in blood.

"Ben, get down!" Sparks cried, trying to line up a shot. He ignored her, standing his ground as the woman screeched towards him. When she was within grabbing distance, he ducked and grabbed her thighs, standing up and slamming her down onto her back. As soon as she hit the floor, Ben leapt onto her chest, stabbing her in the face repeatedly.

"Die, die, *DIE*!" he cried, tears streaming down his face as he continued to stab the zombie long after she stopped flopping around.

Jeff and Sparks shared a worried glance.

"Why don't you clear the house?" the skinhead asked. "I got this." He inclined his head to the maniacal kid and she nodded, moving quietly out of the living room.

As soon as she was gone, Jeff walked over and shoved Ben with all his might, sending him to the floor. The knife clattered and skittered away.

"What the fuck, man?" Ben growled.

"What the fuck indeed?" Jeff asked, kneeling down to get right in his companion's face. "What's wrong with you?"

"I just don't care anymore, man," the boy seethed.

Jeff bristled. "Well you need to start fucking caring."

"Why?" Ben threw his hands up. "Ashley is fucking gone, man. What do I have to live for?"

"Oh, boo fuckity hoo," the skinhead replied with disdain, voice raising an octave. "Like you are the only one who's ever lost someone."

"I…" Ben's lips flapped like a fish. "Uh, but…"

"Yeah, that shut you the fuck up, didn't it?" Jeff snapped. "No more kiddie gloves for you." He grabbed Ben's collar and lifted him from the floor, shoving him down onto the couch before flopping down next to him. "Look man, I know you're hurting. I've been there. When I was fifteen, I watched my brother die, and worse, it was my fault.

"We were dicking around at a construction site and I knocked over a pallet of rebar when I was playing on the second floor. I didn't know my younger brother was below me. That shit just cut right through him.

"I lost my way for a long time after that. Hell, it's how I eventually ended up with these." He patted his chest where his tattoos were. "So I know where you are coming from. Unfortunately, we don't have the luxury of you going through a self-destructive phase, or hell, even a grieving period right now.

"You need to keep your head on straight and focus on the task at hand, which is surviving to see another day. And if you ever start thinking it's not worth it, just remember, in a matter of weeks you could be one of the smartest people on earth. And if we survive long enough that might actually be valuable." He tapped his temple.

Ben sighed. "Thanks, Jeff," he said quietly, nodding.

Jeff clapped him on the back. "Anytime, brother."

"We're all clear," Sparks said, striding back into the room. "Doors are locked and nobody else is in the house. Well, nobody else alive."

"How bad is it?" Jeff asked.

"Let's just say we're sleeping on the couch tonight," she told him. "Unless you want to do a load of laundry for the sheets."

"Couch works for me," he agreed, and stood up. "But first, we need nourishment.

In the meantime, why don't y'all try and dial us up some news."

"I didn't realize you were a gourmet, Jeff," Sparks said in an amused tone as she sank down onto the love seat.

"You should temper your expectations a bit," he admitted as he headed to the kitchen. "However, I do make the best bachelor chow this side of the Red River."

"If it means I don't have to cook, I'm all for it," the redhead smiled, and he returned it just before he disappeared from the living room.

Ben clicked the button on the TV remote, but there was nothing but static. "Damn, nothing," he murmured.

"Try some of the twenty-four-hour news stations, they've gotta have something," Sparks suggested, leaning forward as he flipped through the channels.

"Doesn't look like they have cable or satellite," Ben said as he got through them all. "And all the local channels are out."

"Who the hell doesn't have TV these days?" Sparks scoffed.

"Check that laptop over there, they might have wi-fi," he said and motioned to the desk in the corner.

"Good call," she agreed and strode over, opening it. It was on, but she was met with a password screen. "Well, so much for that." She sighed as she pulled out her phone. "And of course no reception, so we're in the dark."

Ben found another remote on the couch and pointed it at the TV, triggering the stereo system. He flicked to the FM channels and soon Sparks' voice came out of the speakers—her recorded message.

"Tuned in to college radio?" She raised an eyebrow. "That may be a first."

"No, this is 102.9," Ben replied, shaking his head. "So another station must have picked up the broadcast and is replaying it." He hit scan, and every station they found was playing the same broadcast.

Sparks' heart skipped a beat as she sank back down onto the couch. "Well, we did our part, we got the word out," she said as Ben clicked off the stereo.

"Now we just have to hope it did some good," he replied.

Jeff emerged from the kitchen carrying three beer bottles. "I hope y'all are hungry," he said with a grin. "Just put a frozen pizza in the oven. Looked like there were at least four different kinds of meat on there!"

"I'm a vegetarian." Sparks deadpanned.

Jeff stopped in his tracks. "Oh, I mean…" he motioned behind him. "I think there was a head of lettuce in the fridge." He pursed his lips, looking defeated.

Her face erupted into a massive smile and she laughed. "Sorry, Jeff, I couldn't resist," she said as she waved him forward. "I mean come on dude, I'm a police officer. I have a hard enough time being taken seriously in the precinct without opening myself up to a barrage of 'well I got some meat you'd like to eat' jokes."

"Thank fucking Christ," Jeff said with a sigh, extending a beer to her.

The trio leaned back into the cushions, taking a sip of ice cold beer to enjoy a well deserved break from the horrors of the day.

CHAPTER THREE

The sun shone cheerfully down on the dock, illuminating the trio of survivors as they loaded up as much as they could onto the small boat.

"How much gas have we got?" Sparks asked as Jeff hauled two mid-sized cans into the watercraft.

"I siphoned off ten gallons from their SUVs, so that should get us pretty far upriver," he replied. "Although in retrospect, I should have done this before having coffee. All I can taste at the moment is Exxon."

Ben opened the small box of food they'd managed to pack from the kitchen and produced a half fun can of salted nuts. "Here, this should help with the taste some."

"Thanks," Jeff said as he popped the top and took a handful.

"Whoa whoa whoa, easy there," Ben said, putting up a hand. "These rich folk are all about eating healthy, which means there wasn't a lot in the way of non-perishables. We have maybe two days worth of food here before we're out."

The skinhead sighed and dumped half of the handful back into the can, tossing it back to Ben as Sparks untethered the boat from the dock.

"Well, captain?" he asked through a mouthful of nuts. "How are we lookin'?"

"Looking pretty good for the time being," Sparks replied as the boat floated lazily away from the docks. "We got a lot of river ahead of us before we hit any sort of civilization."

"Define civilization," Jeff said, raising a concerned eyebrow.

"Don't know really," the redhead admitted. "The river runs right into a town called Comfort."

He shrugged. "That doesn't sound too bad."

"Well, it's on the I-10 and it's large enough to have a truck stop," she warned. "So it could potentially be trouble."

"Well, that's future us's problem," Jeff replied, propping his feet up on the side of the boat. "I say for right now, we sit back, relax, and enjoy the scenery." He playfully waved her off. "Captain, away we go."

She chuckled and rolled her eyes, firing up the engine.

Sparks killed the motor as the boat approached a dried up portion of river, floating as far as the boat allowed until it bumped into dirt.

"Now what?" Jeff asked.

Sparks studied the GPS app on her phone. "We're still several miles from Comfort, but it looks like if we cut through the woods in that direction we'll come up on a small township," she said. "Doesn't look that big, like the size of a neighborhood."

"Lead on Captain, unless you think the better course of action is to sit in a dried-up riverbed eating snack food until the sun goes down." The skinhead was already stepping out of the boat.

"Alright, let's go experience small town Texas," she agreed, and tried to offer Ben a smile. He avoided her gaze, simply exiting the boat with his knife in his hand.

Sparks led the trio through the overgrowth. They were lucky it wasn't too thick, and soon they came upon a two lane road. There was a tree line on one side and a farm with a white picket fence on the other.

"Stay alert," she instructed, cocking her gun and starting down the farm side of the road. "If something jumps out of the trees, be ready to get over that fence." They moved down the road, eyes darting all around, though the air was still and quiet.

"So, do we want to find a house to bed down for the night?" Ben spoke up, startling the other two. "I don't like the idea of being this exposed once the sun goes down."

"We will, but we need to make sure we aren't in a bad situation first," Sparks replied. "The center of town, if you want to call it that, is at that intersection up ahead. If we don't see anything major, we'll find us someplace for the night."

When they reached the four-way stop, it seemed like there was nothing major. There were no zombies, no people, and no cars save for one truck sitting outside of the country store.

"Looks like the entire town just bolted," Jeff commented.

Sparks shrugged. "Can you blame them?"

"Well what do ya'll say to picking up some beer and snacks from the store before breaking into a home for the night?" he asked, a spring in his step as he moved towards the store.

Ben nodded. "Yeah, I can eat."

Jeff reached for the doorknob, but Sparks grabbed his wrist, raising her gun.

"Hold on, listen," she hissed, and the other two did so. There was a faint banging sound from inside the store, and she left the door to pick up a few metal planter sticks. "Don't waste bullets unless you have to," she said as she handed them to her comrades, holstering her gun. "Follow my lead. Ben, you stay behind Jeff."

They nodded in agreement, and she opened the door, leading the way into the small store. There were four aisles of goods, candy and chips, with a small cooler of drinks to the right. The banging came from two zombies behind the counter, slamming into a closed windowed office door.

Sparks waved to Jeff and held up her metal rod, motioning that he should be ready with his. He joined her at the counter.

"Hey boys," she said, and slammed her hand down on the wood, drawing the attention of their enemies.

The zombies screeched and ran full tilt at them, slamming their torsos so hard into the counter that their heads lurched forward. In unison, Sparks and Jeff stabbed forward, rods boring into brain.

"Bold move there," Jeff commended as the bodies flopped to the floor.

Sparks lifted the hinged part of the counter and skirted behind to make sure the zombies were dead. "Well, after the bridge, it dawned on me that these things aren't that bright. Figured this would work." She winked at him.

The office door slammed open, causing the trio to startle and whip to the sight of a muscular man with white hair holding a pump-action shotgun.

"Who in the ever loving fuck are you assholes?" he demanded, voice gruff.

"Whoa, easy there old timer, we don't mean you any harm," Sparks replied, raising her palms to him. "These are my friends Ben and Jeff. I'm Sparks."

"Aw hell, girl," he lowered his weapon, a huge smile breaking out across his aged face. "I know you."

"Yeah, she's the one from the radio," Ben put in, lowering his own hands.

"Radio?" The man furrowed his brow and shook his head. "What in the hell you talking about, boy? This here's Lacy Sparks. I saw her whoop the Dudek Brothers' asses in that Texas Death Match a while back to claim the championship belt. Man that cowbell's a bitch, ain't it?"

Sparks laughed, scratching the back of her head. "Yeah, you ain't kidding, old timer."

"You did *what*?" Jeff blurted.

She shrugged. "I'm also a pro-wrestler."

"Alrighty then." He simply said, unable to even be surprised anymore.

"Well little lady, you can call me Rufus," the white-haired man introduced. "But before we exchange any more pleasantries, it'd be good to secure the joint. Pretty much everyone has gotten the fuck outta dodge, or they barricaded themselves into their homes to die in peace. But I think we'd all feel a lot safer knowing that we're locked in."

Jeff nodded. "Agreed."

"Now if you fellas wouldn't mind tossing these critters out the front door, I'll get us some beverages." Rufus motioned to the zombie bodies. "And it ain't much, but I have some sleepin' bags in the back. Probably not a good idea to be out after dark. And don't worry ma'am, you can have my cot for the night."

"Oh, that's sweet, Rufus," Sparks said, sincerity lacing her tone. "But you don't have to give up your bed for me."

"Well you done stole my heart after you landed a flying dropkick off of the top rope, so stealin' my bed for the night ain't no big deal," he replied with a wink, and she chuckled.

"Thank you Rufus, you're too kind." She offered him a genuine smile.

He waved for her to follow him. "Come on, let's go get you something to drink."

"Everybody's dinner okay?" Rufus asked, motioning to the microwaved burritos on the table. "I know it ain't Taco Bell fancy, but I hope it works for ya."

Jeff swallowed a huge mouthful. "It's fantastic Rufus, thank you," he said, and Ben simply raised his finger in an *a-okay* sign as he stuffed his face. Sparks nodded in agreement as she chased her own mouthful with beer.

Rufus cracked open a second beer, mouth set in a thin line. "It's getting really bad out there, ain't it?" he asked.

"End of the world bad, Rufus," Sparks said. "End of the world bad."

"It's a damn shame," he replied with a shake of his head. "I know I ain't got much, but I enjoyed most of my life and wasn't quite ready for it to end."

"Most of your life?" Jeff cocked an eyebrow. "What, were you married, too?" A chuckle rippled around the small apartment.

"Ha, I like this one." Their white-haired host waggled a finger at his guest. "Now, never quite made it that far I'm afraid. Had a girl when I was younger, but didn't work out the way I'd hoped."

"So what happened?" Ben asked.

"'Nam happened," Rufus replied with a shrug. "Did two tours in the jungle and didn't come back the same. I didn't blame her for leavin' me. Hell, I'd have left me too. She moved to the big city shortly after then, and my pops brought me into the family business. Been workin' at this little country store ever since. I mean, it ain't the exciting life like being a pro-wrestler, but it worked for me."

"Well Rufus, if you've wanted some excitement in your life, I think you're about to get it." Sparks finished her burrito and wiped her mouth, leaning back with her beer.

"Now Sparks, I gotta warn ya," Rufus continued, "my doctor hasn't given me the okay to do what you are proposing, but I'm totally willing to roll the dice. Frankly I can't think of a better way to go out."

"Had a little something different in mine, but just for the record," Sparks said with a sly wink, "you wouldn't survive the night with me."

"Well, if you ever hear me beg for death, that's what I'm askin' for," he replied with a wink of his own.

"Duly noted Rufus," she said with a laugh, and then leaned forward with a sigh. "Back to my original point however, I think you should come with us when we continue our journey west in the morning."

"I don't know lil' lady, it's tempting." He shook his head. "But I'd really hate to abandon this place."

"You'll get to shoot a lot of things," Jeff interjected.

Rufus stroked his chin. "Will I get to blow shit up?"

Sparks and Jeff shared a look and a shrug.

"If the situation arises, yeah," she agreed. "You're officially our blowing shit up expert."

"Well hell, I'm in," Rufus replied, a grin erupting on his weathered face. "Once the sun comes up, we'll throw everything we can in the truck and head up the road to the truck stop in Comfort. Once we're gassed up, we'll head out on the highway."

CHAPTER FOUR

"Alright, that's the last of it," Jeff said as he heaved the last case of bottled water into the back of the truck. Rufus had a stash of a few months worth of MRE's, which was a godsend for an apocalypse like this.

"Man, this is some good stuff," Ben commented as he sipped at the large cup of coffee in his hand. "Ya'll need to try this."

"Oh ya like that, do ya?" Rufus asked. "It's a Vietnam brand I fell in love with when I was over there. Been importing it since the seventies. It's like crack in a cup."

Jeff snapped his fingers. "I'll have to get in on that."

"And after we're properly caffeinated, are we ready to hit the road?" Sparks asked.

"Almost," Rufus replied. "Need y'all to follow me, if you will." He led them around the store to a separate entrance that was padlocked tight. He unlocked it and tossed the chain aside, opening it into a storage room.

There was a massive gun safe inside, and after he punched in a multi-digit code, he opened it to reveal a cache of weapons.

"Holy shit, Rufus," Ben breathed.

The older man squared his shoulders. "'Murica. Get some." He turned to the trio, whose mouths were on the ground. "Well go on, don't be shy. Get you some weapons. Just leave the M-16 to me. That beauty kept me alive in the jungle, so kinda hoping it does the same for me in this situation."

Jeff reached out and grabbed the AR-15, handing it over to Sparks immediately. "Here, between the three of us, I feel confident in saying that you are going to put that to the best use."

"Not going to argue that," she agreed, giving him a little salute.

He grinned. "Hey now."

"Did you not see yourself shoot the other night at the house?" She raised an eyebrow.

He nodded. "Point taken."

The guys loaded up the rest of the weapons into the back of the truck, stuffing ammo in between cases of water. Rufus hopped up into the driver's seat and Sparks put a hand on Ben's arm as he started to climb into the bed of the truck.

"You ride shotgun," she said.

"Thanks, but I'll be alright in the back," he replied.

125

"It wasn't a request." Sparks shook her head. "I'm a better shot than you are, and if we get surrounded, I'm going to need to be able to get to the target." He nodded, and she clapped him on the back as he hopped into the cab next to Rufus.

Jeff reached down and took Sparks' hand, pulling her up into the bed with him.

"So, when were you going to tell me you were a pro-wrestler?" He asked in a teasing tone as they took their seats against the back window of the cab.

She shrugged. "You're a middle-aged man living in rural Texas, I kind of assumed you already knew."

"Eh, I'll buy that," Jeff agreed. He smacked the roof of the truck, and Rufus punched the accelerator, taking them towards Comfort.

The journey was short, but as soon as the truck hit the I-10 the road wasn't serene and quiet any longer. Sparks and Jeff popped to one knee and readied their guns.

There were several cars on the side of the highway, some burned out, some overturned, but all off to the side of the road.

Rufus drove slowly towards the truck stop, Sparks and Jeff on high alert. There was a large military style personnel carrier with almost a dozen 55-gallon drums that someone was filling with gas.

A shot rang out, causing Rufus to slam on the brakes, and then eight men in camouflage fatigues stepped out from behind various positions of cover. They aimed their rifles, and the tallest of the crew stepped forward.

"What the fuck, man?" Rufus poked his head out of the window. "We just need a tank of gas and we'll be on our way."

"Sorry old timer," the tall dark-haired soldier replied with a shake of his head. "But you aren't going to need that gas. Because we're taking your truck and everything in it." He motioned to the men flanking him and they started to move forward.

Sparks popped up, leaning on the top of the truck, aiming her gun. "You ain't taking shit, soldier boy."

The man who'd spoken—clearly the leader—chuckled. He held up his hand to stop his men from moving any further.

"Oh, isn't that cute?" He sneered. "A woman who thinks she's tough because she's got a gun. Tell me sweetheart, have you bothered to look at your predicament? We have you flanked and outgunned. What do you think you're going to do, exactly? Take me out? Well I hope you're one hell of a shot because…" He smacked his chest. "Kevlar, bitch. So it's headshot or nothing."

Sparks yawned. "You done yapping?"

"By all means," he said with a flourish. "The floor is yours."

"Well, upon further review, I'm guessing you guys are wannabe soldier boys given the physique on some y'all," she said and cocked her head. "Looks like the last thing they took out was the Country Kitchen buffet. And to answer your other questions, no, I'm not aiming to take you out. I am, however, aiming at the dozen barrels of highly explosive liquid you have sitting in the open not ten feet from where you're standing. So if any of these fat fucks take a single step towards me, we all go up in flames."

He contemplated for a moment before signaling for his men to move back. "So, now what?" he asked.

Before she could respond, there was the roar of an engine in the distance, back from the way the quartet had come.

"Given that your boys look like they just shit themselves," Sparks deduced, "I'm going to assume the people coming up aren't on your side. So I'd suggest you take what you've gotten, consider it a parting gift, and fuck right on off."

"B Company, on the truck," the fake soldier barked and they all piled on their vehicle. "Let's move out!" He glared at Sparks as the truck sped off, gasoline tanks sloshing.

Two pickup trucks screeched in on either side of Rufus, and a middle-aged man with a mustache rolled down the passenger's side window.

"Y'all need to follow us," he demanded.

"Come *on* man." Rufus threw his hands up. "We just need a tank of gas."

"It wasn't a request," the man replied. "Now I'm giving you the benefit of the doubt that you weren't with those militia assholes, but Principal Dan needs to confirm it before we can get you refueled."

"It's alright Rufus," Sparks called down. "Let's take a ride. One Mexican Standoff is all I can handle before breakfast."

Rufus sighed. "You the boss."

The mustached man waved his truck forward, and it sped off. Rufus followed, the other wary truck sticking around to set up a makeshift guard post around the gas pumps.

Sparks sat back down beside Jeff.

"You know you're full of shit, right?" The skinhead asked as she joined him.

She raised an eyebrow. "How so?"

"Come on, you're a highly trained officer of the law," he scoffed. "You know that a bullet can't ignite gasoline. Hell, at that range I'd be surprised if you could even get a bullet through those oil drums."

"Well, you know that, and I know that," she replied, a twinkle in her eyes. "But after looking at them, I assumed they got all their explosion knowledge from Schwarzenegger movies, so for all they knew I was able to blow them all to hell."

"I swear to christ I'm stealing you a wheelbarrow for Christmas, assuming we live that long." Jeff laughed.

She raised an eyebrow. "Why a wheelbarrow?"

"Well you need something to help you carry those gigantic balls around," he replied, and Sparks guffawed.

A few miles north of the gas station, Rufus followed their guide into the parking lot of a relatively new looking high school. It was a hive of activity, pickup trucks filled with supplies coming and going, heavily armed people milling about.

They parked at the far end, away from the bulk of the people.

"Alright," the man who'd originally spoken said as he slid out of his truck. Rufus followed his lead, as did Ben, and Sparks and Jeff hopped down. Their four new acquaintances faced them in a line, the two sides standing tall. "Before we take you to Principal Dan, we're going to need your weapons."

"Yeah, that isn't going to happen," Sparks spoke up.

The man put his finger on the trigger. "I'm not asking."

"Look man, use some common sense here." She rolled her eyes. "If we were going to attack you it would have been on the road while you were isolated. All we wanted was a tank of gas, and you insisted we go to the Principal's office first. And that's fine, we'll jump through your hoops to get what we need."

He tapped his finger on the trigger. "Again. I'm not asking."

"You're also not listening," Sparks replied. "We don't know you, we don't trust you, and in case you missed the headline of the day, we're in the middle of the goddamn apocalypse. So the only way I'm giving up my gun is if you shoot me."

They stared at each other for a few moments, and then he grunted. "Fine. Walk in front of us with your hands away from your weapons and we won't have a problem."

"Fantastic," Sparks said, voice lighter. "We're making some headway here. So where we going?"

"Head to the tent in the middle of the lot," he instructed.

She extended her arm in front of her like a courteous date. "Shall we, gents?" The boys started walking, and she kept pace with them as their new acquaintances followed.

A man with sandy brown hair in a bright red polo shirt stood six feet tall barking orders like a General during war time. It looked a bit ridiculous with his khaki pants and the high school crest, but his personality commanded respect as he directed the busy bees around him.

"Alright, the last report I got said that the two teams clearing out the neighborhood east of Highway 87 was running into some problems with the apartment complexes," he said to the group of armed men and women standing around a folding table. There was a map on it and he pointed to the area he was talking about. "They lost a few people securing the houses and the zombie population was way higher than anticipated at the apartments. I need y'all to head up there and back them up."

The oldest male in the group nodded and motioned to the others, who followed him out from under the big patio tent.

"Principal Dan," the mustached man piped up.

Dan sighed, not looking up from his map. "What is it, Cody?"

"Caught these people trying to steal gas from the truck stop," Cody said. "Don't know if they're militia or not."

"Well given we were in a goddamn armed standoff with the militia when you found us, it's a good fucking bet that we're not," Rufus snapped gruffly.

"Cody?" Dan asked.

"We got there as the militia was driving off," the mustached man replied. "But yeah, it appears they weren't exchanging pleasantries."

Dan stepped around the table. "Thanks Cody, I'll take it from here." He put his hands in his pockets and leaned against the table. "Please forgive him for being a little overzealous, it's been a rough few days."

Jeff barked a laugh. "That's an understatement."

"I'm Principal Dan, used to run this High School," he introduced. "Now I kind of run all of this."

"This is Jeff, Ben, and that cantankerous coot there is Rufus," Sparks

133

motioned to her crew. "You can call me Sparks."

"Sparks?" The Principal looked shocked. "Officer Sparks, from the radio?"

She nodded. "The same."

"A lot of people standing here today, myself included, owe you a debt of gratitude," he said, extending his hand to shake. "As soon as I heard that message I got a few teachers and came down here to the school to open it up as a shelter. We started warning everybody we could, and it gave us a fighting chance."

"Well it seems like you've done a hell of a job so far," Sparks replied after she shook his hand.

"Not as good as I would have liked," he admitted. "We're only a town of twenty-five hundred, but we've lost a lot of people in the last couple of days. It's been open warfare in the streets and in homes. We have cleanup crews going door to door trying to secure the town, but as you may have overheard, we're losing people at an alarming rate."

"Dan, it's admirable that you want to clean up the town," Sparks said gently. "But you really need to be focused on moving the survivors out west."

"I'm sorry." He shook his head firmly. "But this is our home, and we aren't leaving without a fight."

"You don't get it, sooner or later, San Antonio is going to evacuate," Sparks replied. "It may be survivors, or it may be a horde of zombies. In either case, they will swallow this town whole."

"We're aware of the possibility, and have taken precautions," Dan assured her. "The first morning of this, we expected to be overrun but nobody came. Finally in the afternoon, three cars pulled off to refuel and some of my men spoke to them. Just outside of Boerne, about twenty miles down the road, a tanker truck flipped and exploded. Complete gridlock in both directions after that.

"So if anybody is fleeing San Antonio, zombie or not, they are going to have a difficult time reaching here in any significant numbers. And just in case, I have a couple of scouts set up ten miles down the road to keep an eye out for anything of significance headed our way."

"Well it seems like your mind is made up," Sparks said. "But you need to understand something. No help is coming. We are on our own."

"Oh no, we understand," Dan agreed. "But we're trying to take this one day at a time. And today's task is clearing out the town."

"MEDIC!" a voice in the distance cried, accompanied by screeching tires.

135

Dan led the quartet from the tent, approaching a black pickup truck brandishing a decal for Ricky's Auto Body Shop. A young couple exited the truck, covered from head to toe in blood.

"Medic!" the woman screamed. "We need a medic!"

"Mary, Ricky, what happened?" Dan asked as a group of people in aprons pulled an older man out of the bed of the truck. They helped him towards the school, holding a bloody rag to his bicep.

"The supermarket is a goddamn shitshow of biblical proportions," Ricky replied, running crimson shaking hands through his dark hair.

"Calm down, talk to me," Dan said, voice steady. The young man began to stutter and ramble until the Principal put a firm hand on his shoulder, effectively shutting him up. "Mary, what happened?" Dan addressed the blonde woman.

"We went in the secure the supermarket like you asked, but we were overwhelmed," she replied, shaking her head. "We didn't see too many of them at first, so we thought we could take them out without backup. Ricky split us into two teams of three, with the other squad trying to flank them to create a crossfire. As soon as that first shot rang out, the three zombies we targeted became thirty. They just started pouring out of the back. We unloaded everything we could at them but it wasn't enough. Chuck was with us and you can see he got his arm bitten."

"What about the other team?" Dan furrowed his brow.

"One of them is dead for sure," she continued. "Couldn't tell who it was, but I saw one of them trip while they ran towards the back of the store. I know he didn't make it because the zombies chasing him jumped on top."

"What about the other two?" the Principal asked.

"I honestly don't know," Mary replied, eyes wide and sad. "We had to pull out, but I swear I heard gunshots coming from the back of the store."

"I used to work there as a butcher back in the day," Ricky spoke up, taking a deep breath to steady his voice. "They have a big ass freezer in the back where they keep the meat. If they were able to lock themselves inside they could survive. At least until they froze to death. They like to keep their meat cold, and them boys weren't exactly dressed for winter."

"Alright, I want y'all to hang tight for a few minutes," Dan instructed. "Go get some water and decompress. I think Grandma Suzie even has some sandwiches made up, so y'all better eat while you have the chance. In the meantime, I'll put something together and we'll go get them out of the freezer."

"Thanks, Principal," Mary said, voice thick.

Ricky nodded. "Yeah, thank you." They grasped each other's hands tightly and walked off in search of sandwiches.

"You need to quarantine that bite victim," Sparks said immediately. "That bite will turn him."

"Yeah, I know." Principal Dan sighed. "Learned that lesson the hard way I'm afraid. In my haste to set up a rescue shelter I didn't listen closely enough to your broadcast. We had a med unit set up in one of the classrooms, but somebody turned the first night. Luckily, a nurse was able to lock the room from the inside to prevent an outbreak."

"So, wait, you have a room full of zombies in there?" Jeff's eyes widened.

"Afraid we do." Dan nodded. "But it's locked up tight and closely guarded."

"Well Principal, it seems like you have your hands full at the moment, so if you'll excuse us, we'll be on our way," Sparks said. "If you can spare us a tank of gas that would be swell, but if not we'll make do."

"So, before I say anything else I would like you to know that I really am a nice guy," Dan said slowly, hand lowering to rest on his belt buckle. "If you had met me any other time I would have gladly invited you over for a barbecue. So it pains me to have to do this." He sighed, and Sparks' stomach sank. "We've confiscated your supplies, and if you'd like them back I am going to need your help."

"You motherfucker," Rufus spat. "I've seen cum encrusted Vietnamese prostitutes with more class than you."

"I completely understand your rage," Dan replied, putting up his free hand. "But I hope you understand the position that I'm in. This is a war, and not one we're currently winning. We're only a few days in and if I had to guess, I'd say that there are more of them than there are of us still alive.

"And worse, when one of us falls they typically get back up and join their ranks. Right now it looks like I have two people trapped in an industrial strength freezer that is surrounded by undead cannibals. If you go with Ricky and Mary and help get my people back safe, you can have your supplies and as much fuel as you can carry. You have my word."

The Officer shared a look with her crew and then took a deep breath. "Alright, but I have conditions."

"Within reason, of course," Dan replied.

"Of course," she said. "For starters, I lead the raid. If those two come along, they follow my orders."

Dan nodded. "Ricky is a mechanic and his wife Mary taught Algebra, so I don't see a problem with them being led by someone who knows what they are doing."

"Secondly, Ben stays here," Sparks said.

"What?!" The young man threw his hands up. "Why?"

"Because you're smart, Ben," she explained, turning to him. "Smarter than any of us, and if we can get you to the right people, you can do a lot of good. Not going to risk your life when we don't need to."

"But," he protested, "goddammit, I can help."

"I know," she replied, swallowing hard. "But please do this, for me."

He growled, but nodded, and took a step back.

"Also, if this shit goes sideways and we don't make it back, I want your word that you'll get Ben to a military post," Sparks continued, turning back to Dan. "He was getting his PhD studying this virus stuff, so he needs to hook up with the right people."

"You have my word," the Principal agreed. "Anything else?"

"Yeah, gonna need a notebook and pens," Sparks finished.

He nodded. "I think I can scare that up pretty easily."

"Alright." She turned to her bald companion. "Jeff, you ready?"

He saluted her with his gun. "Yep."

"What about me?" Rufus furrowed his brow.

"Well, we know you're old," Jeff teased. "Didn't know if you needed to sit this out."

"Hell, the whole reason I came along with y'all is because you promised I'd get to shoot some shit." The old man scowled. "Don't tell me ya lied to me."

"Alright, come on Rufus," Sparks chuckled. "Let's go shoot some shit. No explosives though."

He grunted. "Eh, you're no fun."

CHAPTER FIVE

"Park far away from the building," Sparks instructed. "We don't want to alert them that we're here."

Ricky parked in the last available space furthest from the supermarket and killed the engine.

"Rufus, front of the truck," she continued. "Keep an eye on the entrance. No shots unless absolutely necessary."

He saluted with a nod. "Yes ma'am."

"Everybody else, bed of the truck," Sparks waved the others to the back, tossing a notebook down on the open tailgate. She drew a square and put an X on the bottom of it before handing the pen to Ricky. "Alright, I need to know what we're dealing with. This is the store and the X mark is the entrance. What's the layout like in there?"

He passed the pen to Mary. "Babe, you are a better artist than I am, so why don't you do the honors?"

"Sure thing, hon," she replied and started drawing lines and boxes. "Okay, so when we first come in there's going to be five checkout lines. Registers with low platforms for the groceries. Gonna be a pile of bodies there too, hopefully all of them down for good.

"To the left are the main aisles. Not sure how many, twelve, thirteen, something like that. It's not a whole lot. In the back is where the freezer is and where we assume the survivors are. If we're lucky, those things will all be congregating there."

Sparks leaned forward. "So what else is there in the store?"

"Nothing else in the back that would be useful." Mary shook her head.

"Wasn't my question," the redhead replied, raising an eyebrow. "What else is there?"

"There's a deli counter in the front," Ricky put in.

His wife nodded. "Oh yeah, forgot about that," she said, and drew it in. "It's almost directly in front of the meat market in the back. From the right aisle you can see it from the rear."

"How high are the counters?" Sparks asked.

Ricky put his hand out in front of him. "Ain't too tall, about tit high."

"You can just say chest high," Mary scolded.

Her husband shrugged. "Yeah, but where's the fun in that?"

"You just like thinking of my tits," she retorted.

"Well, it is why I married you," he
replied, and she playfully smacked him.

Sparks pursed her lips, stepping back
from the truck bed.

"What are you thinking?" Jeff asked,
watching the wheels turn in her head.

She looked up at him. "Jeff, how fast
can you run?"

"Oh fuck me," he moaned. "Why do I
have to be the runner?"

"Cause I did it last time," she
smiled.

He scuffed. "It was like eight feet."

"Fine," Sparks relented. "Rock,
paper, scissors?"

"Alright, now you're talking," Jeff
agreed, and they faced each other
intently. He threw a rock to her paper,
and he grunted. "Best two outta three?"

She shook her head. "Nope."

"Goddammit," he cursed. "Okay, fine,
what's the plan?"

"Well, we're going to go in and set
up a firing line behind the deli counter,"
Sparks replied, stepping forward to point
at the map. "Then you are going to sneak
to the back and get their attention. Then
you run like hell to us, hit the deck, and
we'll mow them down."

"From my perspective, that's a
terrible fucking plan," Jeff said. "But if

I was on the other side of the counter, I see the logic in it."

"Ma'am, not meaning to butt in," Ricky piped up, "but wouldn't it be safer for all of us to get behind the deli counter and just fire off a warning shot to get their attention?"

"Yeah, what he said!" Jeff pointed to his new companion.

"If we do that, we run the risk of them scattering and emerging from multiple aisles," Sparks explained. "With Jeff as the decoy, most of them will hopefully follow him up the aisle, creating a nice and tidy kill zone. It'll help us conserve our ammo and hopefully prevent us from being overrun."

"Alright, I gotcha," Ricky agreed. "Sorry bubba, I tried."

"Appreciate the effort," Jeff replied. "Alright, let's get this over with."

As they entered the supermarket, they hugged the right wall, Jeff pulling up the rear and closing the door quietly behind them. Upon reaching the deli counter, the redhead turned to Ricky and Mary.

"If I fire my weapon," she whispered, "run." The couple nodded as she ducked behind the counter to do a sweep. There were no zombies to be seen, and she reached back to tap Rufus to signal clear.

They moved in behind her, and Sparks kept her rifle trained on the store as Jeff knelt down, getting ready. Rufus and Ricky carefully rolled a metal baking sheet cart to the entrance of the deli counter to give them a bit of a barrier should any zombies make it that far.

Sparks nodded down at Jeff, and he returned it with a thumbs up, mouthing *I hate you* at her. She grinned and blew him a kiss.

The skinhead stayed low to the ground as he held his handgun at the ready, moving through the aisles towards the banging at the back of the store. He carefully peered around the corner to see a dozen zombies hammering away at the door separating them from their frozen dinner.

He spotted a shelf of canned goods beside him and carefully placed them one by one in the aisleway, sideways so that they could easily roll. Once his little minefield was complete, he turned to give Sparks the thumbs up.

Jeff gently stepped over the minefield and leaned around the corner, and aimed his handgun at the closest zombie.

The gunshot drowned out the constant drumbeat against the freezer, bullet finding its mark in the base of his opponent's neck.

As it crumpled to the floor, the horde turned and set their eyes on the fresh meat mere feet away from them. He shot two more times, not hitting any heads, before turning and darting down the aisle as fast as he could.

As the zombies gave chase, the first one to hit the cans slipped and fell flat on its face. The rest of them stumbled over it, giving Jeff enough of a head start to get away. Just as he cleared the aisle, he slid hard like he was stealing second base.

"NOW!" Sparks cried, loosing a bullet directly into a zombie's face.

Jeff hit the deli case with his foot and then spun around, putting his back against it and readying his gun.

The others opened fire, bullets tearing flesh wildly. Some of the zombies fell from being riddled, and Jeff shot them in the head as they hit the floor to make sure they stayed down. The barrage went on for a good twenty seconds, zombie after zombie succumbing to the wall of bullets.

"Reloading!" Ricky cried as he and Mary flicked open their shotguns. The others continued to hold the horde.

Two stray zombies came at them from the left and Rufus pulled the trigger, but came up empty. Sparks stepped beside him and casually put a round in the first one's head. But then there was a sharp *click* as her rifle ran out as well.

"Jeff!" she cried, and he reacted quickly to the panic in her voice. The angle was bad, and all three of his shots went into the zombie's chest. He threw his leg up, kicking the zombie in the chest, and it turned towards him, teeth snapping.

Rufus leapt over the counter, plunging his knife into the zombie's head. Sparks shoved the baking tray cart out of the way and jogged around the counter just as Jeff shoved the corpse off of him.

"Holy hell man, are you okay?" she asked as she reached out a hand to help him up.

Jeff took it and nodded. "Let's never do that again."

"Yeah, that didn't look fun," she agreed, letting out a relieved laugh.

"Come on, y'all, let's go get our people," Ricky said, and started towards the back of the store.

"Take it slow there, cowboy," Jeff warned. "I dropped one of them back there but pretty sure I just paralyzed him. His legs may not work, but his mouth sure will."

"Babe," Mary piped up. "Why don't you let Sparks take the lead here."

"Alright baby," her husband agreed, running a shaky hand through his hair. "You're probably right. Sorry, I've just seen too much death this week. Be nice to save someone for a change." He swallowed thickly as his wife squeezed his arm with reassurance.

Sparks led the group down a neighboring aisle to avoid the pile of bodies they'd created. She held her reloaded rifle at the ready, staying alert. Upon investigating the back, there was one zombie still banging at the freezer, apparently stubbornly desperate for human popsicles.

She slung the rifle over her back and drew her knife, motioning for the others to stay behind the shelves. She silently moved up behind the distracted zombie and planted her knife into the back of its head up to the hilt.

The corpse crumpled to the floor and there was finally silence across the supermarket. She tried to open the door, but it was locked, so she knocked the staccato pattern of *shave and a haircut*. A moment later, there were two quick raps in response and the door opened.

Two young men emerged, shaking like leaves. They looked no more than twenty, scared and confused. Ricky and Mary immediately flew forward, each embracing one of them.

"Holy shit, Jason, Donny, you boys alright?" the mechanic asked.

Donny's teeth chattered. "I think my balls are frozen."

"Hate to break it to you bubba, but I ain't warmin' them up for ya," Ricky laughed.

"Come on," Sparks said gently. "Let's get them outta here." She stepped into the aisleway, ushering Mary and Jason.

There was a sudden shot and Jason's head exploded all over the toilet paper. His body fell back, causing the blonde to go down underneath him.

"Mary!" Ricky cried, dropping Donny, but Jeff grabbed him and jerked him back out of the aisleway. Sparks caught Mary's eye and motioned for her to stay put under her human shield.

The officer peeked slightly around the corner to see a militia member taking aim. Rufus took off his head with his M16, the body dropping to the ground. Another enemy continued to pop off rounds in their direction, but they couldn't see him, only hear the clicks and beeps of a walkie talkie.

"Getting really tired of their shit," Sparks growled.

Rufus nodded in agreement. "If you wanna flank him I'm pretty sure I can peg the sumbitch when he's distracted."

"I'm taking this cocksucker alive," she snarled. "We need information about these assholes."

"Alright, whatcha got in mind?" he asked.

Her eyes twinkled wickedly. "Flying knee from the top rope?" She pointed to the top of the shelving.

"Goddamn you are a woman after my own heart." Rufus laughed. "Whatcha need from me?"

"Give me thirty seconds then lay down covering fire," she instructed. "Use the whole mag if you have to. Just aim a little high so he's forced to take cover."

"Yes ma'am," he said with a little salute.

She singled for him to begin his count and then slipped down a parallel aisle. She waited for Rufus to open fire, and then shimmied up the shelves to the top, peeking down at her mark. He ducked behind the deli counter, and as Rufus stopped shooting, he popped back up again, aiming.

Before he could even acquire a target Sparks leapt from the shelves, landing on top of the guy's head with the full force of her knees. His gun clattered to the floor along with his body, and she rolled off of her easily staggered opponent. She kicked him in the chest and then put him in a sleeper hold.

The front door burst open, and Sparks drew her sidearm, pointing it at the newcomer.

"What are you doing there, little girl?" He sneered, taking a step towards her.

Sparks cocked her gun. "Take another step. Please."

"Alright, let's all take it down a beat here," he replied, taking a step back. "Now, what can I do to resolve this situation?"

"You can fuck off to whatever compound you call a home," she told him.

He leered. "I'd be more than happy to, little lady. Just hand over my friend there and we'll be on our way."

"This asshole killed one of our friends, so he's coming with us," she explained.

"Is that a fact now?" He raised an eyebrow.

"Yeah, it is," she replied.

"*Squad six, squad six, sit rep.*" A voice crackled through the shoulder-mounted radio on her opponent. "*Squad six, sit rep. Respond.*"

"If I don't answer them, they are going to send reinforcements," he said calmly.

She motioned slightly with the gun. "Just remember, if I don't like what you have to say, you die."

He nodded and slowly moved his hand to the receiver. "Squad six here, code sixty-two. All clear, returning to base."

"Shoot that motherfucker *now*!" Rufus screamed, and she didn't hesitate, but her bullet grazed him as he dove for the door.

"You and your friends are going to die, bitch!" he yelled, and just as Sparks took aim again, a zombie burst through the door and latched onto his neck.

"We gotta go now!" she cried. "Jeff, on me!"

He skidded behind the counter as she got to her feet, gun trained on the front door. He picked up the unconscious militia prisoner and threw him over his shoulder like a sack of flour.

Sparks moved to the zombie who was still chowing down on her enemy, putting a bullet in his head. She shot the dead militia member too, just to make sure he wouldn't reanimate. Her crew congregated behind her, Ricky and Mary supporting a dazed Donny.

"He called for backup, we gotta go," Rufus said.

"How do you know that?" Ricky asked breathlessly.

"I'll explain later," the older man barked. "Go get the truck." He bent down as the younger man darted outside, grabbing ammo and the handgun from the dead militia man. Sparks led the group out to the parking lot, where they met Ricky halfway. Jeff tossed their prisoner in the back and hopped up behind him, giving Sparks and Donny a hand up as Rufus and Mary clambered into the cab.

"Should be some duct tape in the glove box," Ricky said as he punched the accelerator. "They can tie up that murdering douchebag in the back."

Rufus rummaged and found it, passing it back through the center window. "For the prisoner there," he explained as Jeff took it.

"Alright, so how in the hell did you know he called for backup?" Ricky asked as his passenger closed the window.

"Well, there's only so much porn a man can watch on the internet," Rufus replied with a shrug. "So occasionally I gotta visit other sites. Ended up on some ex-military militia pages and in one of their little training books they mentioned code sixty-two is a distress call."

"How did you know this militia uses that code?" Mary piped up.

He paused. "Well, I guess I don't. But these assholes have been fucking up my entire goddamn day, so even if I was wrong, I still think I'm right."

"Works for me, bubba," Ricky conceded. "They killed Jason and nearly killed my Mary. They can all suck a lead coated cock for all I care."

"You got a romantic here," Rufus nudged the blonde, who cracked a smile. "You hold on to him."

CHAPTER SIX

Ricky pulled into the school parking lot and right up to the front door. Principal Dan rushed out of the tent, worry etched on his face as everyone bustled out of the vehicle.

"How did it go?" he asked, raising an eyebrow at the group in the back.

"We were able to save Donny and clear out the supermarket," Mary explained. "Ran into some militia though." She motioned to the duct-taped prisoner that Sparks and Jeff were unloading from the bed of the truck.

"Is that a prisoner?" Dan asked, noting the eyes and mouth were covered as well as his hands being bound.

"Yep," Sparks replied as Jeff heaved the still unconscious guy over his shoulder. "Figured it would be in our best interest to get some information on these assholes. Numbers, location, etcetera."

"There's a mostly empty classroom just as you enter," Dan said. "It's across from the front office and the only classroom before the main lobby area. If anybody is in there, tell them I said to find someplace else."

The redhead nodded and led her group inside.

"You need to get some people down to secure the supermarket," Mary insisted, hanging back.

The Principal furrowed his brow. "I thought you said it was clear."

"It's clear of zombies, but we think one of the militia boys sent out a distress call before a zombie got him," she explained.

He pursed his lips. "Alright, the teams clearing out the east side of town just got back," he finally said. "I'll send them over right now."

"What about us?" she asked. "Ricky and I can help out."

"No, I want y'all to stay with Sparks," Dan replied. "Hopefully you can try and convince them to stay. It looks like we're going to need the help."

Sparks finished duct taping the prisoner to a chair in the center of the room. She saw the tip of a tattoo peeking out from under his shirt sleeve, and rolled it up, lips twisting at the sight. She straightened.

"Ricky, watch him for a minute, will you?" she asked.

Ricky nodded. "Sure thing."

Sparks grabbed Jeff's arm, pulling him outside into the hallway.

He stared down at her. "What's up?"

"Recognize his tattoo?" She asked.

He unconsciously rubbed the German military tattoo on his bicep. "Every time I look in the mirror," he replied.

"Do me a favor," she said, "stay out of sight while we interrogate him. I don't want him knowing that you are working with us."

"Whatcha thinking?" Jeff asked, crossing his arms.

"I'm thinking that those matching tattoos might come in handy if we get into a tight spot," she said.

"You're the boss," he said, "I'll hang back."

"What have you found out?" Dan asked, approaching with Mary and Rufus.

The redhead turned to him. "Just about to start. You want to sit in?"

"These guys have been murdering my people, so yeah, I'd like to hear what he has to say." The Principal nodded.

"I don't think this chat is going to be for me," Mary spoke up, face pale. "Can I go check on Chuck? I want to see how his arm is doing."

"Sure Mary, he's on the second floor next to the outbreak area," Dan replied. "Just tell the guard I said it was okay."

"I think I'll tag along if you don't mind," Jeff said.

Dan furrowed his brow. "You're not going to help with the interrogation?"

The skinhead simply motioned to Sparks, signaling for her to explain.

"Just trust me, it's better he stays out here," she said simply.

"I think you've earned some trust," Dan replied. "Okay Mary, take Jeff with you."

"Come on, I'll give you the nickel tour," the blonde said.

Jeff laughed. "Well, that's good, cause it's about all I can afford."

Sparks led the other two into the room, where the prisoner was struggling like mad to get free. She admired her secure handiwork and then ripped the tape from his mouth and eyes. He screamed in pain and then blinked in shock as she got nose to nose with him.

"Before we get started, I'm going to be very clear." The redhead's voice was low and menacing, and sent a shiver up the prisoner's spine. "I'm your only friend in this room. That boy you killed in the supermarket? He was their friend. If it was up to them, you'd already be dead, or at the very least, wishing for death.

"So here's what's going to happen. I'm going to ask questions, and you're going to answer them. The first time you don't give me what I believe to be a truthful answer, Ricky here is going to go out to his truck and get his tools. The second time you don't give me a truthful answer, I'm going to let Ricky show you some of his tools, and describe how he's going to use them on you. The third time you lie will be the last time you ever see me, because I'm walking out that door and letting Ricky do whatever he wants to.

"Have I made myself clear?" She cocked her head.

The prisoner, sweating, glanced to Ricky, whose eyes were wide with insanity. He nodded in the affirmative.

"Great, so the first question is going to be easy," Sparks began. "What's your name?"

"You can call me Bryan," the prisoner replied, clearing his throat.

"Not sure I entirely believe you, but I'm willing to roll with it," she said. "Now, next question. Why did you shoot their friend in the head?"

"Well, I was just looking for some food and I thought y'all were some of them dead cannibals," Bryan replied.

Sparks paused. "Ricky, go get your tools."

"Yes, ma'am!" Ricky bounced out of the classroom, letting out a maniacal laugh as he went.

"You wanna try that one again, Bryan?" the officer asked.

"Um, I mean," he stammered. "Okay, I'll level with you."

"Probably in your best interests to do so," she agreed cheerfully.

"Elijah, the militia leader, sent some of us out to scout the town for supplies," Bryan began. "Him and some boys got chased off from the truck stop this morning, so he figured it would be easier to send scouts in to see what was left and get a sense of how strong the resistance was before committing troops."

Ricky burst back in, carrying a greasy toolbox and slamming it down on the table with a wide grin on his face.

Sparks snapped her fingers, demanding her prisoner's attention. "How many troops?"

"I don't know," Bryan shot back, seeming to shrink away.

She sighed. "Ricky, show and tell time."

"Wait, I honestly don't know!" the prisoner cried. "My cousin is a part of the militia and when this shit went down a few days ago, he told me to get my gun and we're going someplace safe. Well, he *was* a part of the militia, y'all killed him in the grocery store."

161

"Well he shouldn't have been aiming his weapon at my friend here," Rufus growled.

"Look, I ain't even mad," Bryan protested. "But I'm telling you the truth that I don't know how many soldiers he has. From the time I got to the compound I've been running missions with my cousin. The first day we rolled over Center Point and picked the stores clean. Then we got sent up here."

"Well, take your best guess," Sparks suggested. "How many people have you seen at the compound?"

"Thirty, maybe forty?" He shrugged. "Could be ten times that number, though."

Sparks waved Dan to the far side of the room.

"What do you think?" he asked quietly.

"I think it's time for you to evacuate," she replied. "Even if his numbers are remotely close to being accurate, this isn't a situation you are going to come out ahead in."

"We have armed men at the gas station and the supermarket, and they have cover." He crossed his arms in protest. "They can handle a militia assault."

Sparks sighed. "And what about here?"

"What about here?" He threw his hands up. "There are over a hundred people on campus."

"And how many of them are trained to use guns?" she shot back. "Ten? Fifteen? And never mind the fact that half the people are exposed out there."

The weight of the situation seemed to sink over Dan's features like a ton of bricks. "Ricky, please go tell Grandma Suzie and the others out there that they need to quickly move inside."

The younger man made a beeline for the door. "I'm on it."

"So what's the play, lil' lady?" Rufus asked, turning to the duo.

"Well, that depends on the Principal here," Sparks replied. "You finally ready to listen to me and evacuate?"

"In the morning," Dan replied firmly. "It's too risky to move this many people at night."

She turned to her white-haired friend. "Okay, so Rufus, this is what we need to do," she began, but the sound of gunfire cut her off.

CHAPTER SEVEN

Sparks and Rufus rushed to the door, guns at the ready. She took a knee and peeked into the hallway, seeing two of Dan's men take bullets and fall on the other side of the lobby. Within a moment four militia members emerged, moving in combat formation.

"Militia," she hissed as she ducked back into the room.

"Principal, we'll handle this," Rufus said. "You keep an eye on *him*." Sparks leaned back into the hallway and looked through her scope.

"I have the trailer dead to rights," she said. "On my mark, move across the hall to the office." Rufus got in position as she waited. "Now!" she commanded, and he jumped across the hallway. The trailer whipped around and raised his weapon, and Sparks put a bullet in his chest.

The other three opened fire while taking off around the corner, one staying to cover behind a row of lockers.

"Covering fire," Rufus said, "move up."

Sparks nodded. "Go," she said, and then bolted from her position as her companion started shooting. She got to the lobby and slid behind the wall, Rufus jogging behind her as the corner guard took off. Sparks peered around and pulled back at the gunfire, waiting for a break to leap out to shoot.

The trio had made it to the stairwell, and disappeared inside, one staying behind to chain and padlock the door shut.

"What the hell is he doing?" Sparks asked.

"Looks like he's padlocking it," Rufus replied. "What the hell are they doing? Creating a hostage situation?"

Jeff was ready as a militia member eased the door open to the makeshift infirmary, and fired off a quick round into his enemy's head. The man behind him burst through, knocking the skinhead backwards. His gun skidded across the floor and he took a page from Spark's book, wrapping his arms around his enemy's waist. He flung himself sideways and then slammed down, his enemy's neck snapping with a sickening crunch.

Mary winced from her vantage point next to the nurse, but Jeff quickly recovered, grabbing his gun and moving to the door. There was a man by the locked door down the hall, the room housing all the zombies from the original first outbreak of people in the school.

Jeff cocked his gun and the militia man fired back at him, driving the skinhead back into the infirmary. He popped back out as the man finished whatever he was doing and managed to get a shot off into his enemy's back.

Jeff looked back and forth down the hallway to make sure nobody else was there and narrowed his eyes at the black device attached to the locked door. Movement out of the corner of his eye as the man he'd shot fumbled with something in his hand, and it all clicked into place.

"Bomb!" Jeff screamed, slamming the door behind him and locking it.

The zombie door blew open with a *crack* and zombies poured into the hallway, immediately feasting on the injured militia man. His screams turned to gurgles as they sunk their teeth into him.

Rufus and Sparks recoiled as they heard the explosion above them. They stared at the ceiling for a beat, confused, and then cold dread fell over them both.

"What was that?" the Principal asked as he barreled out of the classroom.

"Are there stairs down that hall?" Sparks pointed across the lobby, in the opposite direction of the locked stairs.

"Yeah!" Dan replied, confused, as the two sprinted in that direction. They threw themselves against the doors just as the echoing snarls made it to the doors. They grunted with effort as they struggled to hold them shut, and in desperation, jam the stocks of their weapons between the door handles.

Gunfire erupts outside, the sound of screaming and then more shots.

"Christ, now what?" Sparks huffed. The front doors slammed open and a group of Dan's men scrambled into the lobby.

"What's going on?" Rufus barked.

One of the men turned to him, wild eyed. "They're killing everybody!" he cried.

"You!" Sparks pointed at him. "Come here!" He immediately approached her. "There's a horde of zombies on the other side of that door, so for the love of fucking christ, don't abandon your post," she instructed.

"Frankie! Paul! Teddy! Give me a hand!" the man yelled, and the other guys bustled over to help barricade the doors. Rufus and Sparks reclaimed their weapons, rounding the corner just in time to see more people flooding inside.

A few of them dropped from bullets and Ricky backed in, firing off some cover shots to try to get more people inside.

167

"Ricky, get everyone into the classrooms, and shut and lock the doors!" Sparks demanded. "Stay there until we come and get you."

He ducked behind the door. "Where the hell are y'all going?"

She cocked her gun. "Out." Sparks and Rufus moved down the other hallway, to the side door, weapons raised. They crept out onto the pavement and she immediately shot a running enemy in the chest.

"Nice shot," Rufus commended. "Could have used you back in the day."

They skirt the spot where the fallen militia member was, a tent with boxes stacked behind it. Blood poured out of his mouth as he struggled to get to his fallen gun.

Rufus stabbed him in the skull and joined Sparks behind the boxes. "Don't know about you, but I'm done playing with these motherfuckers," he said. "If they want a war, they're gonna get one."

"Agreed." She nodded. "How you doin' on ammo?"

"Got half a mag loaded in, another full one in reserve," he replied. "You?"

She ejected her mag to check it and tossed it aside. Empty. She loaded up a fresh one with a sharp *click*.

"Last one," she said.

Rufus nodded grimly. "Well, let's hope there ain't too many of them."

Almost as if on cue, five full sized Humvees pulled into the parking lot to form a barricade. Two dozen armed men poured out and started setting up a perimeter.

"Guess we just got the advance team," Sparks muttered.

A dark-haired man stepped out of the passenger side of the center vehicle, and they recognized him as the leader of the pack from the truck stop. He reached into the backseat and pulled out a heavily beaten man with his arms bound behind him.

"Whoever is in charge," the leader bellowed, voice carrying across the parking lot. "You have thirty seconds to get out here before your friend loses his head!" He put a revolver to his prisoner's temple.

"Shit," Sparks hissed.

Rufus shook his head. "I think the Principal is out of his depth here."

"Ya think?" She ran a hand over her crimson locks. "You stay here. If this shit goes sideways, you take that motherfucker out first."

"Twenty seconds!" The militia leader yelled.

Rufus rolled his eyes. "If he does a countdown from ten I might jump the gun," he said.

"And you'd be justified," Sparks replied and patted him on the shoulder. She sprinted back into the school, skidding around to the front entrance where Principal Dan stood, wringing his hands.

"Ten seconds!" The militia leader called, and Rufus took aim. "What, do you not care about the fate of your man, here?" He looked down at his hostage. "Well, looks like you'll be joining your family shortly."

The man's eyes were glazed, in shock from witnessing his family's demise.

"Five seconds," the leader yelled. "Four. Three. Two."

"I'm here!" Principal Dan burst from the front doors with his hands up. "I'm here!"

"Ah, you're the one giving me so many headaches," the leader greeted. "Who are you?"

Dan swallowed nervously. "I'm the Principal of this school."

"I wasn't aware today was a school day," his opponent chuckled. "You'd figure zombie apocalypse would be like a snow day, only more common in these parts."

"Be that as it may," Dan continued, "why don't you let my friend there go and we can talk things out?"

"Now, why would you want him back?" the militia leader wondered. "He's the one who told us about this place, how to get in, the zombie room. Everything. Now before you get too mad at him you should know he did hold out for quite a while. Took a hell of a beating. Didn't break until we started executing his family."

"Why would you do that?" Dan asked, desperation in his eyes. "There are plenty of supplies in this town."

"That's the thing, Principal, there aren't," his opponent replied with a sneer. "At least not enough to sustain everyone. Hell, there's barely enough to sustain me and my men for more than month or so. But as you can tell, I'm willing to do everything in my power to give my men that month."

"Take it and go, then!" Sparks demanded, exiting the front doors with Bryan in front of her at gunpoint.

"Ah, the girl from the truck stop this morning," the militia leader said. "Somehow I'm not surprised to see you still alive and kicking."

She raised an eyebrow. "More than I can say about some of your men I've come across today."

"I *have* lost quite a few troops today, but it's for the greater good," he replied in a jovial tone. "Fewer mouths means the provisions will last longer."

"Look." Sparks sighed. "I can sit here and insult your troupe of wannabe army boys til the sun comes up, but frankly I have shit to do. So let me spell out what's gonna happen. First, we're gonna do a prisoner swap. I got one of yours, you got one of mine. Easy peasy.

"Then, you're gonna take your boys back to whatever rock you crawled out from and you're going to give us a day to evacuate. You win, the town is yours. We're keeping the supplies we have here at the school, and you're gonna let us gas up. By the afternoon tomorrow we'll be out of here."

"Wow, that is quite the little fantasy you have weaved for yourself there." He laughed. "Literally the only part of that you got correct is that the town is ours. Given that you are severely outgunned, let me lay out what's going to happen. For starters, your little prisoner swap idea wouldn't really be fair to me, since we have five more of yours."

He pointed to the last SUV in the row, where a few of the troops were shoving hostages inside. Rufus and Sparks both managed to catch a glimpse of Ben's defiant face as he disappeared inside, stomachs sinking.

"Plus, generally speaking, if you are going to take a hostage, make sure it's one that has value," the leader continued. "This isn't one of my men."

"Come on, Elijah," Bryan stammered. "I did everything you asked of me."

"No, young man, you did everything your *cousin* asked of you," came the retort. "*He* was the man I trusted. I don't know you."

Bryan's wrists writhed against their duct tape bonds. "Motherfucker!"

"Now, what's left from your fantasy that still needs addressing," Elijah pursed his lips in mock thought. "Oh, yes, that's right, your evacuation. You have until sun up to vacate this town. Anyone still here will be shot on sight. If anyone approaches the gas station or the supermarket, they will be shot on sight. And just to show you I mean what I say-"

The gunshot took off the top of his hostage's head, and Sparks immediately fired back, using Bryan as a shield. The militia opened up as Principal Dan tackled the redhead back through the doors of the school.

Rufus took out a few of the men from his position, causing more than one to turn towards him, but they were quickly distracted by Jeff shooting with his handgun from the second floor window. The assault was enough to spook the militia into retreating.

"You alright?" Dan moaned, rolling off of Sparks in the front lobby.

Her eyes widened at the blood pouring from his shoulder. "Holy shit, are you?" she asked.

"Looks like they got me," he grunted.

"Thank you, for saving my life there," she said as she rolled him over to inspect the damage.

"I don't deserve all the credit." Dan chuckled hoarsely, motioning to Bryan's twitching, bullet-riddled corpse. "That murdering asshole there deserves some."

"Well, nothing wrong with your sense of humor," Sparks replied. "Here, put pressure on the wound. Looks like it's a through and through. It's gonna hurt like hell, but you'll be alright."

"Help here!" A panicked voice cried from down the hallway.

"Fuck the zombie horde," Sparks muttered.

"Go help 'em." Dan waved her off. "I'll be fine."

"Ricky!" she cried as she ran towards the stairwell, and he poked his head out of a classroom.

"Where the hell is Mary?" he barked.

Sparks pointed up. "Upstairs with Jeff."

"Oh God." He blanched.

"First things first," she said, "we gotta secure this door. You got chains in the truck?"

"Yeah got it," Ricky ran to the front doors, peering out just in time to see the last Humvee disappear around the bend. He darted out into the parking lot and flung open the door of his truck.

"Ricky!" Mary's voice called out and he whipped around. "Look up!"

He saw the blonde and Jeff hanging out of the infirmary window, waving at him. "Baby, are you safe?" he asked.

"Yeah, can you get us a ladder?" she asked.

"I gotta help Sparks, so people don't die, but Rufus there can," Ricky held up the chain and shook it for effect, disappearing back into the school.

"Hang tight, be with you in a minute," Rufus called. He moved from dead militia man to dead militia man, jabbing each skull with his knife to make sure they wouldn't reanimate.

Sparks waved Ricky impatiently as he rounded the corner inside with the chain, and together they wound it around the handles and secured it. The four men that had been holding the doors shut collapsed with exhaustion, huffing against the walls of the hallway.

The zombies in the stairwell smacked against the doors angrily, the chains allowing barely any give.

"Mary and Jeff are safe," Ricky said. "Rufus is getting a ladder for them to get down."

Sparks nodded in relief. "Well at least something went right for us."

"So what are we gonna do now?" he asked.

"When Rufus gets them down, bring them to the interrogation room," Sparks instructed. "These assholes took our friends. We're gonna get them back."

"Okay, we're here," Sparks said, leaning forward and marking an X on the map. "Both times we've seen them leave and they've been driving south, so we can rule out anything north of us." She looked to Principal Dan, who was sitting in the chair next to her, holding a compress against his shoulder.

"If they didn't get on the I-ten, we can rule out anything east of us as well," he added.

"Well, couldn't they just take the eighty-seven and pick it up?" Ricky spoke up. "You know, to throw us off and stuff?"

Dan shook his head. "Exit's been closed a week for construction," he replied.

"Well, if that's the case, then they took the twenty-seven out of town." Ricky shrugged.

Sparks leaned forward. "Wait, what was the name of the town Bryan said they hit?"

"Center Point," Dan said. "It's about eight miles up twenty-seven, straight shot."

"They got Center Point?" Mary bent over the map and ran a finger over the area, prompting Sparks to circle it. "Had a friend who worked at the gas station. I hope they didn't hurt her."

"I'm sorry Mary," the Principal said. "I hope she's okay."

"Okay," Sparks cut in, leaning on her hands. "If they hit Center Point then came at us, we have to assume they're somewhere on that road. Does anybody have any ideas?"

"Well, why do you think they're off that road?" Ricky furrowed his brow, motioning to the paper. "I mean look at all this empty land, they could be anywhere."

"See all that land out here?" Rufus inquired. "You know what it doesn't have? A river running through it." He pointed to the Guadalupe River.

"Rufus is right," Sparks agreed. "If they are building this to be a survivalist compound, having a source of water would be vital."

Mary made a noise of excitement. "The thirteen-fifty turnoff."

"What about it, Mary?" Dan raised an eyebrow.

"That's where they've gotta be," she said. "It's just before the quarry, there's a huge wooded area right after the turnoff, and the river runs right through it."

"It's where I'd build," Rufus agreed.

"With them coming back at dawn we really only have one shot at this," Sparks said firmly. "Does anybody have a reason to think they'd be elsewhere?"

"I'd be surprised if they were on the other side of Center Point since it's only a mile or so until you hit the Kerrville Airport," Dan pointed out. "Way too much government attention when you get that close to airplanes."

"Alright, that's our target," she confirmed. "Now all we need is a plan."

The Principal shook his head. "I'm going to leave that in your capable hands. I have an evacuation to facilitate."

"Any idea where you're headed?" Jeff piped up.

"There's a farm with a lake up eighty-seven about five, six miles," Dan explained. "It's west of the highway and just before the racetrack. It's not terribly far off the main road, but should be far enough away to give us a chance to regroup."

"Well, hell, I've heard worse plans today." Jeff nodded.

Sparks laughed and playfully smacked him. "Hey!"

"Hey Jeff," he replied, voice a high falsetto, "how fast can you run?"

She pouted. "Point taken."

"Principal Dan, if you can spare us I think Mary and I are gonna stick with these guys," Ricky cut in. "This looks like it's gonna be bigger than a three man operation."

Dan raised an eyebrow. "Sparks?"

"We're happy to have them," she replied.

"Good luck, see you soon," Principal Dan took his leave and exited the classroom.

"So." Sparks leaned over the map again, lips in a thin line. "Anybody have any grand ideas on how to raid a militia compound? Cause I'm open to ideas."

"Ricky, you got a pair of wire cutters I can borrow?" Rufus asked suddenly. "Big ones."

"Yeah, I got a pair in the truck," Ricky replied, brow low in confusion.

Sparks crossed her arms. "You aren't thinking of going in there alone, are you?"

"I did this shit back in the sixties," Rufus replied, "so I don't see why I can't do it when I'm in *my* sixties. I can get in there and secure the hostages, but getting out's a whole other story."

Jeff tapped his chest. "I think I might have an idea on that."

"That could work," Sparks agreed.

"What the hell you talkin' about?" Ricky asked.

"Jeff has a way to get their attention," she replied. "If nothing else it will distract them and give Rufus a chance to find the hostages. Only question though is how are you gonna be able to signal us? We're not exactly flush with communication technology at the moment."

Rufus grinned. "I could whip up some hillbilly dynamite."

"Well, I did say you were our resident blowing shit up expert," Sparks conceded. "This seems like a good a time as any."

Rufus clapped his hands. "Awesome, y'all got a science lab here?"

"A surprisingly well-stocked one," Mary said. "Come on, I'll show you."

"Well, thank you, ma'am." Rufus tipped an imaginary hat at her. "Ricky if you don't mind, while she takes me there, could you run out to the maintenance shed and see if there's any fertilizer?"

"Come on, I'll give you a hand," Jeff said.

"I'll meet y'all at the truck," Sparks told them. "Gonna collect some ammo from those militia douchebags we took out."

"Rufus, can I ask you a question?" Mary piped up as they entered the science lab.

"You can ask me whatever you want, lil' lady," he replied.

She took a deep breath. "What's hillbilly dynamite?"

"Well, in a nutshell, it's fertilizer mixed with a variety of common chemicals in the correct portions," he explained. "There's a lot of different ways to do it, I mean I myself have a proprietary blend that I'd like to think gives it an extra kick. I would share the specifics with you, but pretty sure doing so would result in you being put on a government watch list."

"Why would that matter?" Mary raised an eyebrow. "The world is ending."

"You're right, we're dealing with the apocalypse, so the last thing you need is Big Brother giving you headaches." He winked.

"Well, is there anything I can do to help?" she asked, motioning around the lab.

"You know what, there is something you can help me with," Rufus replied with a snap of his fingers. "You have an art room?"

Her brows knit in confusion. "Um, yeah?"

"Good, good," he said. "If you can go down there and bring me back some red, white and blue paint and a big ole brush, that'd be great."

She couldn't help but ask. "Why do you need the paint?"

"Why?" Rufus straightened. "Cause this is America, goddammit! And if there's one thing we do, it's blow shit up real nice. So whenever I make hillbilly dynamite, I feel it's my patriotic duty to pay tribute to the red, white and blue by painting it on the bomb."

She shook her head. "I… yeah, I'll be right back."

Mary pointed from the backseat. "Gonna be about a half a mile up on the left," she instructed, leaning beside Sparks' shoulder in the passenger seat.

Ricky nodded. "Got it," he said.

"Stop the car!" Sparks cried, and he slammed on the brakes.

"What the hell?!" Rufus cursed as he and Jeff smacked into the rear window from the bed of the truck. He glared inside at her, and she held a finger to her lips, pointing past Ricky. On the side of the road was a cattle pen, full of a few dozen zombies. His jaw dropped.

"What the fuck is that?" Jeff breathed.

"Looks like their secret stash of zombies," she replied. "Given the fatigues, I think it's some of their own men."

"Well, why in the ever loving fuck would they keep them?" Rufus asked.

"Who knows?" Sparks shook her head. "Maybe they want to set up traps around their compound, you know, chain them up and stuff like a guard dog."

Jeff shrugged. "Or use them as cannon fodder."

"What do you mean?" Sparks raised an eyebrow.

"They could set them loose on their enemies," the skinhead replied. "Why fight against gun toting people when you can send a wave of zombies at them? I mean hell, I'd rather face off against ten zombies than one guy with a gun."

"Hey, Rufus," Sparks asked, suddenly getting an idea. "How much of that hillbilly dynamite you got?"

"Had enough material to make two bombs," he replied.

She smiled. "Remote detonation?"

"Timed, and it's not very accurate," he admitted. "Pretty much once I dump the mixture into the fertilizer you got about twenty minutes before it goes *boom*. And there's a two to three minute margin of error in there too."

"I can work with that," Sparks decided. "How long you think you're gonna need to get into the camp?"

Rufus shrugged. "Assuming their compound is in that tree line there, I could be on site in five minutes if there's a chain-link fence."

"What if they have something sturdier?" Jeff asked.

Rufus held up his hillbilly dynamite canister, painted red, white and blue. "Twenty."

"Alright Rufus, this is what I'm thinking," Sparks said. "Put one of those bombs at the zombie pen gate. Three minutes later, I want you to mix the second bomb."

Jeff gaped. "Are you crazy?"

"Hey now, this is your plan," she retorted.

He blinked at her. "Mine?"

"Yeah, you're the one who suggested zombies could be used as a weapon," she said, shooting him a sweet smile. "We're gonna open that gate then signal them."

Jeff shook his head. "My brilliance is a curse…" he moaned.

"Rufus, you on board?" Sparks asked.

Rufus grinned. "Eh, what the hell, sounds like a party."

185

CHAPTER NINE

Jeff strolled up to the front gate of the compound, hands in the air, completely unarmed. He took in the simple chain-link fence that was about eight feet high, topped with barbed wire.

Two spotlights flicked on, and a trio of armed men aimed their weapons.

"Don't take another fucking step," one barked.

"Whoa whoa whoa," Jeff countered, spreading his fingers to accentuate his palms. "Easy there, cowboy."

The guard shook his head. "You need to find someplace else."

"I heard this was the place for me," Jeff replied, grasping the hem of his shirt.

The guard cocked his gun. "You don't wanna do that!"

"Easy," the skinhead cooed. "I'm just taking my shirt off to show you what I mean."

"Do it slow," the guard sounded confused but intrigued. When Jeff revealed the German military tattoos riddling his chest, the guard grasped his radio. "Tower one to Elijah, Tower one to Elijah, over."

"*What is it?*" the militia leader replied through the mouthpiece.

"Some trouble at the front gate," the guard replied. "Gonna need you to come up here."

"*On my way.*"

"Just wait there," the guard instructed Jeff, "and no sudden movements."

The skinhead nodded. "Yes, sir," he said, and then tilted his head side to side, to signal Sparks that the distraction was on.

Rufus slipped into the river, snipping the chain-link fence that bridged the gap between two metal siding walls. He stayed low in the water until he was inside the compound, behind an outbuilding. He silently moved to the corner to peer out, slipping back into the darkness as a guard approached.

The guard turned the corner and Rufus bum rushed him, slamming him against the wall with a hand to his mouth and a knife to his throat.

"You in a whole mess a trouble, boy," the older man whispered, planting his knee on the assault rifle to prevent it being raised against him. "Now, you're gonna answer a question for me, or else you're gonna choke on your own blood. You understand?"

The guard nodded, eyes nearly popping out of his head at the feel of the knife against his jugular.

"Good," Rufus hissed. "Now, you assholes took some of my friends from the high school. I wanna know where they are. Do you know?" The guard nodded. "You're doing good. Now where are they?"

The guard tried to speak, mouth muffled by the older man's hand.

"Hold on there," Rufus cooed. "Now listen very carefully. I'm gonna remove my hand from your mouth. If you so much as think about speaking above a whisper, I'm gonna slit your throat, then I'm gonna cut your dick off and throat fuck you with it. We clear?"

The guard had lost four shades of color in his face and nodded ever so slightly to agree to the terms. Rufus moved his hand very slowly away from his mouth.

"They're close," the guard whispered, so quiet it was almost inaudible. "Two buildings away. Not the one directly behind you, but the next one."

"Guards on the door?" Rufus asked.

His prisoner nodded. "Should be two, but there's a back way in, I can show you." He gasped as the blade pressed harder against his throat. "Or I can just tell you."

The older man grinned. "That's the right answer."

"There's an access panel on the back of the building where you can put in firewood for the stove," the guard explained.

"Really?" Rufus raised an eyebrow. "A wood burning stove?"

The guard nodded. "Elijah wanted to be prepared for everything, including running out of fuel."

"Speaking of that, where did all that gas go to from this morning?" his captor asked.

"It's at the end of this row," came the shaky reply. "No more than thirty yards."

Rufus smiled. "Boy, I want you to know you've done well."

"So are you gonna release me?" the guard asked shakily.

"In a manner of speaking," Rufus replied, and covered his prisoner's mouth again, quickly slitting his throat. The guard struggled for a moment, before losing too much blood and going limp.

The older man set him down in the shadows and wiped off his knife, checking his watch. "Shit, eight minutes, gotta move," he hissed to himself.

He moved through the shadows, checking each corner for more guards before clearing the space between the buildings. At the end of the row, he spotted the fuel truck. There was one guard at the tailgate, watching the rest of the compound.

The door of the building behind him opened, and half a dozen armed men wandered towards the front gate.

Well, looks like whatever Jeff is doing is working, Rufus thought to himself. As the guard by the fuel turned to watch the group approach the gate, Rufus lunged out of the shadows, planting his knife into a fresh throat.

They fell to the ground, and the only thing the guard could think of to do was reach up to his neck. It was an effort in futility, and he bled out before Rufus managed to spring up and drag the body behind the truck. He peeked back out to make sure nobody had noticed him.

"Half a century later and still got it," he murmured, and stabbed the militia guard in the head for good measure.

Rufus took out a small container from his pack and set it next to the gas cans, darting back into the shadows to get to the hostage building. He skirted the outside and was amazed to find that the access panel actually existed.

Wow, guess that kid actually thought I was gonna let him go, he thought, and slipped into the storage room. He peeked through a door frame and surveyed the space, one guard sitting at a table reading a magazine with five hostages bound and sitting against the wall.

Rufus knew he wouldn't be able to make it undetected, so he broke off a small chunk of wood from a nearby box and tossed it at Ben. The kid didn't notice, so he did it again, until he finally glanced at the door.

When it dawned on him who it was, he cocked his head as Rufus put his finger to his lips, followed by pointing to the guard.

"Yo guard," Ben piped up.

Their captor grunted. "Keep your mouth shut."

"That's fine and all, but do you really want it to smell like piss in here?" the kid asked. The guard threw his magazine onto the table with a huff and got up, stomping over to grab Ben by the collar.

He growled as he shoved the kid against the wall. "You piece of fucking shit-"

Ben head butted him directly in the nose, and the guard staggered back. Rufus leapt out and grabbed his face, stabbing his opponent in the gut. The guard went limp as he attempted to stare down his attacker, but soon the life was gone and Rufus stabbed him in the skull.

"Rufus!" Ben blurted. "What the hell are you doing here?"

"We ain't leaving anybody behind," the old man replied gruffly.

"How are we getting out of here?" the kid asked, turning around so that his rescuer could cut his bonds.

"Transport is gonna be here any minute now, so we need to get y'all ready to move," Rufus replied, and when Ben was free he handed the kid a second knife. "We gotta hurry."

"Why?" Ben asked.

"Because any minute now, we're going to be sending a huge signal that we're here," the older man replied with a grin. The kid's eyes widened at the thought of the potential mayhem his ex-soldier companion could have planned.

"So, what do we have here?" Elijah asked, approaching the fence. Jeff stood on the other side, hands still raised.

The guard stiffened. "He says he wants shelter."

"And you decided the best course of action was to disturb me rather than shoot him in the head?" Elijah snapped, narrowing his eyes.

"He's got some relevant ink," the guard explained quickly. "I didn't want to assume anything, sir."

"Really?" The militia leader raised an eyebrow. "Okay, that buys you… let's say thirty seconds to explain how you came to be on our front doorstep."

"Look, I did a stint in Bexar country lockup a while back, and some of the boys in there told me about y'all," Jeff replied. "When shit hit the fan I figured the best place to be was among brothers. That's why I'm here."

Elijah crossed his arms. "And who were these boys exactly?"

"I'll be honest with you, it was so long ago that I've forgotten their names," Jeff admitted with a well placed wince. "Really tried to block out that part of my life, if you know what I mean."

"And exactly how long ago was that?"

"Five, maybe six years ago," Jeff replied.

"Is that a fact?" Elijah raised his chin. "That's funny, seeing as how we didn't start this compound until three years ago."

"Shit," Jeff muttered. "Hey, look man, I don't know what to tell you," he said louder.

"Can somebody please shoot this asshole so I can go back to bed?" Elijah asked, almost sounding bored, but there was an explosion in the distance.

Jeff put his hands out in front of him. "Whoa now, if you shoot, you all die!"

"Explain." The militia leader held up a finger to signal his guards to hold their fire.

"That sound you heard was a homemade explosive that opened the gate at your zombie pen just on the other side of those trees," the skinhead explained with a wry smile. "So right now, there are a few dozen zombies milling about just looking for a place to run to. They hear the sound of your guns, they're gonna pay you a visit."

Elijah sighed. "I don't know what your game is, but one shot echoing through the air isn't going to attract much of anything."

With perfect timing, the second batch of dynamite exploded, taking the gas canisters along with it. A fireball shot forty feet into the air, taking the two buildings on either side with it.

"How about that, asshole!" Jeff cried as Sparks opened fire on the distracted guards. The skinhead turned and barreled back to the tree line as the guards dropped like flies.

He reached her tree and started to climb beneath her as the camp descended into chaos. Ricky's truck plowed through the front gate, forcing Elijah and his remaining stunned guards to dive out of the way. One militia member wasn't quick enough and caught the front grill with his face, ending his apocalypse adventure in a brutal fashion.

Elijah pulled out his handgun and aimed at the truck with wild eyes as men staggered out of the barracks in panic and confusion.

The thunder of zombie feet caught everyone's attention, however, and Elijah whipped around to face the front gate.

"Open fire!" he screamed.

A few guards tried to climb the tower by the front gate, but Sparks took their heads off as they tried. Their bodies fell down into the zombie mosh pit happening below, caught up in a river of rotting flesh.

She aimed back down at the leader, but he and a few of his men disappeared into a storage building. They slammed the door on one comrade left outside, and he pounded on the glass as the zombies descended onto him. They tore him apart, covering the window in fresh crimson.

Ricky sped around the compound, looking for some kind of signal. "Where in the hell is Rufus?!"

"There!" Mary cried and pointed at a white-haired man hanging out of a window with a high powered flashlight. The guards giving chase to Ricky turned to concentrate on the horde instead, giving him time to skid to the opening door.

"Everybody in, quick!" Rufus shouted, brandishing an assault rifle as he waved the hostages forward. Ben led everyone into the bed of the truck and the older man covered them, firing at the remaining militia men so they would be easier zombie food.

"Rufus, let's go!" Ben screamed, and he leapt up into the bed, pulling the tailgate up behind him. The kid smacked the roof hard, and Ricky punched the accelerator.

Bullets flew everywhere, zombies feasting on fallen militia, those not wounded attempting to retreat to the buildings that weren't on fire. Rufus looked down at one man that reached up to him as they drove by, eyes beginning for a bullet as three zombies gnawed at his lower half. The older man simply smiled as a fourth zombie bit into the man's cheekbone.

Just as they were clearing the gate, Rufus caught sight of Elijah peering out through the glass door of the storage building.

"Ben, smack the roof," he instructed.

The kid did a double take. "Why?"

"Just do it," Rufus demanded. He did, and Ricky slammed on the brakes as Mary slid open the back window.

"Did we lose somebody?" Ricky asked.

Rufus shook his head. "Back up ten feet," he said.

"Are you crazy?" the driver snapped.

"Just fucking do it!" Rufus cried, and Ricky sighed, backing up.

Elijah narrowed his eyes, wondering what the hell these terrorists were doing, but then he realized what was going on as the old fuck in the back raised his assault rifle.

"Eat it, motherfucker," Rufus declared as he let the bullets rip into the building. The glass shattered and Elijah's head disappeared.

Ricky looked in his rearview mirror and saw the zombies change course at the sound of the rifle. "Hang on, we're outta here!" he cried, and sped off, pausing at the tree line so that Sparks and Jeff could hop into the bed.

"Holy shit." Sparks let out a relieved laugh. "Did we pull that off?"

"Oh yeah, missy," Rufus replied with a grin. "We hit em so hard their grandkids'll feel it."

"What about Elijah?" she asked. "I had a shot on him but had to take out the guards first so they wouldn't get Jeff."

The skinhead saluted her. "A move I approve of."

"He was in some storage building near the entrance," Rufus explained. "I shot it up pretty good and took out the glass on the door. I don't know if I got him or not though."

"Well, if he does survive, he's going to have a hard time making much trouble now." Sparks shrugged.

"That's for damn sure," Rufus agreed. "Ain't gonna be a whole lot of them boys left."

Ben nodded. "Ain't that the truth. Ole Rufus here is a cold-blooded motherfucker."

"Slittin' throats and blowin' shit up," the older man said wistfully. "It's like I'm back in 'Nam."

CHAPTER TEN

The sun was just peeking over the horizon as Ricky pulled into the driveway of Principal Dan's new farm. There were a few school buses parked to the side of the massive farm house. The leader himself came out, arm in a sling with his shoulder bandaged, followed by a few other townsfolk.

"Is everybody safe?" he asked as Jeff opened the tailgate to let the passengers out.

"Yep," Sparks said as she dismounted. "We were able to get out all the hostages, safe and sound."

"And the militia?" Dan asked.

"Rufus did a number on them," she replied. "IF there are survivors they aren't going to be looking for a fight anytime soon."

He let out a deep sigh. "That's a relief."

"I still wouldn't recommend going back to the school," she added.

"As it turns out, that's not an option anyway," he replied.

Sparks furrowed her brow. "What do you mean?"

"Well, we had an encounter on our way up here." He scratched the back of his head with his non-wounded arm. "I… um. I need you and Ben to come with me. Someone wants to talk to you."

"Dan, what's wrong?" The redhead's pulse quickened.

"Nothing's wrong," he assured her. "In fact, you might actually want to hear this news. So grab Ben and come on."

"If you want us, you're getting my team," she shot back.

Dan put his hand up in surrender. "Fair enough."

"Hey guys, somebody wants to meet us," Sparks said, and waved her companions after them.

The Principal led them inside to the dining room. There was a military man sitting there in proper fatigues, flanked by two soldiers.

"Captain Evans, I'd like to present Officer Sparks," Principal Dan introduced, and the Captain stood, extending his hand.

"Officer Sparks, you are one difficult woman to track down," he said, though not unkindly.

She chuckled as she shook his hand. "What can I say? It's been a hell of a few days."

"Can't argue with that, ma'am," he agreed.

She straightened up and looked him in the eye. "So, Captain Evans, what can I do for you?"

"Well, Officer Sparks-"

She put up a hand. "Just Sparks."

"Okay, Sparks," he corrected, "I'm based out of Camp Bullis in San Antonio. When shit went bad, my orders were to follow up on your radio message. I led a small team that raided Doctor Alvison's lab and secured his notes."

"How useful was the info?" Sparks asked.

"The basis you covered in your radio broadcast were incredibly useful," he told her. "Last I Heard they were quarantining people on the coasts, but the belief among a lot of us is that it will be like putting a bandaid on a bullet wound. I don't want to dismiss what you did, it undoubtedly saved lives, however it remains to be seen how many or if it will matter at all."

She furrowed her brow. "What about his notes and research?"

"To be honest, we can't really make heads or tails of it," Evans admitted. "Which is why I had to track you down. The top page of his report said that two of his research assistants, Ashley and Ben, were escaping with you. My hope is that they were still with you."

"I'm Ben." The kid stepped forward. "But my girlfriend Ashley didn't make it."

Captain Evans bowed his head. "I'm sorry for your loss, son."

"Appreciated," he replied, "so what can I do for you, Captain?"

Evans straightened. "My orders are to take you back to base."

"You want to take me back to San Antonio?" Ben deadpanned. "Are you fucking crazy?"

"Camp Bullis got overrun yesterday," the Captain explained. "Lots of good men died in the process. So no, I'm not crazy and I'm not taking you to San Antonio."

"I'm…" the kid stammered. "I'm sorry Captain."

"It's alright," Evans replied gently. "No, I'm taking you to our mobile base. We have a few ships stationed in the gulf and have set up a research lab so you can work."

Ben swallowed. "Why me?"

"Look Ben, I'll level with you." Evans sighed. "We know you're not the best of the best, but you could very well be the best we're gonna find. We have satellite uplinks on these ships, so if we are able to secure more experienced researchers in this field, you'll be able to help relay the Doc's findings.

"Look, the bottom line is, we need you. Your country, and hell, the entire world needs you."

"You should go, Ben, if for no other reason than you can escape this madness," Sparks cut in.

"So that's it?" The kid clenched his jaw. "Y'all just kicking me to the curb?"

Sparks put a hand on his arm. "Come on, Ben, it's not like that."

"Gotcha!" A grin erupted on his face. "I'm just fucking with you. After being kidnapped I think I've had my fill of apocalypse world."

She smiled in relief. "I'm glad you're going."

"And hey, if it's not too much trouble," Jeff added, "can you find a cure for this shit there, Chocolate Thunder?"

"Sure thing, white bread," Ben replied, and extended his hand. Jeff took it and they did a surprisingly warm bro-hug. The kid turned and embraced Sparks proper, and she gave his shoulder a reassuring squeeze as she pulled back.

"Well, Captain Evans, what about us?" she inquired. "Can you get us out, too?"

"Unfortunately I can't," Evans replied, having the grace to look regretful. "We're barely going to have enough fuel to make it to the ship as it is. Any more weight and we're swimming."

"No worries, Captain," Sparks replied. "Just had to ask."

"I can offer you some advice, though," he said. "Get as far west as you can. Austin is on fire, and San Antonio is completely overrun. Those hordes are going to be moving out sooner rather than later."

She nodded. "That's the plan."

"Is there anything you need that I might be able to provide?" he asked.

"Gear," Sparks replied immediately. "Specifically, we need communication gear. Even if it's a carrier pigeon."

Evans laughed. "Don't worry, the US Military is a little more advanced than that. And yeah, I can hook you up when the chopper gets here. Should have a few sets we can spare."

"Appreciated, Captain," she saluted him.

"Sir, chopper inbound," one of the soldiers touched his ear. "Two minutes."

"That's my cue," Evans said. "Let's move out."

"Well, at least we can talk to each other now," Jeff said as the chopper flew off into the distance, carrying Ben with it.

Principal Dan sighed. "So, what's next?" he asked.

There was a long moment of silence, the only noise the fading blades of the helicopter.

"Well hell," Ricky piped up. "I could go for some breakfast."

Sparks laughed. "That's the best idea I've heard all day."

END OF BOOK TWO

DEAD TEXAS
BOOK THREE: LONESOME ROAD
BY DEREK SLATON
© 2018

CHAPTER ONE

"Everybody," Rufus said as he got to his feet, holding up his full cup of coffee. "I'd like to propose a toast." He looked around at the breakfast table, meager servings of toast and half-pancakes on plates in front of his friends.

"Wait, aren't you supposed to have alcohol to make a toast?" Sparks raised an eyebrow. He simply smiled and winked down at her. "You wily old bastard. Holding out on us, for shame."

The white-haired man pulled a flask out of his back pocket and handed it to her. She poured a nip into her coffee and passed it to Jeff, the skinhead to her left.

"Now, as I was saying," Rufus continued as Principal Dan added a little to his cup and passed it to Mary, who poured for both her and Ricky. "I'd like to propose a toast. To our fellow traveler Ben, who at this moment is flying high above the shitshow that each and everyone one of us is trapped in. May that smart little bastard enjoy his new life at sea."

Ricky snorted. "And maybe he can come up with a cure, and stuff."

"Hell I'd settle for a can of zombie spray," Rufus replied. "Take them bitches out like roaches."

Jeff chuckled, imagining the sight. "Realistically that's probably the best we can hope for at this point."

Silence fell over the table, and they all contemplated the fact that this little breakfast was likely the best thing in their lives for the foreseeable future.

"Well, that got kinda dark quick." Sparks pursed her lips. "Who needs more of Rufus' special coffee?"

Jeff and Ricky both shoved their cups forward emphatically, and Rufus put up a hand. "Hey now, I got a limited supply."

"Don't worry there bubba, I got a bottle of Jack in the glove box," Ricky replied, wiggling his cup expectantly. "I'll hook you up."

Rufus grinned and produced his flask. "Round two it is!"

Principal Dan knocked on the table as everyone passed around the booze to get their attention once again. "I'm glad everyone is having a good time, Lord knows we need it after the last five days or so, but we can't be getting drunk."

"Looks like someone is underestimating our alcohol tolerance," Jeff retorted.

Sparks glanced at him with a raised eyebrow. "Be that as it may, Principal Dan is right. So this is the last round of the morning."

"Last round of the morning," Mary said good-naturedly. "Man, feels like I'm back in college again." There was a round of chuckles.

Rufus clapped Ricky on the back. "You gots yourself a keeper there, bub."

"Don't I know it," Ricky said with a grin.

"Pretty sure you left that one off of your job application, Mary," Principal Dan said, leaning on his elbows.

She blushed. "Sorry, Principal Dan."

"I mean, I would have still hired you, but if I had known that I would have toasted your hiring," he replied with a glint in his eye. Another round of chuckles.

"Alright y'all," Sparks said, clapping her hands together. "Let's get serious. Dan, what's the situation with the survivors and transport?"

"As far as transport goes, we have two busses that have about three quarters of a tank, so that should get us to at least Junction," he replied. "Not including the people at this table, we have a head count of thirty-eight."

Jeff blew air through his teeth. "Holy hell, that's a lot of people to take care of."

"It gets worse," Dan cut in. "We only have food and water for about four or five days, and that's with heavy rationing. We may be able to get to Junction with that, but we aren't getting much further."

"Not meaning to sound ignorant and all," Ricky piped up. "But where exactly are we headed?"

"Not ignorant at all," Sparks assured him. "Unfortunately I don't think there's an answer yet. Once we get past Junction it's about two hundred miles of nothing. Just spit balling, but maybe we should target a place like Fort Stockton?"

"Not a bad idea," Dan said, chewing over it. "Small town, isolated from pretty much everything, and enough buildings that we could set up some greenhouses and get a sustainable source of food."

"So my choices are: get eaten by zombies or become a vegetarian?" Rufus looked horrified. "Man, that's a tough one, anybody got a coin?"

"Wait, wait, back up a second," Jeff cut in, putting up a hand. "Greenhouses sound like a great idea, but do we have the material to pull them off?"

"It could be difficult," Dan admitted. "But I think there's enough ingenuity at this table alone to pull it off."

Jeff nodded. "So I guess we need to add seeds to our shopping list?"

"More seeds wouldn't be a bad idea," the Principal agreed. "I packed everything they had at the school for the horticulture club, but it might not be enough."

"Jeff does bring up a good point," Sparks added. "Before we head west we're going to have to do some shopping."

Mary shrugged. "Well, we know we need food, water and seeds. What else could we need?"

"Bullets have gotta be at the top of that list," Rufus spoke up. "We can handle a couple of them fuckers with blades, but if we run into a pack or a horde, we're gonna need somethin' with a little more punch."

"We need medicine," Dan added. "Cold and flu medication especially. We're all going to be living in tight confines with unsanitary conditions. One severe flu outbreak could wipe a lot of people out, especially the older ones."

"Speaking of the older ones, how many senior citizens and young kids do we have in the group of survivors?" Rufus wondered. "Just tryin' to get a feel for our operational capacity."

"Out of the thirty-eight?" Dan pursed his lips. "About thirty of them wouldn't be much help in a fight."

Rufus deadpanned. "Jesus H motherfucking christ, you telling me there's only eight people in that group that can handle themselves in a fight?"

"Afraid so," the Principal admitted. "Between the militia and the zombies, a lot of good people have died in the last couple of days."

"Christ man, do we need to add wheelchairs and kiddie leashes to the fucking list?" Rufus barked, running a hand through his snow-white locks.

"Well, there are some medications," Dan replied.

Rufus scrubbed a hand down his face and tittered a humorless laugh. "Of course there are."

"We have a couple of people with heart issues and they need nitroglycerin," the Principal continued. "It's not exactly a popular recreational drug, so I'm hoping that the pharmacy at the grocery store in Fredericksburg will have some."

"Well, looks like you have our target picked out for us," Jeff said with a sigh.

"I'm totally open to different ideas," Dan protested. "But I think this is going to be our best bet. Fredericksburg is about ten miles north of here, and the grocery store is in the southern part of town. My hope is that

213

you'll be able to sneak in and secure the store without much resistance."

Jeff leaned back in his chair. "How big of a town is it?"

"About twice the size of Comfort," Dan replied.

"So we have what?" the skinhead scoffed. "The potential for a few thousand of these things? Yeah, that sounds like a breeze."

"Well, it's either that or we starve to death," the Principal snapped.

Sparks put up a hand. "Not necessarily."

"What do you mean?" Dan raised an eyebrow.

The redhead took a deep breath. "I mean the militia compound."

"Holy hell girl, you wanna go back there?" Ricky blurted. "I know we put a whoopin on 'em and all, but they might not take kindly to us showing back up."

"It's not going to be an *us*," she said firmly. "It's going to just be me."

"Sparks, are you joking?" Jeff burst out. "We beat them and they don't know where we are. Let's just do the Fredericksburg run and get the hell outta Dodge."

"I agree that y'all should do the Fredericksburg run, but the reality is we don't have a lot of time and we can't dismiss a potential source of supplies," she said calmly, putting both palms on the table and standing up. "They raided Center Point *and* Comfort and presumably had stockpiles of stuff when we hit. If we can get our hands on that, we'll have enough to get us to Fort Stockton or wherever the hell we're going. Plus, I don't know about you, but I want to make sure we don't have to spend this entire trip looking over our shoulder, wondering if Elijah and his wannabe soldiers are after us."

"Sparks is right," Dan piped up. "If they have supplies, we can certainly use them."

"Well hell, girl, if you're gonna go," Rufus said, eyes softening, "let me come with. If you run into those tiny dicked militia bastards, you could use another gun."

"These guys need your infiltration skills, Rufus," she said to him. "And besides, once I hit Comfort I'm going to be hiking on foot. If they are still out there, it's too dangerous to be driving around. Last thing I want is to end up in a car chase in the country."

The older man sighed. "I see your point, and would just like to add that I appreciate the fact you complimented me before taking a giant shit on my ability to keep up with you."

"Don't take it personally Rufus," she said with a glint in her eye, "not too many men out there can keep up with me."

"Like I told you girl," he said with a playful wink, "I'm willing to give it a go if you are."

She couldn't help but crack a smile. "Not until you're ready to die."

"Well, according to our current plan, it'll be when we get out to Fort Stockton and I have to eat salad for every meal," he muttered, and everyone chuckled, breaking the tension.

"Well, looks like we have us a plan," Dan cut in. "So, this is what I'd like for y'all to do. Go to these locations and secure the supplies, then radio back and I'll send a couple of trucks to load up what you have and bring it back here.

"Thanks to our military friends, we have the ability to communicate with each other now. Looks like I'll have the command module and each team can reach me on their earpiece. Unfortunately, you won't be able to communicate with each other."

Jeff furrowed his brow. "So how are we supposed to let you know where stuff is?"

"The cell service looks like it finally crapped out a couple of hours ago, so the maps on the phones won't be much help," the Principal explained. "There are a couple of dedicated GPS systems in the busses, so we'll grab those. Might be a good idea to program in this place just in case the path you came from gets blocked."

"Which brings up the next question," Sparks piped up. "What's our timeline? I mean based on what the military guy said, San Antonio is going to be emptying out soon, if it hasn't already."

"I'd say we go as soon as we're ready," Jeff said.

Dan nodded. "I agree with that wholeheartedly, but I also think we need a drop dead departure time."

"Forty-five hours," Sparks declared.

Ricky blinked at her. "Well, that's an odd choice of time there."

"Not really." She shrugged. "It's nine AM now, so in forty-five hours it'll be six AM. The sun will be coming up and we'll have the maximum amount of daylight to make it to our next destination. Which I know we said is Junction, but it might be prudent to stop at the exit before it."

"That's a good call," Dan agreed. "It's the last stop for gas for a long while, so everybody who has the same idea we do is going to be stopping there."

"And as them militia boys found out," Rufus added, "we don't really play nice with others."

The Principal eyed him warily. "Ideally, we'd like to avoid bloodshed if possible."

"But if it comes to that, we'll be ready," Sparks added.

"So as a contingency, how long are we staying at the meeting spot in Junction?" Jeff asked. "We're all essentially going into a war zone, so some shit can happen that will throw us off schedule."

The Principal took a deep breath. "Even the best case scenario is that we're going to have limited supplies, so I wouldn't recommend staying longer than necessary."

"Stay one day," Sparks decided. "If nobody is there by six AM the following morning they'll be on their own, with the ultimate plan to reach Fort Stockton. The good news is that once you get past Junction, there are only so many places the group can go, so even if we get separated it'll be easy to find them." She downed the last of her lukewarm coffee and set the cup on the table. "Alright, we should get ready to head out."

"Sorry, but I have to veto that idea," Dan argued, putting up a hand. "You are all exhausted and need rest."

"We don't have time for that," Sparks countered.

"Yes, you do," he said firmly. "Sleep for two hours, that's all I ask."

She pursed her lips. "I'll give you one."

"Fair enough," he conceded. "In the meantime we'll get your travel pack ready to go. Food, water, and whatever else you may need."

"Cell phones," the redhead added.

"Why?" Dan furrowed his brow. "The cell system is shut down."

"That may be," Sparks agreed, "but they still have alarms on them. Those things are attracted to noise, so having a phone can potentially save a life."

"I'll collect all that I can," he said, "is there anything else?"

The officer nodded. "I need duct tape and a pair of binoculars."

"Should be able to dig up the tape, but I'll be surprised if I have a set of binoculars." He cocked his head in thought. "Although, if you are going through Comfort, that truck stop is pretty well stocked. They might have a set for you."

"That was going to be my first stop anyway," Sparks told him. "If the militia is still active, they'll probably have men stationed there. Guess I'll do a little shopping while I'm there."

"You ladies and your shopping," Rufus cut in with a laugh, "not even the apocalypse can keep you from it."

She punched his arm playfully. "Watch it, old man."

"Alright, everybody, there are a couple of rooms upstairs with some beds and cots," Dan said loudly, pushing his chair back from the table.

"Everybody be safe," Sparks said as the group rose to their feet and shuffled towards the stairs. "I'll see y'all in a couple of days."

"We've got a full strike team," Jeff replied, smiling though his eyes were concerned. "*You're* the one who needs to be safe."

"Aw hell, Jeff, you've seen the shit this woman can do." Rufus clapped the skinhead on the back. "If I had to bet, I'd say she's gonna have to come rescue us before it's all said and done."

Sparks laughed. "Appreciate the confidence there Rufus."

CHAPTER TWO

Sparks strolled out of the house, shaking off the grogginess behind her eyes from the too short sleep. She secured her sidearm and slung the AR-15 over her shoulder.

"Hey Sparks, over here!" Dan called, and she turned to see him waving at her from the back of Ricky's truck.

"What's up Dan?" she asked as she walked over to him. "You got my bag ready?"

"Yeah, I got you food and water for the next couple of days," he said. "And some duct tape, and a couple of cell phones."

She pursed her lips. "Only a couple?"

"Yeah, it was slim pickings on those, so I gave each group two of them," he explained.

She nodded. "It'll have to do."

"Need you to do one more thing for me," Dan said, turning fully towards her.

Sparks looked up at him expectantly. "Sure."

"Need you to give the boys here a lift down to the school," he motioned to three men heading over from the nearest bus. "There are a couple of pickup trucks we need to secure. I know you're going on foot, so Hale here is going to drive Ricky's truck back."

She nodded again. "Shouldn't be a big deal to do that." She took the bag from him and opened the driver's side door, tossing it inside before climbing up herself. After closing it up she reached out the window and smacked the outside a few times to signal to the guys to get in.

Two men hopped into the bed, waving to Principal Dan, and Hale climbed into the passenger seat. Sparks nodded to the robust middle-aged farmer.

"You be careful, Sparks," Dan put a hand on the truck, looking her straight in the eye. "And stay in touch."

"Will do, Dan," she agreed. "Once I scope out the gas station and the grocery store in Comfort, I'll give you an update." She leaned out the window. "You guys secure back there?" she called, and both replied in the affirmative. "Alright then, we're moving!" She waved to Dan, who stepped back to allow them room to bustle off.

She punched the accelerator and sped off towards the school.

"Thank you," Hale said, clasping his hands together in his lap.

Sparks furrowed her brow. "For what?"

"For everything you did for us yesterday," he replied, swallowing hard.

"If you and your friends weren't there, then we probably wouldn't be here right now."

"No thanks are necessary." She shook her head. "I'm doing the same thing you're doing, just trying to survive this nightmare."

"Still," he said, "thank you."

She nodded as opposed to replying, and soon they were pulling into the parking lot of the school. She stopped next to two sitting pickup trucks, and hopped out of the driver's seat, leaving the vehicle running.

"All yours, Hale," she said as she slung the backpack over her shoulders. He slid over to the driver's seat and leaned on the window as their passengers hopped down and manned the other two trucks.

"You sure I can't give you a lift into town?" he asked.

She shook her head. "Safer if I go on foot. If the militia are there, I don't want them to know I'm coming at all."

"Alrighty." He nodded. "Well, you be safe, ma'am."

Sparks gave him a little salute and stepped back to allow them room to peel out of the parking lot and took a deep breath. As the truck engines faded from earshot, she closed her eyes for a moment, letting the light breeze kiss her skin and ruffle her hair.

She savored the brief moment of peace —before what was sure to be a non-peaceful day.

Sparks crept towards the gas station parking lot, taking cover behind a dumpster. The place was mostly quiet, except for a few figures moving on the other side of the building. The windows on both sides allowed for her to watch their shadows.

"Well, either you're zombies and I'll have to kill you," she muttered to herself, "militia and I'll have to kill you, or civilians in which case I just might have to kill you." She checked her assault rifle and slung it back over her shoulder. It was a last resort weapon, not just for the noise attracting unwanted attention, but because of her dismal ammo situation.

She took a deep breath and broke into a combat run across the parking lot, crouching at the brick pillared corner of the store. She peered around the corner, and finding it clear, she darted to the glass doors. Staying low to the ground, she kept her eyes on the figures outside, and pushed open the door as quietly as she could.

Dingdingddddingdingdi-ding. The bell attached to the top of the door cheerfully announced her presence.

"Fuck." Sparks dove behind the nearest shelf as three men hurried around the building and through the tinkling door.

"Spread out, see what that was," a voice barked, and the redhead's blood ran cold at the authoritarian voice.

"Yes, sir," two voices responded in unison, and her stomach sank. Militia.

She couldn't see the front of the store well enough to make a move on the enemy there and glanced to the back. The steps were closer now, and she weighed whether or not she'd be able to make it to the back bathrooms and bottleneck the militia members in the hallway.

She popped into a squat, preparing to make a run for it, when a zombie ran headfirst into the front door. It smacked so hard against the glass that the doorbell trilled, and the guy at the front door snorted.

"Just a zombie," he said. "Peg that motherfucker."

The member closest to Sparks turned and fired, shattering the front door and the zombie's head, leaving a mess of broken glass and guts on the concrete.

"Man, what the hell time is it anyway?" the third guy asked, wandering towards the front of the store.

"Damn near noon," the guy at the front replied.

"Why in the hell haven't we been relieved yet?" the shooter asked.

"Good question, they're nearly an hour overdue," front door agreed. "I'll give them a call." There was a crackle as the static of his walkie talkie filled the dank air. "Camp freedom, camp freedom, unit two checking in. Request status update on relief squad." Static. "Camp freedom, do you copy?" Static.

"Could the coms just be down?" the shooter asked.

"Unlikely," the third guy made it to the front and sounded worried. "Maybe them high school folks hit back."

"You wanna talk about unlikely." The shooter laughed.

"Whatever it is, we gotta go check it out," the first guy pocketed his walkie talkie.

"Okay, you two go, I'll stay here and hold down the fort," the worried guy offered, and Sparks rolled her eyes.

"You stay frosty," the front door guy said, "we'll be back soon."

The bell dinged twice, and then a truck started up and peeled out.

Sparks peeked around the corner of her hideout, watching the remaining militia member stroll over to the drink cooler. He opened the door, letting the cool air waft over him as he popped open a soft drink. As the glass fogged up from being open in the heat, she used that as cover to move up the aisle with her weapon raised.

When he closed the door, he stared down the barrel of her AR-15.

"Tasty beverage?" she asked, and he threw the drink at her before tearing away from her. She dodged and stuck her foot out, tripping him up so that he hit the tiles face first. She kicked him in the nuts, and as he recoiled into the fetal position she toed him onto his back, resting her foot on his chest.

He groaned in pain, holding his sack and sputtering through the blood running from his busted nose. She pointed the rifle down at his wide-eyed face.

"You may be a young one, but don't pretend for a second that your youth is going to cut you any slack with me," she warned. "You and your buddies there did a number on me and my friends yesterday, so as far as I'm concerned, every single one of you is marked for death."

"Oh please, nonono," he moaned, "it wasn't me, I swear!"

She cocked the gun. "Save it," she demanded. "All I see when I look at you is that uniform. Now, how do you feel about answering some questions for me?"

He nodded furiously, eager to comply.

"Good," she said, "first question. How many men you have in town?"

He took a deep breath. "I'm it right now."

"I don't belieeeeve you," Sparks singsonged.

"It's true!" he protested.

"So you don't have anybody over at, say, the grocery store?" She raised an eyebrow.

"No, we cleaned that out yesterday and took everything to the farm," he explained hurriedly.

"The farm?" she asked. "Don't you mean the compound that's out in the woods?"

"No, it's some sort of safe house for the senior members," he replied, spitting some blood from his mouth. "When people are running missions they can't always make it back to the compound."

She leaned forward. "So where is this farm?"

"I don't know." He visibly trembled.

She pressed the barrel against his forehead. "You literally just said that you cleaned the grocery store out and took it to the farm."

"I just helped load it up in the truck!" he cried. "They don't trust me enough to share the location!"

She lowered the rifle and cocked her head at him. "Alright militia-boy, I just have one more question for you," she purred. "What's your blood type?"

"Uh, it's b-positive," he stammered. "But why do you need to know that?"

"Just checking to see if I needed to waste a bullet or not," she said, and in one fluid motion, drew her knife and slashed his throat. He reached for the wound, gurgling, but she kicked his hands away from trying to staunch the bleeding.

She watched the panic in his eyes, and her heart skipped a beat. A week ago, this was just a kid. Granted, a racist kid with some bad friends, but still just a kid. She knew she had made the right choice in ending his life, because if the other members came back he could warn them about her. But she still didn't feel great about what she had to do.

This was war. But it wasn't a war she had started.

When the last of his life left his eyes, Sparks knelt down, wiping the blood on her hands on his pants. She reached to take his ammo, but then realized that if the others found him like this it would give her away.

"Fuck, now what?" she muttered to herself.

She took a deep breath and then used the serrated edge of her knife to hacksaw his neck wound raw. It didn't look exactly like a bite, but it could pass for one at a quick glance. She took his handgun and put it in his hand, put it to his head and pulled the trigger. Brains splashed against the drink cooler, and she let him slump, hand falling to his lap.

She eyed the gun, but the need to stay undetected at this juncture was greater than the need for ammo.

She drew her weapon and moved to the front of the store, checking both directions to make sure the gunshot hadn't attracted more zombies. Upon deciding the coast was clear, she hopped over the counter and checked the back wall of electronics for sale. She scooped a pair of cheap binoculars and four disposable cell phones.

Sparks approached the supermarket, taking a position about a hundred yards away to break out her new toy. She gazed through them, adjusting the focus. There were a few dozen figures roaming the entrance, all zombies. A few of them were in militia fatigues, showing her that their conquest of the store wasn't without its costs.

She zoomed in as far as she could, tutting quietly at the sight of empty shelves through the front door. She tapped her earpiece.

"Good to hear from you, Sparks," Dan's voice came through into her ear. "What's the situation?"

"Comfort is a bust," she said quietly. "There were a trio of militia men at the gas station, but from the sounds of it they had no idea we took out their compound."

"What about the supermarket?" he asked.

"Picked clean and overrun with zombies," she replied. "But according to the militia douchebag I interrogated, he said they moved it to their safe house. Some far, but he didn't know where it was."

"Well, I'll send Hale and the boys down to pick him up," Dan offered. "Maybe we can get it out of him."

She swallowed the lump in her throat. "I had to eliminate him, couldn't risk him signaling the others.

"Understood," Dan paused, "you okay?"

"About as okay as I'm gonna be," she replied thickly.

"You don't have to push on if you don't want to, Sparks," he reassured her.

"Yeah I do." She cleared her throat, firming up her voice. "We need that food and medication, especially if the other target is empty or has a horde occupying it."

"In that case, as soon as I get confirmation they got it secure, then you can come back," he declared.

Sparks lowered her binoculars. "How are the others doing?"

"Just got off the horn with them a minute ago," he told her. "They were about a mile from Fredericksburg."

"Keep me posted," she instructed. "I'm headed to the compound."

He took a deep breath. "Be safe."

"Yep." She clicked off the earpiece, gave herself a little shake, and began the long hike to the compound.

CHAPTER THREE

Ricky rounded the bend a mile outside of Fredericksburg and Mary gasped at the giant plumes of thick black smoke rising out of the city.

"What in the fuck is that?" her husband blurted, and Rufus leaned in the back window from his perch in the bed of the truck next to Jeff.

"Looks like some shit went down in Fredericksburg," he drawled.

Mary shook her head. "It looks like the whole city is on fire."

"Well, hopefully it looks worse than it is," Jeff put in. "And *really* hope that the fires haven't reached the grocery store."

"Well, we're about a mile from the store, so we'll find out soon enough," Ricky replied solemnly.

"Slow down to about twenty miles an hour there, Ricky," the skinhead instructed. "Rufus and I can stand up then, we really need to be on guard from here on in."

"Will do," the driver nodded.

The comrades in arms stood up once the truck was slowed right down, leaning over the roof with their assault rifles. Mary rolled down her window, but her husband grabbed her hand as she reached for her shotgun.

"That shotgun's gonna be too much to handle from the window," he protested. "Don't worry though, them boys in the back got you covered."

She pulled her handgun from its holster on her thigh. "Just in case."

He smiled at her, admiring the schoolteacher's toughness.

As they entered the residential streets, the homes sat quiet. It looked like a massive battle had gone down in the suburbia cul du sac, zombie corpses littering the road next to a row of cars that looked like they'd been used for cover. There were no civilians to be seen, however.

"Hanging a right in two blocks and we'll be there!" Ricky called back through the rear window.

"Ten four," Jeff called back.

However, when Ricky made the turn, he slammed on the brakes. "Motherfucking fuck."

"Well, that's not good," Jeff muttered.

The massive grocery store stood a hundred yards ahead, with reams of thick smoke pouring out of it.

Jeff smacked the roof. "Get a little closer?"

"Why?!" Ricky cried back. "The fucker's on fire!"

"We need to see how bad it is," Jeff protested. "We might be able to sneak in a salvage something before the flames overtake it."

Ricky shook his head but crept forward, pulling into the parking lot. The fire seemed to be contained in the back half of the store, where the majority of the smoke plumed out of. The front part looked moderately clear.

"See?" Jeff hopped down from the truck bed. "We can get in there and get some stuff if we hurry."

"Fire ain't the only thing we gotta worry about," Rufus reminded him. "Ricky, give the horn a good long honk."

The mechanic complied, the horn echoing throughout the parking lot. Within a few seconds, half a dozen flaming zombies emerged from the shattered door at the front of the store. They shambled slower than normal, but still faster than anyone would have assumed a body on fire could move.

Before they were halfway across the parking lot, another ten emerged from the smoke.

"Man, that's a whole lotta nope right there," Rufus declared.

"Goddammit," Jeff conceded. "Okay Ricky, get us back to the edge of town and pull in behind that cul de sac fortress we passed."

"Will do, bubba," Ricky agreed, happy to get away from this scene, and peeled back through town. He parked behind the cars, and Jeff hunkered down, touching his earpiece.

"You guys keep watch, I'll call in to Principal Dan," he said. Ricky and Mary jumped out of the truck to take defensive positions behind the cars, while Rufus watched the houses from atop the vehicle.

"Hey baby, watch where you step," Mary said. "It doesn't look like it ended up too well for these people."

Ricky shook his head. "Judging by how crappy these houses are, they didn't have a whole hell of a lot to lose, but what they did have, they lost in a big way."

"Hey Principal Dan, you there?" Jeff asked.

"Man, you guys are quick," Dan replied. "You have the grocery store secured already?"

"It's a no go on that," the skinhead admitted. "It's currently burning to the ground and is infested with flaming zombies. So we got nothing."

"Sparks struck out in Comfort, too," the Principal replied with a sigh.

"Well, have you got any bright ideas?" Jeff asked. "Because starving to death isn't exactly high on my list of things to do."

Dan took a deep breath. "Where are you guys now?"

"We retreated to city limits on the route we came in on," the skinhead replied.

"Perfect, I need you to get to the GPS and look for a place called Colonial Court," Dan instructed.

Jeff raised an eyebrow. "Alright, hang on." He reached through the window and grabbed the GPS, fiddling with the touch screen. "Okay, I got it, looks like it's a couple miles east of us. So what the hell is it?"

"High end gated community," the Principal replied.

"In Fredericksburg?" Jeff scoffed. "Are you shitting me?"

"Little known fact," Dan said, "but Fredericksburg has a large number of wineries. Turns out a lot of the winery owners want to live in nice houses, so they bought up some land in the middle of a working class neighborhood and put in Colonial Court. Complete with an eight foot high brick wall that surrounds the entire thing."

"Even in the apocalypse you learn something new every day," the skinhead replied in wonder.

Dan chuckled. "Happy I could educate you."

"So what's the play?" Jeff asked.

"You guys get in, go from house to house, and raid the hopefully well stocked pantries," came the reply. "Stage it and I'll send the boys to pick everything up you can find."

"Sounds like a better prospect than flaming zombie land," the skinhead admitted. "Alright, we're on it, I'll touch base when we have it secure."

"Be safe," Dan instructed.

"Yep." Jeff switched off the earpiece. "Alright y'all, we have a new target."

Ricky and Mary made their way back towards the truck.

"Where we goin' now?" Rufus asked.

"Someplace I don't think any of us have ever been to before." Jeff grinned. "A rich ass gated community."

"Oh, I like it." Rufus mirrored his expression. "Hopefully these Richie Rich types will have some high end alcohol."

Jeff barked a laugh. "Good to know you have a one track mind there, Rufus."

"Hey now, I think of boobs too," he defended.

"Whoa there," Mary piped up.

"Well, not yours, Mary," Rufus said quickly, a blush creeping up his cheeks. "I mean, not that they aren't nice, but I mean… ah, fuck it, let's just go shoot some rich zombies in the face." He cocked his gun, and she playfully smacked his shoulder through the window, cracking a smile.

Colonial Court was hidden from view by a red brick wall tied together with an ornamental wrought iron gate. A brick guard booth sat in the middle of the driveway, and Ricky and Jeff skirted it to take the gate in their hands.

After giving it a good shake, it rattled and moved about six inches in each direction.

"Well hell, they spent all this money on the wall, but skimped on the gate," Ricky said with an amused grin. "Sure it looks pretty and all, but man I've seen some beaver dams that were sturdier than this piece of shit."

"So, it shouldn't be a problem to remove it?" Jeff asked.

"Looks like this thing is motorized," he replied, "so let's not get ahead of ourselves just yet." Ricky popped into the guard booth to look for the switch, but the controls were badly damaged. "Well shit, looks like someone went all Babe Ruth on the control panel there," he said as he emerged. "Busted it up good."

Jeff shrugged. "So, plan B?"

"Yeah, the gate won't be a problem for the winch on my truck." Ricky nodded. "Although we probably wanna do that when we ready to get the hell outta here."

The skinhead furrowed his brow. "Why?"

"Well, when that big bitch comes down, it's gonna make a hell of a racket," his companion explained. "From the looks of it, this is the only way in or out, so if we attract unwanted attention before we're ready to go…"

"We'll be fucking ourselves," Jeff finished. "Yeah, great." He looked around and noticed a small parking lot to the right, against the wall. "Why don't you park your truck over there, and we'll hop the fence and just borrow someone's ladder when we're ready to hop back."

"Sounds like a plan, bubba," Ricky agreed.

After moving the truck, Jeff climbed up first, peering down the other side and dropping in an awkward manner. He jumped back up, hoping the others hadn't seen his bad landing, and scanned the immediate area for zombies or people. There were none, so he waved for Rufus to follow him.

Once everyone had landed, the quartet
moved quietly into the backyard of the
first house. The yards were mostly open in
the ritzy neighborhood, with no fencing to
separate them. Though the houses were so
close together it would have been hard to
have fencing as it was. They wandered
under the mid-sized trees in the first
yard and up onto the back porch.

Jeff jiggled the handle of the patio
door. "No luck, we'll have to break it,"
he said, and as if on cue, a zombie
slammed into the glass from the inside.
The skinhead tumbled backwards in shock,
drawing his handgun at the same time. The
zombie thrashed against the glass, but it
didn't budge or crack. "Thank christ these
rich folk sprung for the safety stuff," he
breathed.

"You alright?" Rufus asked, helping
his companion to his feet.

"Yeah, let's just put this house on
the *maybe* list," Jeff replied.

Rufus chuckled. "Plenty of houses
left to hit," he assured him.

The group moved towards the next
house just as a shot rang through the air,
snapping into the tree next to Ricky. He
shoved Mary behind it, Jeff and Rufus
taking cover at the edge of the patio. The
older man aimed over the top, the younger
around the bottom. They made out a middle-

aged man in jeans and a white tee standing on his back porch with a shotgun.

"That's far enough, assholes!" the guy bellowed.

"Yo, chill the fuck out, man!" Jeff cried. "We ain't gonna hurt you!

"Nah, you just want my shit right?" he called back. "Well you can't have it!" He fired off another shot, blowing off the wooden railing six feet away from where they were crouched.

"Man, this guy is a shitty fucking shot," Rufus said quietly. "Pretty sure I could walk into the middle of the yard and he'd still miss."

"Let's not tempt fate, shall we?" Jeff suggested.

Rufus pouted. "Eh, you're no fun."

Another shot rang out, but didn't appear to hit anything.

Jeff glanced over at Ricky and Mary, who were perfectly safe behind their tree. "Look man, we don't want your shit," he called gently. "We won't even come into your house, I swear. You won't even know we're here!"

"You don't get it, this entire neighborhood is *mine*!" the guy yelled. "I took it. When the mayor rounded up everybody to take them to the old church downtown, I said he could go fuck himself. When he persisted, I shot a few of them.

Finally, they realized I meant business and left me alone.

"And guess what, I was fucking right! I don't know what went down at the church, but I'm guessing by the smoke it wasn't good. Now why don't you do yourself a favor and fuck off before I have to shoot y'all too." His next shot hit the ground a few feet away from Rick and Mary.

"Can I shoot this motherfucker yet?" Rufus raised an eyebrow.

"You have a shot from this angle?" Jeff asked.

The older man inclined his head to the tree. "I like Ricky's vantage point better."

"Okay," the skinhead gave in, "I'll lay down some covering fire and-" He was cut off by the sound of shattering glass and the unmistakable screech of zombies.

A couple of houses up, a small pack of zombies poured out of the back patio door that had finally given way under their onslaught. They raced towards the standoff, undeterred by the neighbor's panicked shots that missed them entirely. He tried to dive back inside, but they got there first, tackling him into his house. Another shotgun blast pinged around his kitchen as Jeff waved to Ricky and Mary.

"Get across the street!" he screamed, and the quartet tore between two houses,

Rufus pulling up the rear. When they got to the other side, he whipped around to fire a few rounds back at their pursuers, hitting the lead zombie in the head to trip up the two behind it.

"It's locked!" Ricky cried from the front door of the first house, an elegant wooden number with a glass panel in the middle.

"Move," Jeff instructed, and when his companion did so, he fired his assault rifle, shattering it. "Everybody in!" he cried, and they all hopped through the hole. "Rufus, clear the house, Ricky, help me with this table."

They grabbed the dining room table, flipping it on its side, and slammed it against the hole in the door. Mary sat on the ground with her back to it, wedging herself up against it to keep it from moving.

She drew her handgun to keep watch as Rufus cleared the house. The two pursuing zombies slammed into the waist-high barrier, squealing, and Jeff punched his rifle over Mary's head, pushing back one of the attackers. Ricky drew his handgun, but Jeff shook his head.

"Save your bullets," he directed, "use your knife."

Ricky nodded and dispatched the two zombies, each with a stab to the head. They crumpled onto the front steps.

Meanwhile, Rufus set his handgun on the kitchen counter and picked up a thick wooden cutting board, smacking a wayward zombie in the face with it. It staggered and he knocked it over, bashing the corner of the board into its forehead repeatedly. Once it stopped moving, he finished his sweep, coming back around to the front door.

"Outside secure?" he asked.

"For the moment," Jeff replied. "And the house?"

"Ground floor is cleared," the older man said. "I'll take the second floor."

Jeff nodded as Rufus moved up the staircase. "Alright, Mary, if you want to go inspect the pantry and medicine cabinets, your husband and I are gonna see if we can attract any more zombies to our little trap here," he instructed.

"Sure thing," Mary agreed. "Can I bring you boys anything from the kitchen?"

Jeff nodded. "Could use some water."

"And a towel," Ricky piped up. "That last dead fucker leaked all over me."

His wife nodded. "Coming right up."

"You good for another assault?" Jeff asked his partner.

Ricky took a deep breath. "Yeah, let's get it over with."

Jeff put two fingers in his mouth and let out a piercing whistle. "Well, once those zombies across the street are finished with lunch, hopefully that will get their attention."

"If not, then they must be deaf, holy fuck that was loud." His companion winced.

"Sorry about that." The skinhead laughed. "I'll warn you next time."

"That would be appreciated," Ricky confirmed.

Mary reappeared with bottled water and a towel. "Here you go, boys," she said.

"Thanks, babe." Her husband smiled at her and accepted the towel.

Jeff grinned. "Thanks, Mary."

"Took a quick peek into the pantry, and it looks like it's loaded," she told them. "Like Costco loaded."

"Alright, maybe we won't starve to death after all," Jeff said. "Hey Ricky, can you keep watch for a minute? I'm gonna call Dan."

"Have at it, bubba," his companion replied.

Jeff nodded in thanks and hit his earpiece.

"Jeff, what's the story?" Dan asked immediately.

"Well it's actually good news for once," the skinhead replied. "We got into Colonial Court and the first house has a lot of goods."

"That's great news," the Principal gushed. "I'll let the boys know."

"We ain't gonna need them for a while though," Jeff cut in. "Some of the houses have zombies in them, so it's gonna take us a while to get everything secured."

Dan pursed his lips. "How long you think?"

"Let's see, there looks to be fourteen houses in here," Jeff guesstimated. "Maybe fore hours for us to work our way through? It'll go faster once we get the straggler zombies taken out. Speaking of which, hang on a sec." He leaned out the door, let out another loud whistle, attracting the attention of one of the zombies from across the street. "Sorry, had to stay on top of it."

"Ow, Bubba," Ricky muttered, poking at his ear.

"No worries," Dan replied. "Do what you gotta do and touch base with me in a couple of hours for an update."

Jeff nodded. "Ten four." He clicked the earpiece and jabbed forward with his rifle to stop the latest zombie, just like last time. Ricky stabbed it in the head just as Rufus descended the stairs.

"Upstairs is clear," the older man declared.

"Good," Jeff commended, clapping his friend on the back. "Mary is taking care of the pantry, so if you wouldn't mind checking the bathrooms for medication, that'd be great."

"You got it," Rufus agreed. "I'll check the bedrooms for weapons and ammo too."

The skinhead nodded. "Good call."

"Hey guys," Ricky piped up. "We may have a problem."

The two men turned to the door, following Ricky's finger at the sight of smoke seeming from the windows of the house across the street.

"Fuck, is that smoke?" Rufus blurted.

Ricky nodded solemnly. "Looks to be."

"That dumbass must have started a fire with his final shotgun blast," Rufus grunted.

Jeff shrugged. "Well, there's not a whole lot we can do about it except hope it doesn't attract a lot of attention."

CHAPTER FOUR

Sparks touched her earpiece as she hit the walking trail about fifteen yards off the highway.

"Hey Sparks, made it to the militia compound yet?" Dan asked.

"Not quite," she replied. "According to the GPS thing I have about a mile to go before I hit the turnoff. Figured this would be a good time to touch base."

"I'm glad you did, as I talked to the other group about an hour ago," the Principal said. "Happy to report I have promising news."

"Did they secure the grocery store?" she asked hopefully.

"Unfortunately it went up in flames, however they made it to a rich gated community," he replied. "The homeowners apparently loved Costco because the pantries are well stocked."

"That's great, Dan," Sparks said with a smile. "Hopefully there will be enough there for the journey."

"We have our fingers crossed," he assured her.

The redhead stretched her arms above her head as she hiked. "How's morale at the farm?"

"Everybody is scared, obviously, but people are holding up pretty well," he told her. "Some of the older folks are keeping the young children entertained with stories, and a few of the older kids are throwing a football around. If I took a picture of it you'd swear it was someone's family reunion." He chuckled and paused, but there was only quiet on the other end. "You okay, Sparks?"

"Yeah, just daydreaming about better days," she admitted. "I mean a week ago I was fighting against an old boys network to get onto the SWAT team and my biggest worry outside of my work was getting prepared for my next wrestling match to defend my title."

"Did you ever dream of making it to the show?" he asked.

"I was never at that level," she told him. "I mean don't get my wrong, I could hold my own in a ring, but there were so many others out there that were bigger, faster, and stronger. And to be frank, I was happy where I was. Nothing wrong with being a big fish in a little pond."

Dan chuckled. "I can relate, believe it or not."

"Were you a wrestler too?" the redhead asked, shocked.

"Baseball player," he said. "Man, I chased that dream hard too, but just couldn't quite make it to the show. Spent about six years in a triple-A before calling it a career."

"Six years isn't that long, especially in baseball," she mused. "Why did you throw in the towel?"

"Combination of things, really," he said with a shrug. "I played third base and the big league team traded for an all-star third baseman that was two years younger than me, which didn't exactly bode well for my chances of moving up. When I asked for a trade they said no. Couple that with the fact I had gotten married the year before and I decided to call it a day. There were more important things going on in my life other than baseball."

"I can respect that." Sparks nodded. "And, please forgive me if this is insensitive, but were you still married when all this went down?"

"You're good," Dan assured her. "No, my wife Katie passed away in a car accident late last year. One second she was here, and then next, just, gone. I mean I would have loved to have had the last year with her, but she had A-blood type and I think that would have been much worse than what happened."

"I'm sorry Dan," the officer replied sincerely, "didn't mean to bring down the conversation. I mean any more than it already was since we were talking about failed dreams."

He chuckled. "As crazy as it sounds, it's nice to talk about the old world."

"The old world?" She laughed too. "It's barely been a week, not quite ready to be referring to it as the old world."

"Fair enough," he conceded. "Well, anytime you want to shoot the breeze about the good ole days, I'm around."

"Thanks Dan." She reached the end of the path where it forked into two. "And with that, I need to jump off com for a bit," she said regretfully. "I've reached the woods at the compound."

"Be safe, and give me an update as soon as you have one," he instructed.

Sparks nodded. "You got it." She clicked off the earpiece and readied her assault rifle.

The officer of the apocalypse crept up to the road, taking a good long look in either direction to make sure the coast was clear. Once she was confident that nobody was around, she sprinted across the street and into the woods, immediately going back into a combat walk with her gun up in a crouched position.

She wove her way through eighty yards of trees before spotting the compound.

From where she was, she couldn't see much except that the front gate was open.

She shimmied up a tree not far from her vantage tree the last time she'd been there, and braced herself in a V branch. She pulled out her binoculars and maxed out their range, scanning the compound. She didn't see any movement as she scrutinized the area and slid back down to ground level.

She touched her earpiece as she approached the gate. "I'm at the compound and it appears to be deserted," she told him. "I want you to stay on com while I go through."

"Understood," he replied.

Sparks swept the courtyard, a couple dozen corpses littering the ground. None were standing, though a few were twitching. She wondered vaguely if the zombies didn't leave enough of the militia members that they could be mobile upon reanimation.

"Looks clear, heading in," she reported, and headed to the storage building first. She poked her head through the window that Rufus had shattered shooting at Elijah, noting a pile of zombie bodies piled up in front of the door to bar it shut. "Looks like Rufus was able to shoot Elijah, but it doesn't appear as though it was a kill shot."

"How do you know?" Dan asked.

She scanned the small space. "Not enough blood."

"If he's still alive, you should get out of there," he warned.

"Not until I check the back storage buildings," she countered.

She headed across the courtyard, careful to keep her distance from the corpses lying about just in case they were animated enough to bite her ankles. A zombie moaned from the storage buildings ahead of her, and she raised her weapon. It was in civilian clothing, so not a militia member, and she waited for it to sprint towards her.

"That's odd," she commented when it didn't.

Dan made a noise of curiosity. "What is it?"

"There's a zombie, but it's not running," she explained. "It's like she wants to, but just can't."

"Well don't admire it too long before putting it down," he advised, and she slung her rifle back over her shoulder. She was about to draw her knife, but the glint of a machete caught her eye. It was strapped to the leg of a fallen militia member and she reached down and snatched up the severed leg, drawing the machete and tossing the leg in one fluid motion.

The zombie staggered as the leg hit it, and Sparks shoved the blade directly through its face. It twitched as dark blood poured from the wound, and the zombie collapsed as she jerked the machete free, shaking off the excess blood as she moved towards the building.

"Approaching the storage building now," she said, reaching for the doorknob.

"Wait!" Dan cried suddenly.

Sparks jerked back, heart pounding. "Holy hell man, don't do that," she said.

"It might be a trap," he explained.

She furrowed her brow. "A trap."

"You said these guys had a zombie pen," he said. "They'd have to know someone might come looking for their supplies."

"I gotta give it to you Dan." She let out a deep breath. "You are absolutely right." She contemplated for a moment, wondering how to approach this situation in the event that he was right. She finally shrugged and simply knocked on the door, figuring if anything was in there it would stir them up.

The knock echoed through the empty shell of a building. When nothing followed the knock, she cracked open the door and peered inside.

"Building one is totally empty," she said. "They took everything. Checking building two now."

She repeated the knock on the second building, and this time it was returned by moans. Rather than tempt fate, she ceased and backed away from the door. The banging from the inside was quick and loud, but the large metal door stood fast.

"Good call on the trap," Sparks commended. "The second storage building was filled with zombies."

"Well I'm glad you're okay." Dan sighed with relief. "And really glad I thought of the trap."

"Not nearly as glad as I am," she admitted. "Thank you."

"If my count is correct, this is the second time I've saved your life," he said wryly.

She chuckled. "Well, I don't like owing favors, let alone life debts, so I'll need to even up the score soon."

"Well, you coming back safe should be worth at least one of the life debts," he continued. "I mean, you can't really fulfill it if you're dead."

She shook her head. "Well, I still have another day out here."

"Where else are you going to go?" he asked, confused. "The compound was a bust."

She took a deep breath. "I'm going to go Center Point."

"It's an unnecessary risk, Sparks," Dan said quickly and firmly. "The militia said they hit Center Point on the first day."

"Yeah, they hit the food," she agreed. "But they didn't say anything about the drugstore. I mean, they have a drugstore, don't they?"

"Yeah they do, right on the main stretch in the center of town," he confirmed.

"Alright," she said, "well, that's where I'm headed next. With any luck, they'll have the nitro there for the heart patients in the group."

"You're a few miles from Center Point and it's going to be getting dark soon," he worried. "You should think about finding a place to hole up for the night."

"Well it sure as hell isn't going to be here." She shivered at the thought. "So I'm open to suggestions."

"The airport might not be a bad idea," he suggested.

Sparks paused. "The airport? You mean the airport that's on the other side of Center Point? Doesn't really make much sense to huff it on foot through my destination so I can rest up."

"Have you checked the docks?" Dan asked.

She furrowed her brow. "The docks?"

"Sparks, the militia compound is built on the river," he explained. "Chances are they might have a boat floating around."

She wanted to smack her forehead. "Just for the record," she declared, "I'm chalking that one up to sleep deprivation."

He chuckled. "Alright, I'll buy that."

She headed to the river side of the compound and unlatched the door that lead out to a small dock area on the water.

"Well I'll be damned," she said. "There's a boat."

"It shouldn't be too long of a trip," he said. "The river runs right by Center Point and the airport. You should be able to see the air traffic control tower from the water. In fact, that would probably be a good place to hole up for the night."

"Isolated, one entrance, and elevated so that I can see trouble headed my way," she agreed. "Good call."

He chuckled. "I get them every now and then."

"Alright, I'll give you a shout when I get to the airport," she said. "Sparks out." She clicked off the earpiece and untied the boat before hopping in. After checking the engine, she gave it a crank, starting it right up. As she motored away, she flicked to the left at a movement out of the corner of her eye, but it was too quick.

She didn't know if it had been human or zombie, but she was not in any mood to stay around and find out.

CHAPTER FIVE

"Alright, that's the last of the food," Ricky declared, plonking the last few canned goods onto the living room floor. Mary stuffed as many as she could into the last bag and stacked up another case of bottled water.

"Got some cold medication from the bathroom, nothing in the bedroom," Jeff said as he emerged from the hallway and Rufus descended from upstairs.

"Rufus, you find anything?" Ricky turned to the older man.

He shook his head. "Just some cold and allergy meds," he said. "Looked through the bedroom and didn't find any weapons, unless you count a riding crop. I did take their handcuffs, though."

"Gotta love rich folks and their kinks," Mary said, earning a curious raise of the eyebrow from her husband.

Jeff shoved the table out of the way of the door, leading everyone outside. "Alright, five more houses on this block, but really we can only hit two of them. I don't want to get too close to the burning one."

Rufus headed up to the next door and knocked on it as a zombie check before working on getting it open.

"You know, I think we'd be alright to hit the neighbors houses," Ricky said and crossed his arms. "I know these houses are close together, but it doesn't look like the fire is spreading."

"I still think it's too big of a risk," Jeff replied with a shake of his head. "If we encounter zombies we can only flee in one direction."

"Man's got a point," Mary agreed. "I don't really feel like running through flames, do you?"

"Nah, you're right," Ricky conceded. "Only gonna be about half a day's worth of food for the group in those two houses anyway."

"Hey Rufus, how's the door coming?" Jeff called up the walkway.

"Couple more minutes," the older man replied. "Gonna try and pick the lock before I kick the fucker in."

The skinhead nodded. "No worries brother, we have plenty of-"

An explosion suddenly racked the neighborhood, a giant flaming SUV flying out of the garage and landing with a metallic screech in the middle of the street.

"Holy fuck knuckles man, what the hell was that?!" Ricky exclaimed.

"Looks like it was that asshole's car," Mary replied. "Gas tank must have exploded."

Moans permeated the air, and Jeff sighed. "That doesn't sound good." The trio headed towards the front gate, checking around the flaming wreckage. There was a small horde of zombies reaching through the wrought iron, apparently attracted to the noise.

"Aren't you glad we didn't open the gate?" Ricky asked smugly.

"Yeah, that was a good call there, bub," Jeff admitted.

The horde grew larger, more zombies adding pressure to the gate. The trio watched with horror as the top dislodged from the motorized track and fell to the asphalt with a deafening *clang*.

"Back to the house!" Mary screamed, and they fled back towards where Rufus was still attempting to pick the lock.

"Open the door!" Jeff cried. "Open the door!"

Rufus glanced back to see his comrades running full tilt towards him, a horde of zombies hot on their heels. He rocketed to his feet and forcefully kicked the door, twice in succession, loosening the knob. The third kick broke the deadbolt, the door slamming open, and he dove inside just in time for the trio to barrel in.

Jeff threw his weight back into the door, closing it on a zombie arm and leg. Ricky and Mary joined him, but the old man stood, looking around the expansive front lobby.

"What the fuck are you doing Rufus?!" Jeff barked.

"Making a plan," his white-haired companion replied calmly.

"Well can you speed it up a bit?" Ricky grunted, trying to get a good foothold against the door.

Rufus took note of the indoor plants, specifically the four foot long metal planting spikes, jerking a few from the soil and heading back to the door.

"Ricky, Mary, get upstairs to the master bedroom," he instructed. "Get ready to slam that door shut and try to find something heavy to move up against it."

"Jeff, you braced?" Ricky asked.

"As much as I'm gonna be!" Jeff grunted. "Just go!"

The couple barreled up the stairs as Rufus set to slamming the metal spikes against the door. He grabbed a solid wood cabinet from the wall and dragged it over, putting it against the spikes.

"Alright, that's gonna act like a doorstop," he declared.

"Pretty sure that ain't gonna hold them once I let go," Jeff said.

Rufus sighed. "How fast can you climb stairs?"

"Goddammit," Jeff growled, "I really wish people would stop asking me how quickly I can do athletic shit!"

Rufus cocked his head. "All I heard was *fast*."

"Fucking hell," Jeff panted.

"Alright, when I'm in position at the top of the stairs, I want you to run up them and get to the master bedroom as quickly as you can, you got me?" the older man asked.

The skinhead groaned. "Got it."

Rufus stood at the top of the stairs with two of the metal spikes in hand. "Go!"

Jeff leapt away from the door and dove for the stairs, hitting the second step before the front door gave way. He reached the top of the stairs and turned to the master bedroom. Rufus shoved his spikes forward, catching the lead zombie in the chest. He flung the corpse back and forth with it, stopping the rest of the horde from getting up the stairs.

The zombie pushed forward, the spikes going further through him and piercing the dead ones behind it.

Jeff emerged from the bedroom, shotgun in hand. "Get ready to run," he said, and shot the zombie point blank in the face.

The blast took its head clean off, causing the body to fly back into the horde, knocking them down the stairs.

The duo sprinted down the hallway and slammed the door to the master bedroom shut. As soon as it latched, Ricky and Mary dragged over a heavy dresser. There were moans and bangs from the other side of the door, but it didn't budge.

"Goddammit," Ricky groaned. "It would be nice if we could catch a motherfucking break today."

"Hey, look at the bright side," Mary huffed. "At least they weren't flaming this time."

Ricky let out an exasperated laugh. "Thank god for small motherfucking miracles."

"Give me a minute y'all, I gotta let Dan know," Jeff said, tapping his earpiece.

"Jeff, you ready for us?" The Principal asked immediately.

"Hold off on sending the boys," the skinhead replied. "A horde broke through the gate."

Dan swallowed hard. "Is everybody okay?"

"Yeah, for the time being," Jeff said. "We're holed up in a bedroom and have the door secure. I think we're going to lay low for a bit and hope they get bored and leave."

"If there's anything we can do, let me know," came the reply.

"Thanks Dan, I'll keep you posted," Jeff said, and hit the earpiece again.

"Well, good thing this is a king-sized bed," Rufus said as he patted the cushy four-poster, "cause it looks like we're gonna be here for a while. At least we can get a nap in."

Mary gaped at him. "How in the hell can you think about sleep with that noise?"

"My dear, when you can catch some z's in a foxhole during a Vietcong bombardment, a little banging on the door doesn't really do much of anything," Rufus drawled and stretched out on the bed. "Holy hell, these rich fuckers know how to live," he moaned as he sank into the soft mattress.

"Rufus is right," Jeff agreed. "Go ahead and lie down, get some rest if you can. I'll take watch. We'll give it an hour or so."

Ricky and Mary nodded, climbing up onto the massive bed. Before they'd even grabbed pillows, a deep snore came out of

Rufus' open mouth. Jeff chuckled as he ascended the other side, stretching out across the foot of the bed.

Mary shook her head. "Are we sure he's not narcoleptic?"

CHAPTER SIX

The air traffic control tower grew taller as Sparks motored down the moonlit waterway. The bright light on top of the tower acted as her North Star in the darkness. The river began a lazy curve, so she ran the boat right up the embankment. She got out and took the rope in her hands, dragging it clear out of the water and tying it tightly around a thick tree.

She slipped through some tall underbrush, reaching the deserted highway. She stayed off to the side, ready to dive back into the trees if she needed to. The only obstacle between her and her goal was an eight foot high chain-link fence. As she climbed it, she couldn't help but think about climbing the fence at her grandmother's house as a kid to get to her friends in the woods. The memory brought a smile to her face.

She dropped to the asphalt on the other side, keeping an eye out for trouble, but all seemed quiet. There were a few puddle jumpers parked at the end of the runway, but no other vehicles nearby.

The door to the control tower was shut tight, but there was a key dangling from an elastic key chain on the knob. Sparks pulled it off and then realized there was a message scrawled across the

door in permanent marker: *ONE DEAD INSIDE*.
She was thankful for the foresight of
whoever had left this to think somebody
might need refuge.

She opened the door and drew her
handgun, moving inside and locking it
behind her. The interior was bare, just
grey concrete walls and a spiral staircase
that led fifty feet in the air. A
shuffling sound echoed down from the top,
and she pulled her machete, not wanting to
risk a fight on the stairs.

She banged the handle against the
metal handrail, letting the metallic *clang*
reverberate upwards. She readied herself
at the dead screech of a response, but the
zombie simply dove for her, flipping over
the top railing. It plummeted the whole
way down, only smacking wetly off of the
railing once, hitting the ground head
first with a sick *crack*.

The zombie's neck was a complete
ninety degrees, and it stopped twitching
quickly. Sparks leaned over to make sure
it was dead, and noticed the official ATC
badge clipped to its shirt. The name read
Stevie Johnson, and the photo somewhat
resembled the mangled face in front of
her.

"Looks like you knew you were going
to die, but wanted to go out doing
something important," she said quietly.

"You did good, Stevie. You did good." She nodded at the corpse and took a moment of silence before slamming the machete into his forehead just for good measure.

She made the long trip up the stairs to the main area of the tower. It was a ten by ten foot box with a single row of equipment along the floor to ceiling windows. She tossed her bag down on the desk at the end of the room and took a seat in the massively comfortable office chair, enjoying the three hundred and sixty degree view of the airport.

Sparks touched her earpiece. "Hey Dan, I'm in the tower."

"Glad you made it safe," he replied.

"Me too," she admitted. "So look, I won't keep you. I'm going to have a snack and get these cell phones I picked up at the gas station charging, and I'm passing out."

He nodded. "Get some rest, Sparks."

She touched the earpiece again, reaching into her bag for a sandwich and a bottle of water. Just as she wrapped her lips around the bready treat, the tower radio crackled.

"Kerrville tower, do you copy?" a male voice asked, and Sparks swiveled around, wide eyed. "Kerrville tower, is anybody home?"

She set the sandwich down on the desk and headed over to the mic. "This is Kerrville tower, who is this please?"

"Hey, what do you know, there *is* someone alive down there," the man said, sounding relieved. "My name is Winston Conroe."

"Well Winston Conroe," she replied with a tone of playfulness in her voice, "you can call me Sparks. What can I do for you on this fine apocalyptic evening?"

"I'm just calling to let you know that you need to warn your pilots to stay out of San Antonio airspace," Winston told her. "We just flew through there and barely made it out alive."

Sparks sombered quickly. "What the hell is going on in San Antonio?"

"The military is bombing the hell out of it," he replied. "We got buzzed by a fighter jet that nearly knocked us out of the sky."

She gaped. "A fighter jet to take on zombies?"

"Yeah, things must be terrible on the ground in downtown," he mused, "because the jet fired every missile it had into the high rises down there."

Sparks leaned on the machine, biting her lip. "My god."

"You ain't kidding," Winston added. "From our vantage point, the entire city was on fire, and not just the downtown area. It looked like a group of pyromaniacs had started a thousand bonfires. So yeah, you need to let your pilots know."

"Well Winston, I'll level with you." She took a deep breath. "I don't work at the airport, but the good news is the place looks cleaned out so any pilots that could have been warned must have taken off a while ago."

There was a pause on the other end. "If you're not airport staff, then who are you?"

"I'm an Austin police officer," she replied. "Or at least I *was*."

"Wait," Winston cut in, "are you that woman from the radio?"

She smiled. "Live and in person."

"Ha, what do you know?" he asked, amused. "Good to see you're alive and kicking! You helped a lot of people with that message."

She shrugged. "I did what I could, Winston."

"So if you don't mind me asking," he drawled, "what in the world are you doing at the Kerrville airport?"

"I don't mind at all," she assured him. "This is just my home away from home for the evening. I'm out here scouting for supplies with a group I fell in with."

"Well, I hope the journey has been quiet and uneventful," he replied thoughtfully. "At least as much as they can be given the circumstances."

She sighed. "Well, today was easier than yesterday, so I'm moving in the right direction."

"Best you can hope for, right?" he asked.

"Yep," she agreed. "So Winston, if you don't mind me asking, where are you flying off to? As fate would have it, I'm looking for a new home."

"Well, I got a buddy who works for the railroad up in Dalhart, it's this little down way up in the panhandle about an hour north of Amarillo," he explained. "He sent me an email shortly after this all started and said that the town was going into lockdown mode."

She furrowed her brow. "How does a small rural town go into lockdown mode?"

"It's funny, I asked the same thing." He chuckled. "He said they were rounding up every potential infected person and putting them in the prison that's on the outskirts of town and blockading the only main routes in.

"It's also a big farming community, so they'd have food long term. I told my wife about it and decided it sounded better than being within a stone's throw of San Antonio. So we grabbed the couple next door, headed to the airport, and took off."

Sparks nodded. "That sounds like a winner if you can get there."

"Yeah, we caught a good tailwind shortly after taking off, that should help with the fuel," Winston agreed. "Shouldn't be a problem to make it to their airport." There was a bit of a crackle on the last few words.

"You're breaking up a little bit, Winston," she informed him.

"Guess we're getting out of range," he said. "Just so you know, I would totally offer to come pick you up, but we're full up in here. I mean, unless you wanna hang on to the wing."

"I appreciate the thought." She laughed. "It's all good though, I have some unfinished business here to attend to."

"Well if you do make it up to Dalhart, be sure to look me up," he insisted. "If I have any say in the matter, I'll make sure someone at the Dalhart airport awaits your call."

She nodded gratefully. "Thanks Winston, y'all be safe."

"Hell girl, we're a mile above the action," he replied. "It's *you* who needs to be safe."

"Will do," she promised. "Until I make it to the panhandle."

"Look forward to it." There was a click as the communication broke, and she flicked off the mic. She shook her head in wonder, heading back over to her comfy seat, and put her feet up on the desk, taking her sandwich back in hand.

CHAPTER SEVEN

Ricky dug through the closet in the corner as Rufus' snores provided the overture to the still present soundtrack of moans and bangs on the other side of the bedroom door.

"Man, all this money and not a single t-shirt?" Ricky groaned. "Are you kidding me?" He pulled out a couple of expensive looking dress shirts before tossing them back into the closet. "You'd figure rich folk would know how to relax, or at least be able to hire somebody to teach them."

"Who knows," Jeff piped up from where he sat on the floor, back against the dresser barricade. "Maybe these fuckers banging on the door aren't actually after us, and are just really desperate for fine clothing."

"Yeah, well, they can have it," Ricky muttered.

Mary sighed from her perch in the windowsill, tearing her eyes from the stars to look down at the red brick wall. "Hey guys," she said as a lightbulb went off in her head, "I think I may have a way for us to get out of here."

Rufus startled awake. "Alright, you got my attention."

"Everybody come here." She waved them over.

"I'll wait until someone can tag in," Jeff replied. "Not sure this thing is going to hold without someone pressed up against it."

The other two joined Mary at the window, Rufus rubbing sleep out of his eyes.

"It looks like these people wanted the bigger floor plan," she said, "because that wall can't be more than ten feet away."

Rufus shrugged. "And?"

"And we jump for it," she explained. "We're high enough and the wall is low enough, I mean we should be able to reach it with a good enough jump. Hell, one of us could jump over with a bedsheet and the others could climb over."

"Lil' missy, I'm touched you think I'm an athletic god." Rufus put a hand over his heart. "But I assure you that my bones would disintegrate upon impact if I attempted that."

Mary shrugged. "Well, it was a thought."

"And one we shouldn't dismiss yet," Ricky piped up.

The old man raised an eyebrow. "Did you miss the part about my bones disintegrating?"

"No, not jumping to the wall," Ricky explained, "I'm talking about jumping over

277

there." He motioned to the window beside the closet and led them over there. The house next door was only about six feet away, with another window facing them.

"I'll never understand how people can spend this much money to live that close to someone else," Rufus mused.

Mary ignored him. "So how do we get in?"

"We've got a shotgun," Ricky said simply. "We just blast out the window and hop over."

"Yeah, but how does that help us get out of the neighborhood?" Rufus asked. "The front gate to the place is wide open, so god only knows how many of those things are in there."

Jeff shifted in his position. "What about a ladder?"

"What do you mean?" Mary furrowed her brow, turning to him.

"I mean one of us goes over there, gets down to the garage, grabs a ladder and we use it to reach the wall," the skinhead explained. "I mean these are two story houses, so they have to have some twenty footers in there."

"Assuming these prim and proper folk do their own yard work," Rufus retorted.

"Eh, they're rich," Jeff said. "They buy shit they don't need all the time."

"He's right, did you *see* that closet?" Ricky put in. "Who needs eighty button-down shirts?"

Rufus took a deep breath. "So, who's jumping?"

"I'll do it." Mary raised her hand.

"What? No." Ricky shook his head. "I should do it."

"Don't pull that patriarchal bullshit with me," she snapped. "I'm in better shape than you, I mean when's the last time you did a pull-up?"

Her husband blushed. "I'm gonna plead the fifth on that one."

"Exactly," she said, squaring her shoulders. "I'm strong enough that if I short the jump, I can pull myself up. Now do you wanna stand here and argue some more, or you want to grab the shotgun?"

Ricky nodded. "Shotgun it is."

Rufus patted him on the shoulder and then opened the window. He stood back as Mary did some stretches behind him. The thunderous blast of the gun shattered the window across the gap, and they waited with bated breath to see if there were any zombies inside that were attracted to the noise.

"Damn, that window is toast, but it looks like there's some jagged glass sticking up from the base," Rufus worried.

"Hey guys, lift up the mattress," Jeff instructed. "There may be some bracing boards underneath."

Ricky and Rufus complied and found a few two-by-fours bracing the king-sized bed. They each grabbed one and then slid them gently through the frame, using them to jab away the rest of the jagged glass. Once clear, Rufus attempted to bridge the gap with the board, but it wasn't quite long enough.

"Damn, thought I had you a bridge there," he grunted as he pulled it back in.

Mary squeezed his shoulder. "It's okay, I'll be fine."

"Wait, before you go," Ricky cut in, "I have an idea."

He grabbed the bedsheet and tied it around the center of the board. He made sure the knot was tight and then reared back, throwing the board like a javelin through the opposite window. He pulled the sheet tight, the two-by-four acting as an anchor braced in the frame.

"There," he declared proudly, "you can climb across if you want."

"Not sure I trust that two-by-four to hold very long," Mary replied warily, "but drop the sheet out so I have a safety."

"You got it, girl," her husband agreed, and tossed the rest of the sheet between the houses.

Mary climbed out of the window, stepping carefully down onto the six-inch brick overhang. She took several deep breaths to psych herself up for the difficult jump, trying to ignore the moans of the zombies below, attracted to the commotion.

She crouched and sprung before she lost her nerve, hands outstretched. She caught the opposing sill, but a small piece of remaining glass sliced into her right hand. On instinct, she tore that hand back, put caught the sheet as she slipped back.

She ignored Ricky's incoherent cry of fear as she nearly plummeted into the horde below, and pushed away the pain, heaving herself up into the bedroom. She stood up and looked back at her husband across the gap, his face pale and relieved.

"I'm good y'all!" She waved. "Be back in a minute!" She drew her handgun and approached the bedroom door, cracking it to peer into the hallway. There was a figure slumped against another door in the hallway, unmoving.

She approached carefully and then relaxed at the sight of half of the corpse's head missing. There was a handgun at the dead woman's feet, and as she bent to pick it up, she noticed a fallen sign from the door. *Emma's Room* was scrawled across it in proud crayon letters, and Mary's heart skipped a beat at what this poor woman had probably had to do.

She moved quickly through the rest of the house, clearing it quickly. She knocked on the garage door, and not hearing a retaliatory sound, opened it. She was greeted with the welcome sight of a brand two twenty-foot ladder hanging on the wall. She hooked it over her shoulder and hurried back upstairs.

"Hey boys, look what I found!" she declared proudly, sliding the ladder across to their window.

"All that's missin' is a bow and a decorated tree," Rufus gushed as he and Ricky took the end, holding it steady.

"Hang tight, I'll be right back!" Mary waved once more and darted back downstairs, grabbing a shopping bag from the kitchen and loading it from the mini-bar. Upon returning to the bedroom, she slung it over her shoulder and then made sure the ladder had enough counterbalance for her to climb across.

She took a deep breath, hand over hand, looking ahead instead of down at the hungry enemies below.

"Baby, you okay?" Ricky asked as he pulled her back into the window, holding her tightly.

"Yeah, just a little prick in my hand," she assured him.

Jeff laughed. "Here's hoping that's the first time you've heard her say that, Ricky."

"Goddamn right it is," Ricky declared.

"So what's in the bag?" Rufus asked, and she cracked open the canvas to give him a peek. "Mother of god."

Jeff raised an eyebrow. "What is it?"

"Just a half-dozen bottles of the finest liquor money can buy," the old man replied with stars in his eyes.

"Great, if we survive this we can get toasted." Jeff rolled his eyes.

Mary shrugged. "Well, we can do that, or we can use a couple of them to burn this fucker to the ground."

"You wanna start another fire?" Ricky asked, incredulous.

"Yeah, I do," she replied. "These things don't seem to care if they're on fire or not, so I figured we could take out a good number of them on our way out. At least have a chance at thinning their numbers to the point where we can get the supplies out."

"Hell, sounds like a plan to me," Jeff agreed. "If we don't do something about the horde, we aren't getting to the food anyway."

Rufus nodded. "Alright, let's get that ladder out there." He and Ricky worked the ladder inside and then out the back window, extending it to the wall with a few feet to spare. They took a few more bedsheets and tied the bottom rung to the bedposts to secure it in place.

"Not going to be the sturdiest of holds, but should get the job done," Ricky said.

"Alright, I'm going first," Rufus said. "I'll get to the wall, check out what's on the other side, and motion when I know what we're doin'."

Mary nodded. "Go get 'em."

He climbed along the ladder, hand over hand, frowning down at the zombies reaching up for their meal in the sky. He shook his head as he reached the wall, a good foot thick for him to balance on. He looked down the other side, spotting a broken down car about ten feet away that looked close enough to jump down to.

He waved.

"Alright, that's the signal, Mary you're up," Ricky said, and his wife easily traversed the bridge. He followed her and they stood on the wall, waiting for Jeff. He stood up, keeping his foot braced against the dresser, readying his lighter.

"You got this, easy as pie," he muttered to himself. "All you have to do is sprint to the window, light and throw a molotov cocktail as a horde of zombies chase you across a ladder above a pit of even *more* zombies. Nothing to it."

He took a deep breath and ignited the fabric, immediately pocketing the lighter and making a run for the window. As soon as he let up on the dresser, the zombies were able to slightly shove the door open, just in time to take a flaming cocktail in the face.

The glass shattered and flaming liquid coated the door and wall, spreading rapidly as the zombies struggled to get into the room.

Jeff hurtled out onto the ladder, trying to be quick but careful not to wobble too much.

"Come on Jeff, you got this," Ricky encouraged.

Just as the skinhead was halfway across, a flaming zombie started out after him.

Mary clenched her fists. "Hurry, Jeff!" she cried. He looked back and saw his pursuer and tried to move a little faster. Ricky aimed his handgun, but Rufus pushed his arm down.

"Don't fire," he said. "We're making enough noise as it is and are about to be on foot. He'll make it."

Jeff was about six feet from the wall when the ladder started to shake from the weight of him and the less graceful flaming zombie. Rufus held the metal as steady as he could, but the flames in the bedroom seemed like they'd eaten the makeshift supports.

Ricky grabbed Jeff's arms and helped him onto the wall, and Rufus immediately jerked the ladder towards him, dislodging it from the house. It bounced roughly and slammed into the ground, the flaming zombie taking it down with him into the horde.

As the smell of burning flesh permeated the night air, Rufus sighed. "There's a car about ten yards down, shouldn't be that bad of a jump," he said. "I think that house on the corner is going to be our best bet, as those bars look sturdy. Y'all get in a secure the place."

"What are you going to do?" Mary asked.

"Somebody needs to keep them occupied," he told her, "make sure they don't go wandering off and setting the other houses ablaze. I'd hate to do all this work for nothing."

"Good deal," Jeff agreed. "I'll contact Dan and let him know the situation and that we're holding tight til morning."

Rufus nodded. "I'll be along shortly." He turned to the fiery corpses below. "It's a damn shame I don't have any marshmallows.

CHAPTER EIGHT

Sparks steered the boat along a dock at the edge of Center Point. It looked to be the personal dock behind a small house, and she tied off and headed up the embankment. She pulled out the GPS and looked for the drugstore.

"Six blocks up," she murmured to herself, "one to the left. Let's do it." She double checked her AR-15 to make sure it was easily accessible, and that her sheathed knife and machete were good to go. Confirmed battle ready, she headed off towards downtown.

The streets were eerily quiet, with no movement to be seen. There were several corpses strewn about, and Sparks wondered if they were left by Elijah's militia when they raided the town. She picked up the pace and turned onto Main Street.

She backed up around the corner of a building upon seeing a few dozen zombies milling about the sidewalk in front of the drugstore.

"Fuck," she muttered, pulling out her binoculars. *Not enough ammo… and a full frontal assault would be suicide,* she thought as she surveyed the horde. *A diversion tactic could work, but if even one of them stayed behind they could draw the others back. A double diversion, perhaps? One to get them away and one to make sure they stay away?*

She took out two cell phones, set one alarm for ten minutes and another for twenty-five. It wasn't that large of a drugstore, so she figured if she couldn't find what she was looking for in fifteen minutes, it meant that the drug wasn't going to be found by anyone short of an archaeologist.

She pressed her earpiece. "Do you have a stopwatch?"

"Yeah, why?" Dan asked.

"Set one for twenty-five minutes, starting now," she said as she reset the cell phone.

"Done," he replied.

"I'll be in touch," she said brusquely, clicking off the earpiece again. She turned and placed the first cell phone on a nearby windowsill.

Sparks walked back to the road she'd come from, which ran parallel to Main Street. She moved behind the buildings all the way to the drugstore. She peeked around a corner and made sure the coast was clear before sprinting across the road, skidding into an alleyway. She set the second cell phone on top of a dumpster, admiring the concrete walls that would provide a nice echo for the concert she was shortly going to be putting on.

She made her way back to Main Street, peeking at the milling zombies. In a few minutes, the first alarm bleated loudly from six blocks down, almost loud enough that it sounded like a police siren in the quiet.

The zombies immediately sprinted to action, like a group of racers hearing a starter pistol, and tore off towards the sound.

Sparks cautiously waited until most of them had turned the corner before running cross the empty street. She peeked around a row of cars to make sure there were no stragglers waiting and then managed to reach the door. There was a chain looped through the handles with a padlock.

"Shit, those fucking militia they-" she stopped at the sight of the lock hanging open. "They didn't lock it." She jerked the chain down and dove inside, throwing the deadbolt once she got in. She moved out of view of the street and paused, drawing her machete to assess the room.

There was a shuffling emanating from the back, and she carefully stood on her tiptoes, peeking over the small shelves. There was one figure moving behind the counter.

She ducked back down and combat walked up the aisle closest to the creature. She picked up a bottle of hand lotion from the shelf next to her and tossed it to the far end of the room. The zombie shrieked and went after it, and when he passed her, she flung her leg out to trip it.

As its face smacked into the linoleum, she jammed the machete down into the back of its head. It gurgled blood for a moment before falling still.

Sparks moved to the back of the cleared store to check the shelves. Most of the medication had been snatched up, however a few of the prescription medication remained. She wasn't sure what they were as she checked each one, but was disheartened to see that they were not nitroglycerine. She threw them all in the bag anyway and touched her earpiece.

"Time check," she said.

"Seven minutes," Dan replied.

She sighed. "Well, they don't have any nitro."

"Look for a filing cabinet," he suggested.

She glanced around and skirted a desk, finding one underneath. "There aren't any drugs in here, just file folders."

"Those should be patient files," Dan explained. "A lot of small town pharmacies haven't made the switch to computers yet, which is just fine since the population in these towns skews older."

"There has got to be a hundred files here, I don't have time to look through them," she groaned. "I'm just going to have to take as many as I can carry and check them out when I'm clear."

"Four minutes," he said.

"Thanks," she replied. "My plan is to get back to the boat and regroup at the airport. This means I won't make it back before you have to leave, so I'll just meet you in Junction."

"Be safe and give me an update when you can," Dan instructed. "Oh, and three minutes."

"Thanks," she repeated, "Sparks out." She clicked off the earpiece and pulled a stack of folders from the filing cabinet, stuffing her bag. She was barely able to get it to close and wasn't happy about leaving some behind, but her time was up. She moved to the door and waited for the alarm, cracking the door so she could hear.

The other alarm went off, giving her the kick to move. She bolted from the door and got across the street before the horde got to their next diversion. She ducked behind a car for cover, slamming back against it. The vehicle sprung to life, its own alarm going off, lights flashing.

"Fuck my life," Sparks muttered and took off, the horde now fixated on her position. She pumped her legs as fast as she could, but they were gaining on her by the time she reached the residential areas of town. She glanced over her shoulder to see a dozen or so zombies in pursuit, and she hung a right around a house.

She reached into her pocket for a cell phone, holding down the home button until a digital assistant asked what she needed.

"Ten second timer!" she cried, and the phone complied. As the timer began to count down, she tossed it into a yard and veered to the right, hoping to distract at least some of her pursuers. As the alarm went off she chanced a look over her shoulder to see a trio of zombies still coming after her.

Her muscles screamed and her enemies were gaining, and in a moment of desperation she tore into a backyard with a pool. She threw her bag and guns aside like refuse out of a car and leapt into the water.

The zombies piled in, face planting due to lack of coordination. Sparks wasted no time in swimming to the edge to pull herself out, springing to her feet and drawing both her knife and machete. The zombies seemed disoriented but still trying to get to her.

She crouched by the side, and as their heads crested the water she stabbed them like a zombified whack-a-mole game. Several strikes later, the pool was crimson with three corpses floating face down.

Sparks forced herself to get moving again, ignoring the burning of her lungs as she retrieved her gear. She darted deeper into the neighborhood in search of a place to lie low. A few blocks over, there was a nice house with no car in the driveway and intact doors and windows. She ran up to the back door and knocked, waiting a beat for a banging response.

When there was none, she used the stock of her gun to bust out one of the glass panels and reached into the unlock the door. She flicked the deadbolt and shoved a little wall unit against the broken glass, raising her blades to clear the house.

It was empty. After double checking the front door lock, she collapsed on the couch and smacked at her earpiece with an arm that suddenly felt like jelly.

"Sparks, are you okay?" Dan asked.

"Yeah, just," she huffed, "had some issues getting out of the drugstore."

"Oh my god, are you okay?" he gushed. "You aren't bitten are you?"

She shook her head lazily. "No, I'm good, just an old fashioned chase around town."

"Where are you?" he asked.

"Some random house in the neighborhood," she said, kicking off her soaked boots. "Going to lay low and catch my breath while looking over these patient files." She peeled off a sock and wrung it out. "Besides, I need to let my clothes dry out a bit before moving on."

"Dry out?" the Principal inquired. "Did you go swimming?"

"Nah, just played the worst game of Marco Polo ever." She chuckled as she drew her tank top over her head. "Turns out if you have a machete, it doesn't matter if you're a fish out of water, you still win."

"That…" He couldn't help but bark a laugh. "That is good to know."

"I'll be in touch when I have something," she said. "Sparks out."

CHAPTER NINE

Rufus scrambled eggs on the stove as Jeff poured four cups of coffee, Mary and Ricky keeping an eye out for trouble.

"Come on y'all, breakfast," Rufus called, and the couple joined them in the kitchen of the house they'd hunkered down in.

"How's it looking out there?" Jeff asked.

Ricky shrugged. "Pretty quiet. Nothing on the streets," he said.

"And the smoke coming from Colonial Court seems to be petering out, so it doesn't look like the fires spread," Mary continued.

"Well that's a bit of good news, at least," Rufus replied as he divvied the eggs between four plates. "Now we just gotta figure out how to clear the neighborhood so we can get the food."

"Maybe we can lure them to one side like you did last night, Rufus?" Jeff suggested. "Stand on the wall, make a shitload of noise, and keep them there while the rest of us get the supplies?"

"Sounds risky," the older man warned. "All it's gonna take is one of them bastards to get wind of Dan's boys and they're gonna be overrun."

"You could Pied Piper them sumbitches," Ricky spoke up. "I mean my truck is right by the entrance. We'll get her started up, get their attention and lead em right out into the country."

They all stared at him in awe.

"Ricky, that is a solid fucking idea," Jeff commended, and then shoved the rest of his eggs into his mouth before standing up. "I'm gonna get Dan on the line and let him know."

"Pied Piper them sumbitches?" Mary raised an eyebrow at her husband. "I swear it's a good thing I was a math teacher and not an English teacher."

"Hell girl, you should just be happy the boy made a literary reference." Rufus chuckled.

Ricky grinned. "You tell her, Rufus."

She rolled her eyes and focused on her breakfast, knowing full well this was a battle she wasn't going to win. Jeff sipped his coffee while looking out the window, waiting for the Principal to answer his tap.

"Hey Jeff," Dan finally came through, "sorry about the delay there, I was helping get things ready. How we looking over there?"

"Well, from our vantage point it looks like the fires have burned out," Jeff reported. "But we don't know what the zombie population looks like. Although we do have a plan."

"Great, let's hear it," Dan offered.

"To quote Ricky, the thespian among us, we're gonna Pied Piper the sumbitches," the skinhead replied with a grin. "Ricky's truck is parked by the entrance, so the plan is to lure them out of the neighborhood, and really right out of the city."

"Sounds like as good a plan as any," the Principal replied. "I'll make sure the teams going in know to be ready for any stragglers."

Jeff nodded. "Probably a good idea, since we're going to be moving as soon as the first wave gets to us. We won't have a way to know how successful we are."

"How long do you think you'll need?" Dan asked.

Jeff pursed his lips in thought. "Plan on two hours," he said finally. He pulled out the GPS and zoomed out to take a look at the area. "Based on our position, we're going to go out 1631, and when we get way out into the country we'll leave them behind and circle around to Highway 16 and come back into town. We're not going to be able to go that fast initially, since we don't want to lose any zombies."

"Sounds good, Jeff," Dan commended. "I'll have the boys ready to go in two hours. Let me know if anything changes."

Jeff nodded. "Ten four." He tapped his earpiece and went back into the kitchen. "'Alright, the plan is a go." He puts hands up as the trio started to get up. "Whoa now, finish breakfast. I told him it'd take us a couple hours, so we have plenty of time. Besides, how many more of these good old fashioned hot breakfasts are we gonna have?"

Rufus shrugged. "Man's got a point, eat up everybody."

CHAPTER TEN

Sparks shot awake, sitting up violently on the couch, gun in hand. She steadied her breathing as she remembered where she was, and lowered her gun, rubbing her eyes. She looked around at the file folders and clothes strewn about, yawning as she headed to the kitchen.

She rummaged through the cabinets, finding very little. The previous tenants must have packed everything they had been able to fit in their vehicle when they left.

"Ugh, that's just wrong," she muttered upon finding a single canister of decaf coffee. "Guess this is as good as it's going to get." She fired up the coffee maker as she tapped her earpiece.

"Good morning Sparks, sleep well?" Dan asked.

"Not really," she replied with a yawn. "Up most of the night trying to find the heart meds."

He frowned. "Any luck?"

"Only three patients had a prescription for it," she said. "One of them has an address south of downtown, which after yesterday I don't want to go anywhere near. The second one hasn't had their order filled in two months, which leads me to believe they stopped needing them."

"And the third?" he prompted.

"Picked up a week before the outbreak," she said. "IP address looks like it's fourteen miles northwest of my current position. So after I wake up a bit, I'm going to start hiking."

"Well, at least it's taking you in the right direction towards Junction," he said.

She nodded as she dumped the blasphemous coffee into a filter. "Hopefully they have some transportation there, because this walking is getting old."

"Why don't you just take a car from where you are?" he suggested.

She shook her head. "Still too many of those things around," she said. "I'd much rather sneak out of town on foot than risk setting off another alarm."

"I don't blame you at all," he said.

"How are the others doing?" she asked.

"They're safe," he reported. "They found a good bit of food and now they're going to lead a zombie convoy out into the country so we can go pick it up."

"When you talk to them again, tell them I said howdy and that I'm still kicking," she said.

"Will do," Dan confirmed. "Be safe."

She tapped the earpiece and poured her cup of decaf, grimacing as she did so. "I don't normally wish ill on people, but seriously, whoever lived here can fuck right off."

CHAPTER ELEVEN

The foursome hugged the wall as they moved up the street, guns drawn and at the ready. Rufus led the way with Jeff bringing up the rear, and they met no resistance as they reached the front of the walled neighborhood.

Rufus held up a fist to silently signal for them to stop, and peered around the corner of the wall. There were no zombies outside of the gate, near Ricky's truck from what he could see, but there were lots of blind spots and that worried him.

"Ricky, you got the keys ready?" the old man whispered. When he saw his companion hold them up in confirmation, he nodded. "Wait til everyone is in to start it up."

Ricky nodded, and Rufus gave everyone a thumbs up. He turned, bringing his rifle up into combat ready position, and led them into battle.

When he reached the guard station, Rufus whipped around it, ready to take out any potential threat. The closest zombie was about ten yards away, milling just on the other side of the gate. It seemed more interested in the smoldering house than anything on the group's side of the gate, so Rufus refrained from shooting it and instead motioned for the trio to run to the truck.

Ricky led the charge, the three of them moving at a speed walk to avoid making too much noise, and made it to the truck. They carefully opened the driver's side door and Mary crawled in first, Ricky following. Jeff climbed up into the bed, taking position over the roof to provide cover.

Rufus moved silently across the gap, sideways, with his gun still trained on the distracted zombie. Just as he was about halfway, Ricky gently closed the truck door and the tiny click was just enough to make the zombie turn its head. Without hesitation Rufus put a bullet in its head, but the loud *crack* signaled the rest of the horde that dinner had arrived.

"Start the truck!" he yelled and sprinted towards the vehicle. Ricky fired it up just as zombies began pouring out of the front gate, and he punched the accelerator.

Rufus halfway jumped into the bed, and Jeff grabbed him by the belt, pulling him the rest of the way as the truck bounced violently from running over wayward zombies.

The truck cleared the front entrance with the throng of zombies in hot pursuit. Ricky turned down the road beside the fortified neighborhood, keeping a good twenty yard clearance between them and the enemy.

Mary opened the back window. "You boys alright?"

"Pretty sure I cracked a rib, but other than that I'm good to go," Rufus said, giving her a thumbs up.

"You're lucky you made it in at all with that eight inch vertical." Jeff patted him on the shoulder.

Rufus grinned. "Heh, you ain't kiddin'."

"Yo Jeff, you got that GPS thingy?" Ricky called back. "Need to know where I'm headed."

The skinhead pulled out the GPS and checked their location. "Another mile, then hang a left. After that we'll be out for a leisurely drive in the country," he instructed.

He and Rufus sat back against the cab of the truck and watched as the mass of rotting flesh sprinted after them.

"What do ya think?" the old man asked. "We got about forty of them?"

Jeff shrugged. "Could be fifty."

"Well, whatever it is," Rufus said, "let's just hope it was enough."

CHAPTER TWELVE

Sparks peered through her binoculars at the house, a one story rancher that would run seven figures in the city. There were no signs of movement despite the beat up truck in the driveway. She lowered her binoculars and stepped out of the tree line into the low hanging evening sunlight.

Just as she reached the front door, there was a high pitched mechanical screech in the distance. She whipped around and saw a small black dot in the sky above the trees.

"That can't be good," she muttered, and dove into the house, revolver in hand. A zombie moan echoed from the kitchen, and a rotting corpse in the shape of a teenager ran towards the officer. "Yeah, come and get me girl," Sparks urged, and darted off towards the bathroom.

She barreled down the hallway, opening the bathroom door just in time for the zombie to smack wetly into the other side. Sparks kicked the corpse into the bathroom and slammed the door, trapping it inside. The undead occupant thrashed against the door like a caged animal, but it didn't budge.

"You hang tight, girl," the redhead said, and then did a sweep of the rest of the house. After securing her surroundings, she searched for the medication.

The master bedroom and ensuite came up empty. She worked her way through the kitchen cabinets and the first few contained expensive looking dishes and glassware. The last cabinet revealed a stash that made her eyes widen.

"Holy hell," she breathed, "either someone in the house was feeling really bad, or really, really good." She picked up two bottles from the bottom of the cupboard of drugs and put them in the bag as she checked the labels. Around halfway through she found what she was looking for. "There you are," she said with triumph as she tapped her earpiece. "Dan, I got them."

"That's great news!" the Principal replied excitedly. "And I have some of my own. The boys just got back from Fredericksburg with the food the other group rounded up. There's enough for two solid weeks, so we have enough to get us wherever we need to go."

"That's excellent news," Sparks agreed as she shoved the rest of the bottles into her bag. "Have they gotten back yet?"

Dan made a noise in the negative. "They had to take the long way around to

clear out a horde for us, so we're
expecting them back in a couple of hours."

"Well, I'm going to-" Sparks ducked
at the sight of movement outside of the
kitchen window. "Fuck."

"Are you okay?" he asked.

She pulled out one of the cell phones
and slipped it into her pocket for easy
access. "I have company, I gotta go," she
said and tapped the earpiece before Dan
could respond. She drew her revolver,
aimed it at the figure as they leaned
towards the window, and then jumped up to
fire.

The figure immediately ducked,
prompting Sparks to duck again as well,
saving her ammo and returning to cover.
"Shit, shit, shit."

She couldn't tell if it had been a
militia or not, but as the front door
crashed open she figured she'd be finding
out soon enough. She slid low across the
floor into the hallway and peered around
the corner. There were two militia men
with handguns spreading out in the living
room.

She didn't hesitate, putting a bullet
in one's chest. He collapsed to the floor,
gasping for air as blood gargled in his
airways. His partner opened fire,
shredding the drywall just above Sparks'
head. She made a split decision and jumped

up, running towards the shooter with her gun drawn.

Her opponent immediately hit the ground to prevent being shot, but she leapt and landed a knee on the top of his head instead, stunning him. He staggered to his feet and took a swing at her, but she deftly dodged it, smacking the back of his arm in the process.

As his back exposed itself to her, she wrapped her arms around his lower waist and lifted him, rotating to smack him headfirst into the floor. There was a sickening crack as his neck snapped in two, ending his evening early.

A bullet whizzed by Sparks' ear, hitting the wall behind her, and she dove further into the house as another militia man burst through the front door.

"I'm gonna get you!" he screamed, chasing her down the hall. As she passed the bathroom she dragged open the bathroom door with her, a teenage zombie staggering out to sink its teeth into his throat. His screams turned from a bass to soprano as his vocal chords tore, but Sparks didn't stick around to listen to the concerto as she bolted for the back door.

As soon as her boots hit the grass she hit the ground hard, dazed and dizzy. She tried to refocus her eyes, flipping over onto her back, and her blood ran cold at the sight of Elijah's face. He was flanked by four armed militia members, and he motioned to them as she tried to prop herself up on her elbows.

"You two," he demanded, "go clean up the mess she made. Then we're gonna go have some fun with this one."

His sneer made bile rise in her throat as the remaining two zip tied her wrists in front of her. They dragged her to her feet, Elijah keeping his rifle trained on her.

"So much death and destruction, simply because you wouldn't walk away," he said, clucking his tongue and cocking his head at her.

"So much death and destruction because you and your boys don't know how to share," she replied with steel in her gaze as the other two henchmen exited the house, loaded up with the dead mens' weapons and ammo.

"You still don't get it, do you?" Elijah chided as he motioned for her to walk towards the tree line. "Sharing under these conditions means death. There are no more resources being produced, and once they're gone, that's it."

Sparks swallowed, keeping her voice steady, concentrating on putting one foot in front of the other. "How many people have to die just so you can live a few extra months?"

"Everyone I come across if need be," he replied easily.

"You hear that boys?" She glanced behind her. "You're expendable." The guard directly behind her shoved her hard, and she stumbled down a small embankment into the bushes next to the woods.

Elijah sighed. "Go get her."

"Yes boss," the militia member muttered. Sparks quickly reached into her back pocket, grabbing the phone she'd stashed there. She quickly set the alarm for five minutes and tossed it aside just as the guard made it through the bush to her. "On your feet, bitch," he demanded, and grabbed her ponytail to drag her up.

He shoved her back to the trail, and Elijah and his quartet continued to march her through the trees. Soon they reached a clearing with an SUV parked on the edge of a dirt road. One of the militias ran over to the vehicle and tossed her bag and weapons on the hood before hitting the headlights, illuminating the dusky scene.

Another shoved her down onto her back, gyrating his hips. "Oh, we are gonna fuck you up, then we're gonna fuck you good," he sang to her, licking his lips. "You ever had a train ran on you? Hoot hoot! It's a comin'!"

"Settle down," Elijah snapped. "I have questions before you can have your fun."

The eager young man backed off, as his leader stepped forward, grabbing the front of her tank top in his fist.

"Now, I'm not going to bullshit you," he said firmly, eyes ablaze with power. "Your time is short, however if you cooperate, things will be a little more pleasant. Sure my boys are gonna have some fun with you, but after that there are two options. The first, is a quick and relatively painless bullet to the head. The second, is you get fucked one more time." He snapped his fingers, and one of the men by the truck tossed a machete onto the ground next to them. "By that." He grinned cruelly, running his thumb up her cheek and over her ear. "So, what's it going to be? Are you going to cooperate? Or-" he stopped speaking as his thumb hit the earpiece, and he pried it out. "Interesting," he said as he inspected it, and then pocketed it. "Well, I'll just hold on to that."

He jumped up and walked over to her bag, while the eager young man stood at her feet, rubbing himself through his pants in anticipation for his prize.

"Xanax?" Elijah asked as he dug through Sparks' bag. "I can understand the need to relax in these trying times." He pulled out the GPS with a grin. "Now what do we have here?"

Sparks' stomach dropped, and she swallowed hard.

"Looks like me offer of a quick death has been rescinded!" Elijah laughed, hopping up to sit on the hood of the SUV. "The only thing I wanted to know from you was where you and your friends were holed up. And thanks to your little device here, I have my answer." He hit the saved location and then pocketed the GPS. "I do hope you get at least some enjoyment from my boys, since in a few minutes you'll be wishing for them."

Sparks sighed, rolling her eyes. "Figures you limp dick fucks would be minute men," she drawled. "No wonder you have to play military dress up to feel like real men."

The young horny militia member lunged down, backhanding her across the face.

She sneered. "Didn't think you'd be capable of foreplay."

"You fucking whore, I'm gonna-" he began, but the bleat of the phone alarm cut him off.

"What the hell?!" Elijah screamed. "Find it!"

His cronies ran towards the noise, but none of them could find it, despite how loud it was.

He grew impatient, jumping down from the vehicle. "Forget it, we have what we need, let's go."

The horny militia member pointed to Sparks. "What about her?"

"Leave her," Elijah replied, and jumped in the driver's seat. Before Sparks' would-be rapist could reach the vehicle, a female zombie dove from the shadows and bit him in the shoulder. His leader immediately punched the accelerator, leaving him in the dust.

"Hey bitch, come get some!" Sparks yelled, and as the zombie ambled towards her she flung her legs up, catching the midsection with her feet. The redhead used the momentum to propel the corpse over her, impaling her on a rogue branch.

Sparks popped up, retrieving the machete from the ground and slamming it into the zombie's chest, pinning her further against the tree.

"Don't move, I'll be right back," she winked at the zombie, using the exposed blade to snap the zip tie around her wrist.

She slid down the embankment to find the phone, and silenced the alarm, casually strolling back towards her downed enemy. He held his wound, moaning, blood pooling in the dirt beneath him.

Sparks knelt down, removing his handgun and tossing it aside. "Real good friends you picked there," she said casually. "I mean sure, they were going to let you have your way with me, but at the first sign of trouble? Man they were quick to get out of here. I mean they acted like you were a stripper who told them they got you pregnant, they moved that fast.

"I would give your friends this, however, your boss, Elijah? He does have a way with words. So since you were so find of him, I'm going to give you a similar offer to the one he gave me." She smacked him across the face to make sure he was paying attention, and he whimpered. "Hey, there you are. Now, I wanna know where the farm is. If you tell me, then I'll leave you here to bleed out nice and peaceful. I hear it's a nice death since when you get close to the end, your body releases all sorts of stuff that makes you feel like you're in dreamland."

"And-and if I don't?" he stammered, still clutching his shoulder.

Sparks smiled as she walked back to the zombie. She removed the machete and grabbed the corpse's hair, hacking at her throat until the head was severed. She carried it back over and held it close to his face, the snapping mouth wafting a putrid stench towards his terrified face.

"If you don't, I'm going to make sure you get a little head before you die," the redhead promised, and his eyes bulged out of his head at the horrific realization of her meaning.

"Okay, okay," he gushed. "I'll tell you what you want to know."

She leaned forward. "Where's the farm?"

"It's about three miles away, just go up the dirty road right there and hang a left at the crossroads, you can't miss it," he blurted quickly.

"You sure you're telling me the truth?" Sparks asked, waving the head around. "Cause this bitch looks awfully hungry."

He paled considerably. "I swear, I swear!"

"You know what?" She set down the head, leaning back on her heels. "I got a bonus round question for you. How in the hell did you guys find me?"

"That boat you stole from us had a tracking marker on it," he replied quickly. "We've had eyes on you ever since you took it. We waited until we had a tactical advantage to take you down."

"Eh, that's what I get for stealing I guess." She shrugged. "Okay, you enjoy your death." She got to her feet and turned, taking a few steps. "You know, I have one more question, and it's kind of out of left field." She raised a hand, turning around slowly to face him again. "Do you believe in reincarnation?"

He was shaking at this point. "Yeah, I guess."

"Then I wouldn't be doing my duty if I didn't teach you that being a rapist was wrong," she said, snatching up the head and shoving it down onto the militia member's crotch. The zombie immediately clamped down like a vice grip.

"YOU BITCH!" he screamed, flailing. "Oh please, fucking kill me!"

Sparks smirked as she picked up his gun.. "*Now* enjoy your death."

CHAPTER THIRTEEN

"Slim picking in there, but not a total bust," Jeff said as he wandered out of the gas station, holding up a six-pack.

"Alright, we're gassed up," Ricky replied, holstering the nozzle. "Y'all ready to hit the road back to Fredericksburg?"

Jeff hopped up into the bed of the truck. "Yeah, might as well."

Ricky fired up the truck and they sped off into the darkness. The ride was peaceful, nothing stirring on the roads. Once they approached city limits, he slowed to a crawl, sliding open the back window.

"Holy fuckballs, look at that," he said, and Jeff and Rufus turned and stood up to look over the roof.

"Man, something nasty went down here," the skinhead said, shaking his head. There was a mass of overturned cars functioning as a makeshift barricade across the road, a string of bodies littering the ground.

"So now what bubba?" Ricky asked through the back window. "We can't go back the way we came or else we'll run into that mess of zombies we strong along."

"Hand me the GPS," Jeff instructed, and Mary fished it out of her bag, passing it back to him. He sat down to fiddle with it.

Rufus parked his ass down next to him. "What you thinking?"

"Doesn't look like cutting through town is going to be an option, so I'm seeing how we get to Junction from here," he replied. The device beeped and suggested a route that would take them right through downtown. "Well, fuck. No matter what we do, we're going to have to go through town. The road to Junction is Main Street."

"I got that winch on the front of the truck here, I can get one of them cars moved enough so we can slip through," Ricky suggested.

Rufus pursed his lips. "Then we just gotta hope main street ain't blocked."

"Or that we don't trigger a few hundred zombies," Mary added wryly.

"Oh come on baby, happy thoughts," Ricky suggested.

She shrugged. "A few hundred *was* my happy thought."

"Alright, let's go for it," Jeff said finally. "Ricky, you get the winch set and the rest of us will cover you."

Ricky pulled the truck up to the car barricade and hopped out, grabbing the thick wire while Rufus and Jeff stood, keeping an eye out for any movement. Ricky secured the winch and nodded to his armed guardians that he was ready to flip the switch.

The motor hummed as the wire pulled tight, and the sound of metal scraping against concrete echoed throughout the night. It was almost immediately followed by a chorus of moans.

"Contact!" Rufus cried, opening fire as the first corpse emerged from the fortress of automobiles. Ricky immediately made a run for his seat as several more zombies flooded out to the front of the truck.

Rufus and Jeff were able to peg a few of them in the head as Ricky threw the truck in reverse.

"Hold on!" he screamed, and the two in the back hit the deck as he floored it. The truck rocketed backwards and got a good thirty yards away from the horde before the winch snapped tight, slowing their escape to a crawl as the engine struggled to drag the attached car.

Jeff leapt over the roof, sliding down the windshield and landing firmly on the hood. "Mary, shotgun!" he screamed, and she fed it through her window as Rufus laid down cover fire at the growing group of zombies barreling towards the front of the truck.

It did little to stem the tide, but bought Jeff a few extra seconds to fire shells into the winch. On the third blast, the wire severed and flicked into the horde like a busted rubber band. The lead zombies fell apart as the wire cut them in two at the waist, tripping up the second row.

Jeff scrambled back up over the roof and dove to the bed, grabbing Rufus on the way down. "Go go go!" he screamed, and Ricky floored the accelerator once again, speeding backwards.

A minute later the skinhead sat up, sticking his head into the back window. "Where are you going?"

"Getting us the fuck outta here, man!" Ricky called back. "Where do you think I'm going?"

"We gotta go through them," Jeff instructed, causing the driver to slam on the brakes and look back at him, mouth agape.

"Are you fucking crazy?" Ricky blurted. "There might be hundreds of those things in there?"

"And it's the only way to get where we need to go," the skinhead replied firmly. "We can't go backwards unless you wanna plow through that pack of zombies."

Ricky slammed his hand down on the steering wheel in frustration, and Mary put her hand on his shoulder. "Baby, you got this," she said gently, giving him a squeeze, and he took a deep breath.

"Alright," he said firmly, "where am I goin'?"

Jeff passed the GPS back through the window to Mary. "Once we clear the barricade, it's going to be the fifth street," he explained. "Hang a right and it's straight on til daylight. Mary, you're gonna have to be navigator since Rufus and I are going to be holding on for dear life."

"Alright, I'll make sure he knows where we're going," she confirmed.

Ricky took a deep breath and tightened his grip on the steering wheel. "You boys hang tight," he said, "this is gonna be a bumpy ass ride."

He threw the shifter into drive and hit the gas, tires screeching before gaining traction and screaming ahead. As the grill hit the first batch of zombies, he kept their trajectory straight as corpses flew to the side like rag dolls upon impact.

The commotion attracted more zombies, clogging the path between the cars that they'd made. He accelerated through them, scraping against the side of the barricade as he plowed through the crowd. Bodies flew through the air like bowling pins hit with a sixteen pound ball as they entered the inner sanctum.

"Oh my god, they're everywhere," Mary breathed as a pile of zombies poured out of the nearby church, joining the pursuit.

Her husband didn't break his focus, making it to Main Sreet. "One… two… three…" he counted the streets as they passed.

The horde was a good forty yards behind them, running at full steam. Ricky slowed as he approached the turn, not wanting to risk tipping over or flinging his buddies out of the back.

Said buddies poked their heads up over the tailgate, aiming their guns downrange to make sure nothing was close enough. Ricky turned the corner, hit the gas, and then slammed on the brakes again.

"What now?" Jeff barked.

Ricky sighed. "Look."

Jeff and Rufus clambered over to the window, peering through it to see through the windshield. At least a hundred zombies milled about between them and yet another barricade.

Panic gripped the quartet as the reality set in that they were well and truly trapped.

"Ricky," Rufus demanded, "you floor this motherfucker and aim for where those two cars intersect."

The driver swallowed nervously. "That's a hell of a fucking shot, man."

"Well, it's either that or we get fucking eaten," the old man snapped. "Just do it, goddammit!"

A primal scream tore its way out of Ricky's throat as he punched the accelerator, and his passengers held on for dear life. The truck reached fifty miles per hour before impact against the wall of rotting flesh, vaporizing the front lines at contact. The meat and bones soaked up a lot of damage and slowed the truck down.

By the time they reached the wall, they were only going about ten miles an hour, slow enough that zombies were able to start climbing up onto the tailgate. Rufus and Jeff opened fire, expending round after round in an attempt to keep the climbers at bay. But for each one that took a blast and fell away, another rose to take its place.

Finally the grill reached the cars, and they came to a near standstill. Ricky dropped the truck into four-wheel drive and gunned it, which was enough to get them moving a bit. The barricade groaned and started to give a little.

"Hang on, boys, we're almost there!" Ricky screamed.

Jeff's shotgun gave a sharp *click*. "Fuck, I'm out!" he cried, and Rufus got to his feet, swinging his assault rifle like a baseball bat. Jeff joined him at the tailgate to play whack-a-zombie, smashing the butt of the shotgun into whatever popped up.

The truck finally was able to push through the cars and leapt forward to accelerate to freedom.

"Get down!" Mary shrieked back at them, and Rufus and Jeff dove to the floor to avoid being flung out. They got a few hundred yards clear of the mayhem and Ricky finally slowed down a bit.

"Goddamn, you boys alright?" he asked.

"Never better," Rufus drawled.

Jeff snorted. "Peachy."

"Alright!" Ricky hooted. "Let's get goin, then!"

"Keep it slow for a few minutes," Jeff instructed, "I gotta let Dan know we'll meet them in Junction."

"Well, after what she's just been through, this truck could use a bit of a leisurely stroll," Ricky said, lovingly patting the dashboard. Mary put her hand over his and he interlaced their fingers, bringing her knuckles to his lips.

She smiled at him. "We made it."

CHAPTER FOURTEEN

Sparks made her way down a dusty dirt road towards a fence, jumping off into the ditch to hide her approach. She got to the entrance to the farmhouse property and took a beat to survey it. There was a large barn about forty yards ahead to the left, and a large one story home about fifty yards past that. It was difficult to make out any figures from that distance, but the lights were on and smoke curled from the chimney.

She made her way across the field and up to the backside of the barn. The large doors were sealed shut, but a smaller person-sized door was ajar. She slipped in, handgun raised and at the ready.

There were horse stables built into either side of the barn, blocked metal gates about six feet high. The moon shone in through the rafters and provided just enough light for her to check each pen for enemies. She was so focused on straining her eyes in the dim light that she kicked a metal tool with her boot, causing a little *clang*.

Moans permeated the space, and she raised her gun immediately, taking a fighting stance. Upon closer inspection, however, she realized that the zombies were secure in the last pen, only able to reach through the bars at her. She noted the latch and furrowed her brow.

"What the hell is this?" she muttered, taking in the dozen or so corpses with matching neck wounds. The other thing they all had in common was that they were all of Latino descent, and she shook her head in disgust at the blatant racism of the militia.

Sparks passed the pen and almost tripped over a burlap sack on the ground. She peeked inside and realized it was a severed zombie head, still twitching and snapping and covered in blood. Her confusion mounted until she reached the other side of the barn and saw the reason for the zombie breeding.

The path between her position and the house was littered with wooden posts holding corpses on crude leashes. These evil bastards had created their own vicious guard zombie brigade.

A lone figure sat on the front porch of the house and appeared to be playing some kind of handheld video game. As she watched, two more militia members exited the house, one of them handing a beer to the gamer. They sat around a wooden table, laughing loudly.

She ducked back inside the barn and contemplated her next move. Taking out three guards with only a handgun would be difficult, especially given that she had no idea how many more were inside.

She needed a distraction. A large one.

Sparks looked back at the caged zombies and a devious idea began to form. She rummaged around a workbench and found a length of rope, and attached one end of it to the zombie pen door.

"I guess this is karma for asking Jeff how fast he could run," she said under her breath, backing up as far as the rope allowed. She drew her handgun, took a deep breath, and then yanked hard on the rope, freeing the zombies.

The first of them clumsily reached for her, but grabbed nothing but air. They emerged from the barn hot on her heels with a thunderous announcement.

Forty yards to go.

The guards perked up as they heard more than saw trouble on the horizon. They scrambled to their feet and readied their weapons, screaming for backup as they realized what was headed their way.

Thirty yards to go.

Sparks slid underneath the grasp of a leashed zombie and drew the attention of a militia member with her agility. Before he could raise his weapon, however, she fired at him, the bullet hitting the house but causing the three enemies on the porch to take cover.

Twenty yards to go.

She took the opportunity to break into a sprint for the house, the wide open front door her target. If she could just get inside, she could lock these fuckers out with the dead ones.

Ten yards.

The front porch was within reach as an armed man appeared in the doorway to provide backup to his team. Sparks leapt as soon as she reached the stairs, landing a solid flying knee to his chest. The man fell inside, smacking the hardwood floor with the back of his head.

She immediately launched back off of him, slamming and locking the door. She popped off a round into his kneecap as he attempted to raise his weapon at her.

"I wouldn't try that again," she warned, moving forward to kick his rifle away. "Who else is in the house?"

He shook his head. "Nobody."

She cocked the gun. "Not going to ask again."

"I swear, nobody else," he replied.

There were screams from outside and a smattering of gunfire as the Latino zombies exacted swift revenge on their racist captors. Sparks turned her attention back to her prisoner, who was holding his leg wound tightly. Before she could resume questioning, another man emerged from the back room with a double barreled shotgun.

She dove into the front room, just missing the last from the mighty weapon.

"You missed her, she's on the flo-" Mister No-Knee began, but his warning was cut short by Sparks shooting him in the lung from beneath the couch. As he gasped for air, his partner turned the corner and fired blindly, hitting nothing but floor.

He popped the weapon open to reload, and Sparks took the opportunity to leap from behind the sofa and smash her boot into the side of his knee. His joint bent sideways, shredding every ligament, and he fell to the ground in a heap.

"If your hands so much as move I'm going to end you, are we clear?" she demanded.

He hissed in pain. "Yeah."

"Anybody else in the house?" she asked her new prisoner.

He shook his head.

"If I hear so much as a footstep, you die," she promised. "Now, where's Elijah?"

He took in a deep breath. "He's gone."

"Where?"

"He was here about a half hour ago, dropped off some stuff and loaded up with heavy weapons," he explained, and her heart sank.

"Where's my stuff?" she demanded.

He furrowed his brow. "What?"

"My stuff!" she growled. "The fucking shit he brought in. Was it a big bag?"

He nodded. "Back bedroom."

"You did good," she said, "so you die quick."

"What? No-" he pleaded, but she cut him off by shooting him directly in the face. She didn't even give him a second thought as she ran to the back bedroom.

Her bag was strewn across the bed, the drug bottles dumped everywhere, some of them empty. She scoured through the contents, looking for her only connection to the group.

"Where are you?" she gasped to herself as she searched, panic gripping her chest. "Come on, please, where are you?" She sighed in relief when she found the earpiece underneath a fold in the comforter, and shoved it in her ear, tapping it.

"Sparks, is that you?" Dan asked immediately.

Her blood ran cold. "Oh god, are those gunshots?"

"The militia's here and it's bad," he replied. "They're… they're just killing everyone."

A sob racked her throat. "It's my fault, it's all my fault!"

"It's okay, Sparks," he assured her, not sounding afraid, just sad. "Look, I don't have much time left. The others are safe and going to be in Junction. Go meet them."

In the background, there were more gunshots, and a voice that she was sure belonged to Elijah yelled, "They're in the house!"

"I'm so sorry Dan." Tears streamed down her face, and her gun fell to the bed, her hands suddenly useless.

"I told you, it's okay," he said gently. "You did everything you could to help us. Now it's time for me to go home to Katie."

She cried out at the sound of a loud clatter through the comm, and Elijah clear as day, "Good to see you again, Principal."

There was a hail of gunfire and she screamed, tearing the earpiece off of her and throwing it across the room. She scrubbed her hands up her face, burying her fingers in her hair and jerking at her scalp.

"I'm so sorry," she whispered through gasping sobs, her heart pounding in her ears, *bo-boom*. "I'm so sorry. I'm so sorry."

Bo-boom.

"I'm so sorry."

END OF BOOK THREE

DEAD TEXAS
BOOK FOUR: THE JOURNEY WEST
BY DEREK SLATON
© 2018

CHAPTER ONE

Sparks winced at every gunshot faintly emanating from the earpiece on the floor. Each one of those shots claiming the life of an innocent member of Principal Dan's group. The group she had worked so hard to protect.

She took a deep breath and lifted the earpiece with a trembling hand. She slipped it back on as she clenched her jaw. However painful, she needed as much information as she could get.

"Sir!" A male voice. "There's a fire at the supply trucks!"

"Kill everyone, and do whatever you have to do to save those supplies!" Elijah barked orders in the distance.

"Sir, it's all gone," another voice said with reluctance.

"Goddammit!" Elijah screamed in frustration, and the gunfire died away in the background. "Alright. Let's regroup at the farmhouse." There was the sound of a door slamming and then silence.

When Sparks was sure that there was to be no more intel, she tore the earpiece from her head and threw it across the room. Anger pulsed through her veins like napalm, and she wiped away the last tear she was willing to shed because of these assholes.

She tossed the canvas bag of meds
over her shoulder before doing a sweep of
the house. She nabbed a few handgun mags
from the dead militia members and two
handguns. Her eyes locked on a pump action
shotgun on the kitchen counter next to a
set of keys.

"Not really idea," she picked up the
large weapon and turned it over in her
hands. "But it'll do."

She came upon a large storeroom full
of food and water, and stuffed her bag
full before returning to the living room.
Zombies stood on the front porch, banging
on the door, and she carefully peeked out
the window off to the side. There were a
dozen or so clustered there, and past them
no vehicles that the keys could belong to.

A zombified militia member suddenly
struck the glass with its face, gnawing at
the window. She gave it the finger before
moving to the back of the house. The back
porch was clear, with no movement in the
backyard that she could tell through the
window. There was a pickup truck about ten
feet from the door, and she drew her
handgun.

A thought niggled in the back of her
brain just before she exited, and she
turned to face the store room of supplies
that Elijah and his surviving men were
coming back to enjoy. She holstered her

weapon and rummaged through the kitchen cupboards. She set a bottle of whiskey on the counter and shoved a rag down the top of it. She carefully stowed it in the side pocket of her bag before heading back to the front of the house.

She yelled and banged on the front door. Originally she'd just wanted to rile up the front porch zombies, but she drew on every ounce of her pain and frustration and sadness and injected it into the primal scream escaping her body. It was cathartic, popping the cap on the shaken up bottle of tension in her guts.

Once finished, she stalked to the back door again, feeling lighter and ready for action as she drew her gun. She gently opened it, slipping outside with the keys at the ready and running to the truck. She unlocked the vehicle and grabbed the bottle from her bag before tossing it into the passenger's seat. She clambered up into the driver's seat and closed the door behind her as silently as she could.

She slid the key into the ignition and then set her gun on the dashboard before lighting the molotov in her hand. She turned the key, wanting to make damn sure that her only means of escape worked before burning down her only shelter. It purred to life, and she smiled thinly.

She hung her hand out the open window of the truck and chucked it through the back door of the farmhouse. It shattered in the hallway, coating the walls in liquid flame.

She punched the gas and sped around the house, the zombies oblivious to her escape.

The flickering flames consumed the house quickly and faded into the rearview mirror. The white hot rage within Sparks, however, remained.

CHAPTER TWO

"What do you think?" Jeff asked Rufus, the two leaning over the roof of the truck. All was quiet on the streets as they squinted in the darkness of the interstate exit ramp.

The older man inclined his head. "I'm thinkin' that gas station across the street probably has a bathroom."

"Good to know you're focused on the important things." The skinhead rolled his eyes.

Rufus shrugged. "Spoken like a man who's never had to dig his own hole to take a shit in."

"Just be sure you check under the stall door before you go busting in," Jeff warned.

"Good call," his companion agreed.

"What you think boys, we good?" Mary called through the back window.

"Yeah, head over to the gas station," Jeff instructed.

Ricky put the truck in drive. "You got it," he confirmed. He bumbled slowly across the way into the gas station parking lot. There were a few dead bodies scattered about, all of them missing the backs of their heads. Their clothes were tattered and encrusted in blood, so it was

clear that the head wounds were the
killing blow in their second, undead life.

As soon as he pulled up to the pumps,
the two passengers in the back jumped down
to the concrete.

"You two stay in the cab until we
check the building out," Rufus instructed.
"If you see us runnin', you be ready to
punch it."

Ricky nodded. "I got your back,
bubba."

"You take point," Jeff said, and the
older man led the way to the convenience
store.

"I'll sweep the aisles," he said,
"and you make sure nothin' comes at me
from behind the register or the back
room."

The skinhead nodded. "Alright, let's
do it." He pulled the small door open, and
Rufus burst in, assault rifle at the
ready. He swiftly moved through the front
of the store, aiming down each of the four
short aisles. Jeff followed in and jumped
behind the counter, finding nothing.

"Clear," Rufus called from the back.

"Same here," the skinhead replied.
There was a sudden banging from the back
of the store that startled them both. They
cautiously met at the back hallway towards
the storage room, only to find it heavily
barricaded. Rufus reached forward and

tapped on the door, and a ruckus erupted from the other side.

"Well, that got 'em all riled up," he said.

Jeff yanked on the barricade a bit and shrugged. "It's solid. Doesn't sound like there are enough of them to get through."

"While I tend to agree, you mind keeping an eye on it while I conduct an air raid?" Rufus smirked.

Just as Jeff opened his mouth to reply, the store filled with flashing red and blue lights. "What the hell is that?"

"Whatever it is, we're gonna be ready for it," the older man replied, raising his rifle.

Jeff nodded. "Let's get out there."

"Nah, you stay in here," Rufus said with a shake of his head. "If things get squirrely, it'd be good to have an ace in the hole."

"I'll be ready," his companion replied.

The older man exited the store holding the gun casually but with his finger discreetly on the trigger. There was a fully uniformed police officer standing behind the open door of a cruiser, lights flashing.

"Whoa, that's far enough right there," the officer barked.

Rufus continued his stroll over to the truck, leaning up against the bed. He was happy to see that Ricky and Mary were still inside the cab. "What seems to be the trouble officer?"

"Y'all are in a heap of trouble, breaking into the gas station like that," he snapped, but his voice trembled with false bravado. The older man estimated him to be in his early twenties and wondered how fresh out of the academy he'd been when shit went south.

Rufus laughed. "It's the motherfucking apocalypse and you're worried about breaking and entering? What kind of dumbass are you, boy?"

"Look, the law's the law, and I'm here to enforce it," the officer said, and swallowed hard. "So I'm gonna have to ask y'all to come with me."

"Zombies runnin' wild and you wanna take us to jail for fightin' to survive?" Rufus narrowed his eyes.

"Not gonna take you to jail." The officer shook his head. "The Sheriff has set up a shelter in Junction, so I'm gonna take you there and let him decide what to do with you."

There was a click as Jeff stepped out of the shadows behind the cruiser. "Is this really a fight you want to have?"

The officer whipped around with his gun drawn, prompting both of his opponents to aim at him.

"Easy, buddy," Jeff warned. "I don't want to put you down, but you wouldn't be the first today."

"Alright." The officer holstered his gun slowly. "Now let's just take it down a beat, guys."

"Oh, we're down, bud," Rufus replied.

"How about we do this?" He raised his hands beside his head. "Why don't you guys follow me to the shelter, and I'll tell the Sheriff you flagged me down. Then we're all good."

"Well, it's gonna be a while before we can do that," Jeff replied. "We have some friends coming to meet us and they're a few hours out."

"Some friends, huh?" The officer raised an eyebrow. "How many?"

"A few dozen or so," Rufus said.

"I don't know if we're gonna have the supplies to accommodate that many."

"Don't worry, we're self sufficient," Jeff explained. "Outside of gas, of course."

"Well, hell, bud, why didn't you say so?" the officer asked, and reached into his pocket, producing a set of keys. "Here, I've got the key to unlock the pump

so you can get filled up. I'm Deputy
Carter of the Junction PD."

Jeff gripped his gun tightly, on high
alert. "I'm Jeff, that's Rufus," he
introduced carefully. "The young couple in
the truck are Ricky and Mary."

"Nice to meet y'all," Carter replied
brightly, and headed over to the pump.
"Here, let me get the gas going for you.
You want the hi-test there, bud?"

"Uh, yeah," Ricky replied, brow
furrowed. "That'll work."

"Alright, coming right up!" the
Deputy exclaimed as he opened the gas
tank.

Jeff waved Rufus over to him. "Is it
just me, or did he get suspiciously
friendly when I mentioned we were bringing
food?" he asked quietly.

"Why couldn't this sumbitch be in my
weekly card game?" Rufus replied in a low
voice. "With a poker face like that I
could have been driving a Camaro by now."

"You think we should take him out?"
Jeff wondered.

"Nah," the older man replied with a
shake of his head. "He may be a dipshit,
but I don't think he's lying about the
Sheriff and the shelter. Don't know about
you, but I've had my fill of armed
confrontations for the day."

345

"Alright," the skinhead said. "But he doesn't leave our sight. This motherfucker doesn't get a moment of privacy. If he's not on the up and up, the last thing we need are his friends showing up."

"Agreed."

"There ya go, that'll be twenty-seven fifty," Carter replaced the gas pump and locked it. "Ha ha, just messing with ya!"

Ricky and Mary shared an unamused glance.

"So you know, if you don't wanna sit out here I can run you up to the shelter and send some of my boys back to meet your friends," the Deputy offered, leaning his elbow on the driver's side window. "I mean, no sense in y'all spending the night outside when you can be nice and comfy, right?"

"If it's all the same, Deputy, I think we're gonna stay right here and wait for our friends," Jeff piped up.

"Well, alright then," Carter said, shrugging his shoulders. His eyes darted around as he stepped back from the truck. "I guess I can hang out with you. Hey, any of you want some coffee? I stashed a bag behind the front counter. I can brew us some!"

Jeff nodded. "Sure, let me give you a hand."

"Oh no, I got ya," Carter waved his hands in front of his face.

"Please, I insist," the skinhead replied with a grin. "You're kind enough to take us to the shelter, the least I can do is help out."

The Deputy's big smile faltered. "Alright then, you get the water and I'll get the beans."

"I'll bring Ricky and Mary up to speed," Rufus assured his companion as he followed after the mysterious officer.

"Oh, Rufus, how do you take your coffee?" Jeff called over his shoulder as they walked.

"Like I take my women," the older man called back. "Cold and bitter."

Jeff chuckled. "And here I was thinking you preferred them Irish."

"Ah, you convinced me." Rufus laughed. "I'll take it Irish."

"I'll see what I can do," the skinhead replied as he opened the door for the Deputy.

CHAPTER THREE

Sparks pulled off the interstate slowly as she approached the off-ramp. The combination of sleep deprivation and self-loathing had her in a bit of a daze.

"How the hell am I going to explain this to the others? Everybody is gone because *I* fucked up. Oh god, what if the others didn't make it either?" She shook her head violently from side to side, as if to shake away her demons. "Jesus Christ girl, snap out of it."

She crested the hill of the ramp and nearly burst into relieved tears at the sight of her four friends clustered around the back of Ricky's truck with a police officer. She pulled into the parking lot and before she could even get out of the car, Rufus was right there.

"Goddamn girl, even when you look like hell, you still look amazing." He shot her a lopsided grin. "Bet you have some stories to tell."

She let out a small bewildered laugh before burying her face in his chest.

"Ah, come on now," Rufus squeezed her in a hug. "It wasn't *that* bad of a compliment."

"I'm sorry," she murmured into his chest. "It… it was just a rough night."

"Don't worry about it, girl," he replied, and rubbed her back in slow circles. "We had a hell of a time too."

"Ma'am, I'm Deputy Carter," the officer strolled up, and the redhead straightened up, turning to face him with squared shoulders.

"Officer Sparks of the Austin PD."

"Oh, an officer, huh?" Carter replied. "Good to know." He nodded, but she was already walking past him towards the tailgate.

"Everybody, I… I have news," she said, clasping her hands in front of her. "Last night I had an encounter with Elijah."

Rufus stepped up beside her, eyes blazing. "That motherfucker, did he hurt you?"

"No," she replied, shaking her head. "He tried, but… no. He did get my belongings, though. Including the GPS and my earpiece."

Mary burst into tears, and Ricky wrapped his arms around her shoulders tightly.

"How bad is it?" Jeff asked. "I haven't been able to reach them all morning."

"They're…" Sparks swallowed hard. "They're all gone."

Ricky folded his wife into his chest, glaring at the redhead. "How do you know?" he asked, wiping furiously at his eyes.

"I got my earpiece back and talked to Dan just as Elijah showed up," Sparks explained, eyes downcast. Rufus put an arm around her shoulders, giving her a reassuring squeeze. "All I heard were gunshots, and Dan telling me it was okay. There was apparently a fire in the supplies, too."

Carter stepped forward, rejoining the group. "So there's no food coming?"

Sparks tore away from Rufus and whirled on the Deputy, eyes blazing as she stood nose to nose with him. "That's your fucking takeaway from what I just said?"

His mouth opened and closed like a fish out of water. "I… uh…"

"*My* fuckup killed our entire group, and all you care about is the food?" she demanded.

The deputy stepped back, eyes wide. "Ma'am, I'm very sorry for your loss," he stammered, "and I'm even sorrier for my response. It's just, we have a lot of people at the shelter and the supplies aren't that plentiful…"

The redhead turned away from him, addressing her friends. "This is something that is going to haunt me for the rest of my days," she admitted. "It's my fault that Elijah got a hold of the GPS, and it's… it's my fault that Principal Dan and the others are gone… it's my fault…" She took in a deep ragged breath and Rufus put his hands on her shoulders again.

"Girl, you listen to me and you listen good," he demanded. "You ain't to blame for what that bastard Elijah did. Hell, if you wanna blame somebody then you need to be blamin' me."

"Rufus." Her voice cracked as she looked up at him. "I appreciate the sentiment, but you aren't the one who lost the GPS that led them back to the camp."

"No, but I am the one who missed an open shot on the sumbitch when I had it," he replied. "If I didn't fuck that up, then he wouldn't a been a problem for you cause dead men don't walk."

She raised an eyebrow.

"Granted, that saying carried a lot more weight a week ago," he said. "But damn girl, you get my point."

"I do, Rufus," she said, leaning her head against his shoulder. "And thanks."

He squeezed her shoulder. "Anytime, girl."

Carter stepped back into the group. "Y'all, I'm sorry to interrupt… again," he said, raising his hands. "But if nobody else is coming, we really should get up to the shelter. There's a lot going on in town and I really need to get you back."

"Dude," Jeff snapped. "Can you give us a moment here to mourn?"

"It's alright Jeff, he's right, we can't just sit around here all day," Sparks cut in. "Deputy, I'm going to grab a cup of that coffee and gas up the truck here, then we can be on our way."

"I'll take care of the truck," Rufus told her, "you take care of you."

Carter nodded. "Alright, I'll call it in and let them know we're on the way."

CHAPTER FOUR

"A Camaro, huh?" Sparks raised an eyebrow as she took up the rear of their interstate convoy. "You think his poker face was that bad?"

Rufus nodded. "I swear if that goober got pocket aces his face would look like a porn star crawled under the table and-"

"I get the gist," she replied, putting up a hand.

Rufus grinned. "So would he."

"Did you set out to be a dirty old man, or did it come naturally?" Sparks couldn't help but share his contagious grin.

"One hundred percent God-given ability," he puffed his chest out.

"Good to see that God was generous at one point in time." The redhead snorted and shook her head.

"Amen to that."

"So, were you guys able to figure out what Carter was hiding?" she asked.

"Naw." He shook his head. "We threw some questions his way, but couldn't get a full read on him. All we got was that he was really eager to get us to the shelter and way, way too interested in the supplies we were bringing in."

"Yeah, I caught that part," she agreed. "Motherfucker is lucky I didn't deck him."

"God knows the little prick woulda deserved it," Rufus added.

Sparks raised an eyebrow. "So you got any theories?"

"Maybe they're like those militia douchebags and they're stockpiling supplies?" He shrugged. "But that wouldn't explain why they are keeping people alive in the shelter."

"Assuming that part is true," she suggested.

"Ya know..." Rufus sighed. "We really need to find an optimist to add to the group. It would be refreshin' to go into a situation and hear how wonderful it's gonna be."

"I agree, it would be nice to have a laugh at that absurdity before we rush into certain doom." She laughed.

"Well, I know a few jokes from my military days," he said, and put his finger to his chin for effect. "Pretty sure if I think hard enough I can remember one that wasn't entirely racist or sexist."

Sparks rolled her eyes. "Only one?"

"What do you want?" Rufus shrugged. "It was the sixties. The only time we heard someone say P-C was when it was followed up by a P and *'do you have any?'*"

She laughed. "Simpler times, huh?"

Carter flashed his lights and briefly flipped his siren, signaling to two cruisers that were manning their exit. They let the convoy through, and Sparks and Rufus eyed up the two police officers as they left the interstate. There were two gas stations on either side of the road, guarded by several patrol cars. On the far end, cruisers blocked the road coming from the other direction.

"Man, they've got this shit on lockdown," Sparks commented.

Rufus nodded. "Definitely a step up from the last shitshow we were in."

Carter led them down the road and a few blocks into the small town. There were officers everywhere, blocking off all the exits to town centered around a large church auditorium. Beside the building was a commercial grade transport bus with a few people loading up the bottom compartments with supplies.

Carter parked next to the bus, waving the two trucks in next to him.

Jeff jumped down from the bed of Ricky's truck, approaching the greeting officer as his four companions exited their vehicles.

"Sorry folks, I'm going to have to ask you to turn over your weapons," the officer declared.

Rufus fell in line next to Jeff, the two of them gripping their rifles. "And I'm gonna have to ask you to fuck right on off."

The officer's shoulders tensed, and Sparks stepped in front of her men. "Sir, my name is Lacy Sparks, and I'm an officer with the Austin PD," she said. "These are my deputies who have saved my life on multiple occasions since this thing started. They're legally authorized to carry."

"Be that as it may," the officer replied, "if you want to come into this rescue shelter, you're gonna have to disarm."

Jeff shrugged. "Well, looks like we're gonna be on our way then."

"Just be sure you head east on the interstate," the officer replied. "The north is blocked off to traffic and you don't have permission to go west."

"Oh, really?" Jeff clenched his jaw, stepping forward. "I wasn't aware that a small town police officer had the ability to shut down the goddamn interstate."

His opponent's eyes were like ice. "Well we do, and it is."

"Bullshit," the skinhead snapped. "Come on y'all, we're gassed up, I say we blow this joint and continue on our journey west. Officer limp dick here ain't gonna do shit." He flashed their opponent his middle finger and turned to head back to the truck.

"Let me show you what happens if you do," the officer snarled and pulled his baton. Sparks immediately lashed out, landing a kidney punch from the side, catching his baton arm as it dropped and slamming his head onto the hood of the truck.

Rufus pressed the barrel of his handgun into the now subdued officer's temple, leaning down to look him in the eye. "And what would that be, exactly?"

"My, my, my, what do we have here?" A stern voice asked, and the group turned at the approach of a tall man with a full dark beard.

"Your boy here broke free of his leash," Rufus explained. "So my girl and I was takin' precautions in case he turned rabid."

"Officer Sams, were you misbehaving?" the bearded officer asked, a touch of disdain in his voice.

"Just…" Sparks' captive hissed, and she didn't let up on his arm behind his back. "Just protecting the route like you ordered, Sheriff."

"Well, it would appear as though you came on a little strong there, son." The Sheriff clucked his tongue.

"Yes, sir." Sams gasped.

His leader crossed his arms. "Would you like to apologize to these fine folks?"

"I… I…" the officer grunted. "I'm sorry."

"So," the Sheriff addressed Sparks. "Now that my officer has made amends, would you be willing to release him? You have my permission to put him down if he acts out again."

She and Rufus shared a glance and a nod, and the redhead let the rogue officer go. He rubbed his arm and slunk away to his post, red-faced.

"Folks, let me introduce you to Sheriff Hutch," Carter declared.

"Pleased to make your acquaintance," the Sheriff greeted. "Why don't y'all follow me inside and I'll give you the lay of the land?" He led the newcomers into the shelter, and they strolled after him, Jeff and Rufus still holding their rifles in step with Sparks. On the far end, there was a lone basketball hoop where a few teenagers played. Several families were huddled together around large round wooden tables, a few random groups of people scattered about, eating snacks and making small talk.

"This is our temporary rescue shelter for travelers such as yourself," Hutch said.

"Temporary?" Mary piped up.

"That's right, ma'am," he tipped his hat to her. "Junction has long been the final stop before people headed towards El Paso, as there's not a whole lot for a couple hundred miles. While this makes it a great place to gas up, it's not an ideal spot to house survivors."

"So where are you taking them?" Ricky asked.

"There's a little town about fifty miles up the road called Sonora," the Sheriff replied. "My brother is the Sheriff up there, so when all this started to go down, we partnered up."

"I'm guessing it's secure?" Jeff asked.

"About as secure as anyplace can be, given the situation," Hutch grasped his large belt buckle with his bare hand. "We're the closest major town to it, so it's pretty isolated. And my brother did a good job forming a posse and getting it locked down, so those undead creatures have been eradicated."

Mary raised a delicate hand. "How many people have you relocated?"

"Over the past couple of days, we've been moving the citizens of Junction out there," Hutch replied. "So when you factor in the random survivors who stopped in, I'm guessing five, maybe six hundred have found their way to Sonora."

"How are you doing on supplies?" Sparks piped up. "Your deputy there seemed real upset when he heard we weren't bringing in the truckloads of food like originally intended."

"I'll level with you, it's not good," the Sheriff admitted. "Even when we combine the resources of Junction and Sonora, we barely have enough food and water to provide for that number of people for longer than a few weeks. My brother is sending out scouts and hunters to secure everything they can, but it remains to be seen just how successful they're gonna be."

Carter jogged to the front of the group. "Sheriff, tell them about the truck."

"Settle down Deputy." Hutch narrowed his eyes. "I'm getting to it."

Sparks crossed her arms. "The truck?"

"Most of the people in this room came in on that giant tour bus that's being loaded up," Hutch said. "" They were just outside of Austin when things went to shit, and they got forced into the back roads. The driver informed me that about ten miles up the road, they saw a big rig for one of those giant super center stores that had landed in a ditch. It was dinged up but still looked drivable if we could figure out a way to get it back on the road.

"Problem is, we sent a scout to check it out and he said there were a dozen or so zombies surrounding it. Apparently, the driver was still alive when it wrecked, and that held their attention."

Rufus' brow furrowed. "Then why haven't you gone and gotten it yet?"

"Because we're spread pretty thin here," Hutch replied. "Half of my officers have already moved up to Sonora to secure things, so I'm on a skeleton crew here. I have a mechanic, driver and tow truck operator, but they ain't exactly keen to get into a conflict with those things. So I was wondering…"

"If we could ride up there and lay the smack down on some zombies for you?" Ricky finished.

"I was hoping to put it a little more eloquently, but in a nutshell, yes," the Sheriff admitted.

Sparks put a hand on her hip. "Alright, we'll do it, but we're going to need some ammo."

"Of course," Hutch replied with a firm nod. "Deputy Carter will take you by the armory on the way out and get you whatever you need. And I know I don't have a lot to offer you, but when you get to Sonora I can get y'all some prime housing. Hell, I'll even talk to my brother and see if I can't get you a choice security gig."

Sparks put up a hand. "That's appreciated, but one step at a time." She turned to her companions. "We've got some zombies to kill first."

CHAPTER FIVE

Sparks and Ricky drove their respective trucks towards the big rig just outside of town, following Deputy Carter in his cruiser once again. He slowed down to a stop about a quarter mile away from the zombie horde—close enough to see them, but far enough away that they weren't alerted.

"Well, there it is," Carter said as they disembarked from their vehicles. "Looks like they've attracted a few more of those ghouls."

Rufus and Sparks stepped forward, looking through binoculars they'd nabbed from the police armory.

"This looks like fun," the older man said.

The redhead shrugged. "Eh, we've faced worse."

"Why do you think I said *this* looks like fun?" He chuckled. "Only taking on fifteen of those fuckers is an easy day in the office at this point."

"We are living the life, aren't we?" She grinned.

"I get to spend my days hanging out with the South Texas Wrestling Champion, busting heads together." He puffed out his chest. "So from my point of view, you're damn right I'm livin' the life."

She laughed. "Good to know I'm having a positive impact on your life."

"So, how do y'all want to handle this?" Carter piped up.

"What you thinkin', girl?" Rufus asked.

"Let's see," she said, "it's a four lane road so we have some room to work with. What do you think about doing a double barricade?"

"Trucks side by side, cop car up front to break em up?" Rufus asked, miming the motion with his hands. "And we just pick 'em off from the bed?"

"These things don't seem to be able to climb that well," Sparks said. "So we should be pretty safe in the truck bed."

"Just to be safe, we should have somebody on climber duty," he replied. "Given you have a shotgun I think that should be you."

She raised her eyebrows in mock offense. "You wanna put *me* on cleanup duty?"

"Think of it like a vacation day, girl." He winked at her. "I think you've earned one."

"I think we all have," she agreed.

Carter raised his hand. "Sorry, I didn't quite follow that, what are we doing?"

"Deputy," Sparks said, turning to him, "I want you to pull your car up about twenty feet and park it across the center lanes. Ricky and I are going to line our trucks up behind you and we're gonna climb into the truck beds. When we're set, you're going to hit the siren to get their attention."

Carter swallowed nervously. "You *want* them to run at us?"

"It's a lot safer to attack them from a fortified position," she explained. "And besides, we don't exactly have sniper rifles, so it's gonna be a little difficult to pick them off from here."

He shook his head in disbelief and then trudged back to his car.

"Okay Ricky, line 'em up," Sparks said, jumping back into her truck. They parked about ten feet behind the cop car, parallel across the road with the beds touching to form a large platform. "Ricky, Mary, you take the right," she instructed as the five of them climbed up. "Jeff, Rufus, the left. I'm gonna take center position in case any of these fuckers decide they want to climb."

"And remember y'all, ammo is precious, so don't go shootin' off until they are right up on ya," Rufus added.

"Alright, Deputy, hit the siren," Sparks called.

He reached for the button, and then paused, taking a deep breath. He hit the automatic locks first. A round of chuckles rippled through the group.

"Anytime there, Bubba," Ricky said, and Carter glared at him through the back window as he flicked the siren. The wail reverberated across the roadway, and the zombies tore towards them immediately.

"Wait for it," Sparks said, as the zombies tore around the cop car to slam into the truck beds. "Light 'em up!" she screamed, and her companions lined up their shots and fired, easily hitting their targets. Sparks continued to aim around, making sure none of the creatures gained a foothold.

"A little help here!" Carter yelped, his voice muffled through the car as a pair of zombies pounded on the sides of the cruiser. Sparks jumped down to the road with Jeff and Rufus, holding up three fingers and counting down. When she got to zero, both men fired, dropping the zombies in tandem.

"What tha fuck?" Rufus asked, motioning to the remaining zombies slowly shuffling towards them from the big rig. They'd barely made it fifteen feet since the siren blared. "Shouldn't they be running at us?"

"I encountered a couple of these slowpokes yesterday," Sparks replied. "I thought they may have taken a bullet or something. But with this many of them, it has to be something else."

Carter unrolled his window. "They're starting to break down," he said.

"What do you mean?" Jeff asked.

"A couple of days ago, we were taking a group down to Sonora when a pack of those things started following us down the interstate," the Deputy said, and carefully exited the car. "One of the passengers was a doctor who suggested we let them keep pace with us to see if they would tire out. They sprinted at full speed for about twenty miles when they began to slow down, so we decreased our speed to let them keep up. They still moved with the same intensity, but couldn't run nearly as fast. By the time we got close to Sonora, they were moving like these guys here. After we took them out, the doc did a quick autopsy and found that their muscles were shredded."

"Great, so all we gotta do is get these fuckers to run a marathon and life will be peachy," Rufus said.

"Well, we can set up a zombie fun run in a bit." Jeff cocked his gun. "First, we need to take care of our current problem."

"Hold up, save your ammo," Sparks said. "Hey Ricky, you got some crowbars in that truck of yours?"

He knelt down and rummaged in his toolbox. "Yeah, I gotcha covered." He hopped down and handed Sparks and Jeff each a crowbar.

"Let's get in some cardio." She grinned.

"Y'all have fun." Rufus waved them off. "If it's all the same, I'll keep my gun handy in case they get unruly."

Sparks patted him on the shoulder and then stepped forward with her skinhead companion towards the shambling dead.

"I'll take left, you take right," Jeff said.

She nodded. "Yup."

Jeff reached a zombie first, a youngish looking man missing several chunks of flesh from his arms. The skinhead violently drove the tip of the crowbar through its eye socket, and the corpse fell to the asphalt.

"This seems to be pretty effective," Sparks said with a grunt as she caved in another zombie's head with a forceful smack. "What do you think, Jeff?"

"Kind of wishing I had stretched first," he replied as he ripped his crowbar out of another zombie's temple, "but other than that yeah, it's good."

The duo continued to dispatch the mini-horde until a shot rang out, startling them both.

Jeff turned quickly to see Rufus playfully blowing smoke from his gun. "What the hell was that?"

"That fucker was gettin' a little too close to my girl there," the older man replied.

The skinhead raised an eyebrow at the corpses littering the ground. "I'm pretty sure she had it under control."

"Frankly, I'm glad to know my guardian angel here doesn't take any chances with my safety," Sparks replied, giving Rufus a coy smile.

He nodded. "And I never will."

She patted his shoulder again on her way to the truck. "So what do you think, boys? Wanna see the spoils from this battle?"

"Here's hoping it's more than baby clothes and DVDs," Jeff replied as he and Rufus threw open the doors.

"Fun fact," the older man said with a lazy grin. "If you deep fry canned meat, then smother it in ketchup, it tastes just like steak."

Sparks snorted as she peered around him, eyeing up the pallets and pallets of canned goods in the truck.

"Well, provided you've downed half a bottle of whiskey before dinner," he added.

The redhead shook her head and turned to Carter. "What do you think, Deputy?" she asked. "Have we earned our keep?"

"More than you know," he replied, mouth agape at their fortune. "I'll call in the tow truck while we head back to the shelter."

CHAPTER SIX

The group passed a scowling Officer Sams as they entered the shelter, guns in hand. Sparks led the way this time, Carter trailing in last. Sheriff Hutch had his back turned, chatting with some people in the corner.

"Hey, Sparks, glad you're back," Hutch turned and greeted them. "I have some people I'd like you to meet." He stepped aside to reveal three men in militia fatigues.

Elijah smirked at Sparks and crossed his arms as the group froze.

"It's a godsend that they showed up," Hutch continued. "We need all the trained men we can get."

"Sheriff Hutch," the redhead said firmly. "Please, step back."

"Is…" He realized the tension between the two groups and stepped towards Carter, off to the side. "Is there a problem here?"

"Oh, no problem here, Sheriff," Elijah drawled, spreading his arms. "It's just that the lady here goes wild for a man in uniform, and couldn't stand it when I deflected her adva-"

His tirade was cut short by a shotgun slug blowing his face off. The civilians dove for cover as his body collapsed, face a bloody goulash of bone and brain matter. Hutch put up his hands and stepped forward as the redhead's group raised their weapons.

"Somebody want to tell me what the hell that was all about?" he asked.

"These men murdered our friends," Sparks replied, not taking her eyes off of the remaining militia members. "Slaughtered innocent men, women and children simply because they were in the way."

One of the militia members clenched his jaw, remembering the fiery redhead before him. "Please, ma'am, I-"

She cut him off by chambering another shell. "The next word out of your mouth will be your last."

"Okay, Sparks, I tell you what," Hutch cut in. "If you put down the weapon, I'll escort these men from the building and send them on their way."

She glared at them.

"It's your play girl," Rufus said quietly. "Whatever you wanna do I'll back it."

There was a pregnant pause, and then Sparks lowered her shotgun. "Sheriff Hutch, get these assholes out of here before I change my mind."

Hutch motioned to the cluster of officers rubbernecking in the doorway.

"Come on boys, probably best if you go
with Officer Sams here."

"Sir, where should I escort them to?"
Sams stepped forward.

"Take him to my brother in Sonora-"

"Wait a goddamn minute," Rufus
snapped. "They need to find someplace
else."

"Let me finish." Hutch held up a
hand. "Officer Sams, take him to my
brother in Sonora, and tell him these men
need to be put on Special Duty."

"Yes Sir," the officer replied. "Come
on, fellas." He led them away and the
Sheriff turned back to the group.

"If they are there when we arrive,
I'm going to shoot them on sight," Sparks
informed him, fists clenched.

"Calm down and let me explain," Hutch
said, voice frustratingly calm. "They're
going to be put on Special Duty, which
means they will be sent out into the
wasteland to gather supplies. The only
time they will be in town is to drop off
goods and get their next assignment. It's
a hard life, and based on the last week it
has a very short life expectancy."

"I meant what I said," Sparks told
him as she stepped right up to his face.
"If I see them again, they're going to
meet the same fate as their leader here."

"Fair enough," he replied. "When you get to Sonora, please feel free to relay that info to my brother. Deputy Carter will back you up."

Sparks nodded. "Thank you, Sheriff."

"If you'll excuse me, I need to make some final preparations for this group to get on the road," he said. "If you'd like you can leave your trucks here and ride with them on the bus."

"Yeah, that ain't happening, cowboy," Rufus said.

"Fair enough," the Sheriff replied. "Y'all should get packed up then, so you can follow the bus out to Sonora."

"We'll be ready," Jeff assured him.

Hutch put a hand on Carter's shoulder as he walked away. "Deputy, a word?"

Rufus turned to Sparks as their group huddled up. "Goddamn girl, you are cold-blooded."

"Nah, if I was cold-blooded, those other three would have walked out of here," she replied.

"Speaking of them," Jeff piped up, "what do you think about the Sheriff and his Special Duty bullshit?"

"I think you summed it up pretty well there," Rufus agreed. "Sparks, what do you think?"

"That we should hope for the best, but prepare for the worst," she said. "The reality is, we don't have much in the way of supplies, and there's not a whole lot past Sonora until you get close to El Paso."

"So it's either we play nice in Sonora or we starve?" Ricky threw his hands up.

Rufus scowled. "Seems to be about the long and short of it."

"We aren't going in without a plan, though," Sparks cut in. "Ricky, how's your truck doing?"

"Still going strong," he said. "She's a tough old girl."

"Good, because we're all piling into it," the redhead replied.

Mary put a hand on her hip. "Strength in numbers, huh?"

"Yep," Sparks confirmed, "and we need to be prepared for anything."

"So make sure your weapons are topped off and your trigger fingers itchy," Rufus instructed.

She nodded. "Alright, let's get loaded up."

CHAPTER SEVEN

Sparks and Rufus leaned on the roof of Ricky's truck from the bed, the other three getting situated inside as the tour bus loaded up.

"Sparks, Rufus, you guys about ready to hit the road?" Sheriff Hutch asked as he strolled up with Carter in tow.

The redhead nodded. "We're ready whenever you are."

"I was wondering," he said as he shifted his weight on his left hip. "Could you give my Deputy here a ride?"

The two companions glanced at each other, and Rufus sighed. "Eh, what the hell, climb on up," he said.

"Carter," the Sheriff patted his comrade on the back as he hoisted himself into the truck bed. "Be sure to introduce Sparks and her friends to my brother."

"Yes…" the Deputy stammered. "Yes sir."

"Alright." Hutch nodded. "I'm gonna give some parting words to the tour group, then get you on your way."

"Hey, Sheriff," Sparks called.

He turned and looked up at her, tipping his hat. "Yes?"

"Where's the big rig we helped you rescue?" she asked. "Thought it was going to be headed this way too?"

"It's gonna be an hour or so behind you," he told her. "We just got it back to the truck stop and wanted the mechanic to give it a once over. Last thing we want is for it to break down on us."

"Well you know," she said, "Ricky is a hell of a mechanic, he can take a look at it if you like."

"Oh don't worry, we have everything under control." Hutch smiled and put his hands up. "Y'all have done enough. Get to Sonora, kick back, and settle in to your new home."

Sparks nodded and returned his smile. "Thanks Sheriff, I appreciate it."

"Y'all have safe travels," Hutch replied and waved as Carter settled in against the tailgate. "Thanks for your help up here."

Rufus nodded. "Our pleasure."

The Sheriff climbed into the tour bus and climbed in, grabbing the microphone to address his refugees. "Folks, if I can have your attention please," he began. "I know that this has been a very trying week for everyone. We've all faced unimaginable terror, losing our family and friends, as well as our homes. But fate has led you to my doorstep, and now that you're here I'm going to take care of you all."

There was a round of applause and some hoots, and he extended his hand to wave them calm.

"Thank you, but that's really not necessary," he said. "I'm just doing what anyone in my position would do. Now, my brother has Sonora safe and secure, and has a new house set aside for you. Granted, some of you may have to have some roommates for a while, but everybody here is friendly, right?"

There was a louder round of applause this time, with yells to the affirmative.

"That's the spirit, y'all!" he cried. "Alright, kick back and enjoy your leisurely drive to your new home. Driver, just follow that nice officer in front of you and he'll get you to where you need to go!" Hutch handed the mic back to the driver, and exited the tour bus as the passengers whistled and clapped in excitement.

"Off we go," Sparks muttered as everyone started their engines.

Sparks and Rufus leaned against each other as the convoy sped down the interstate, backs against the cab of the truck. They watched Carter, who watched the cruiser following them.

"I can't tell if he's signaling them or if he is just wondering what he did so wrong to have to ride with us," the redhead said into her companion's ear.

"All I know is, if anything ain't right in town, that motherfucker dies first," Rufus declared.

"You caught his stuttering too?" Sparks asked. "When the Sheriff gave him his orders."

"Like I said," he replied, "I would have given anything for him to be in one of my card games."

The truck slowed as they approached their exit, and two armed officers moved their cruisers out of the way on the ramp. They returned to defensive positions once the convoy passed through and turned right towards the northern part of town.

"Any idea where we're headed?" Rufus asked loudly. "Looks like a lot of the houses are the other way."

"Don't worry," Carter turned to him, but avoided eye contact. "We're headed to the airport to get everybody processed."

Rufus pursed his lips. "Uh-huh."

Sparks nudged him to discreetly look at a side street filled with cars sustaining major damage. She got to her knees and stuck her head into the back window of the cab as Rufus leaned forward to distract the Deputy.

"So, looks like y'all have a hell of a traffic jam over there," he said, motioning to the side street.

"Well, you know," Carter laughed nervously, "maybe they were having a block party?"

Rufus raised an eyebrow. "Uh-huh."

Sparks resumed her sitting position and the older man turned to her. "How they doin' up there?" he asked.

"Oh you know." She smiled. "Just anxious to get settled into their new home."

A moment later, the engine revved loudly, and the truck slowed to a crawl. Carter clenched his fists as he saw the bus pulling away towards the airport hangars.

"Come on guys, we gotta catch up to the others," he said, a hint of panic in his voice.

"Relax there Sparky." Rufus waved at him. "It's a small town, we'll catch up easily."

Carter wrung his hands. "Yeah, but-"

"Shh, it's fine." Rufus put his finger to his mouth.

"Sorry y'all," Ricky called back through the window. "She does this from time to time, just gimme a minute!"

His revving was suddenly drowned out by the sound of gunfire, and Sparks and Rufus jerked their heads around to see the tour bus being torn to shreds by bullets. They whipped around just in time for Carter to stand up and draw his weapon, but the redhead was quicker and she kicked him square in the chest.

He hit the asphalt hard on his neck, and Rufus opened fire on the windshield of the cruiser behind them, blood splattering the insides of the windows.

"Ricky, get us the fuck out of here!" Sparks screamed, and the vehicle lurched forward violently. Rufus grabbed her around the waist and threw them down on the truck bed, softening her fall with his body.

"You okay, girl?" he asked into her ear.

She nodded. "Yeah, you?"

"You know me," he replied with a chuckle. "I like it rough."

Bullets ricocheted off of the side of the truck as Ricky made a hard turn onto a side street. A tire blew and he swerved violently from side to side, but he managed to make it a few blocks before he couldn't make it any further.

"Everybody out, we gotta move!" Sparks yelled, her and Rufus leaping over the side of the back. The others piled out of the cab and Jeff busted through the gate of a privacy fence, huddling around the back of a house in tense silence.

Sparks knelt down, staring off into space, looking near catatonic. Mary broke away from the guys standing guard to sit beside her.

"Sparks?" she asked gently. "Are you okay?"

No response.

"I think we're clear," Jeff said quietly, after a few minutes. "At least for the moment."

"Yeah, we got nothing from this side either," Ricky added from the other side of the house.

Rufus knelt down in front of the redhead. "How's she doin'?" he asked.

"Still not speaking," Mary replied, worrying at her lower lip.

"Sparks, you hangin' in there, girl?" The older man searched her face for any kind of recognition. "We're in a bit of a situation and we could use you right about now." He reached out and squeezed her bicep, cocking his head. "Hon? What can I do?"

She tilted her head at this, steely gaze meeting his. "We're gonna kill them all." Her voice was low and deadly.

"There's my girl," Rufus declared, and took a step back as she got to her feet.

"This has gone on long enough." Her voice rose in volume as she paced back and forth in front of her teammates. "The strong preying on the weak. Innocent people just trying to survive another day, only to be cut down by gun toting hillbillies hiding like cowards because they can't find their balls with a goddamn electron microscope.

"Well, no more. This ends right fucking now. I am going to cleanse this town like a goddamn biblical plague. I don't know if my life expectancy can be measured in hours, days, or months, all I know is that I'm going to spend the rest of my time protecting innocent lives and murdering every last goddamn motherfucker that even contemplates doing harm to them." She stopped pacing, took a deep breath, and looked to Rufus. "I could use a hand."

The older man raised his arm like a schoolboy. "Can I loot the dead?"

"If you see something you like, then by all means, it's yours," the redhead replied with a shrug.

He grinned. "Alright, I'm in."

"Sparks," Jeff said reluctantly, "I know you're upset over Principal Dan and the group, but we have no idea how many men we're up against."

Mary nodded. "Shouldn't we just cut our losses and get out while we can?"

"I'm not asking y'all to come with me," Sparks declared. "I know you see this as a suicide mission, but I don't. I became a police officer because I wanted to help people, and now after all this time I finally have that chance. In all honesty, this is the first time I've really felt like myself since this whole thing began. At the very least, I'm going to make some of them pay for what they've done."

"Alright," Ricky agreed, "we're with you in spirit and all, but Mary and I ain't exactly equipped for all out war, ya know? But if there's something we can do to help, we'll do it."

Rufus grinned. "Any of y'all know how to drive one of them big rigs?"

"My daddy drove a route for years and showed me a thing or two." Mary nodded. "As long as you aren't having me parallel park, I should be okay."

"What are you thinking, Rufus?" Sparks asked.

"Well, while the two of us purge this town of douchebags, these three can hijack that truck full of food that's on its way," he replied, squaring his shoulders.

"Yeah, I guess it wouldn't do us much good to get further west if we don't have basic supplies," Jeff agreed. "I think we can handle that."

"How in the hell are we gonna hijack that big-ass thing?" Ricky exclaimed.

"We take out the two cops at the exit ramp," Mary replied, mischief in her eyes. "They had it blocked off when we came in. We pose as them, stop the truck on the interstate, and we're good to go."

Her husband threw his hands up. "And what happens if they have an escort?"

"Wouldn't be the first shootout we've been in today." Jeff shrugged.

"When you get the truck, I want you to drive a hundred miles west, then stop at the next exit," Sparks instructed. "If Rufus and I survive the day, we'll be there by dawn. If we don't, then I hope you guys find some peace and quiet."

"Come on now, don't talk like that," the skinhead said, putting his hands up. "You've walked away from a lot worse this week. Y'all got this."

"Thanks for the vote of confidence," she replied with a chuckle. "Go on, y'all need to book it to the exit ramp if you're gonna catch that truck."

Jeff nodded and moved towards the gate. Ricky peeked out through the slats and then quickly shut it, ducking back in.

"What is it?" the skinhead asked.

Ricky put a finger to his lips. "It's a patrol."

The group crowded around the gate, and Sparks peeked out before turning towards her companions. "Okay, when I give the signal I want you three to take off running," she said.

Ricky furrowed his brow. "Are you crazy?"

"Trust me," she replied. "They might get off a panic shot, but they won't get off any more. Rufus and I will be sure of that."

Ricky scrubbed his hands down his face. "Goddammit."

"You take left, I got the right," Sparks said to Rufus as the trio prepared to sprint for their lives.

The older man raised an eyebrow. "And the center?"

"First come, first served," she said.

Rufus grinned. "It's on then."

Sparks watched the patrol as they carefully moved closer, and when they hit the twenty yard range, she tapped Jeff on the shoulder.

The trio burst from the gate, startling the guards into jumping back before even thinking about raising their weapons. As they took aim, one took a bullet in the head, the other in the stomach. The third barely opened his mouth before two bullets blew through his chest.

"Pretty sure mine hit first," Rufus said.

Sparks punched his arm lightly. "You better get your eyesight checked old timer, cause I think it's fading quick."

"Check the score sweetheart, my guy's dead while yours is still wiggling around," he teased as they strolled out through the gate.

"I wanted to ask him some questions, so I adjusted my aim," Sparks feigned offense at his insinuation.

Rufus rolled his eyes. "You sure you weren't one of them slick politician types instead of a cop? Cause that's some next level bullshit right there."

"Alright, you got me." She laughed. "But you have to admit that my bad aim paid off."

"That it did, girl," he agreed as they reached the moaning cop. "Now let's ask this sumbitch some questions, shall we?"

Sparks knelt down beside their victim as Rufus kicked his gun away. "How you doin there, bud?" she asked. "Looks like you hurt yourself a bit."

He simply moaned, clutching his stomach as blood puddled beneath him.

"Yes, I know it hurts," she said, "but you really need to suck it up and listen to what I have to say."

"Please… I…" he hissed. "I have a family."

"And if you ever want to see them again, you need to pay attention," she demanded. "Now, I'm going to make this as simple as I possibly can. You answer my questions, and my friend and I will be on our way. You refuse, and, well…" She drew her knife, holding the blade up near his face. "I'm going to jam this thing through your eye socket and twist it until you stop moving. Do you understand?"

He nodded furiously, eyes wide.

"Good," she said. "So, let's start with your name."

"It's…" he gulped. "It's Mitchell."

"See, that wasn't so hard, was it?" Sparks wiggled the knife. "Now, how many men do you have?"

"There are…" He coughed, spitting blood all over the sidewalk. "There are a few dozen or so up by the airport. We… we took over the hangars and made it a base."

She cocked her head. "Is that where your family is?"

"No…" he hissed. "The families are in the south of town."

"Families?" Sparks raised an eyebrow. "How many are there?"

He shrugged and then coughed again. "Forty, maybe fifty women and children."

"Jesus Christ," she snapped. "If you are protecting families, then why did you assholes murder that bus full of people?"

"Because that…" Mitchell gasped. "That's what the Sheriff demanded. He puts his people first, and we need the supplies."

"So that means the rest of us have to *die*?" She lashed out and grabbed his throat and squeezed, causing him to sputter as his face turned bright purple. She finally let him go and he gasped and hacked, adding to the pool of blood beneath his head.

"It's nothing personal," he wheezed.

Rufus barked a laugh. "As you can tell, we sorta took it that way."

"The Sheriff came around when this all started… and gave us an ultimatum," Mitchell croaked. "Join him and our families would be safe. Anybody who refused was executed and their families were taken to the hospital."

Sparks clenched her fists. "This maniac attacked the families?"

"No, he locked them in the hospital,"
he replied.

Rufus furrowed his brow. "What's in
the hospital?"

"Zombies… and lots of them…" Mitchell
hacked. "As soon as the first person
turned, the Sheriff locked it up tight to
contain it. When people don't co-operate,
they're forced inside."

"So you selfish maniacs have murdered
hundreds of innocent people?" Sparks took
a deep breath.

"We did it for our families," he
wailed, and coughed violently again. "What
would you do to protect your family?"

She raised her knife. "You're about
to find out."

"Hold up there girl, I got a question
for ole Mitchell here," Rufus interrupted.

She lowered her arm. "Okay… go for
it."

"Who were the thirteen Vietnamese
Generals involved in the Tet Offensive?"
the older man asked.

Mitchell hissed in pain. "How the
hell would I know?"

"Alright, carry on, girl," Rufus said
with a wave of his hand.

Sparks slammed the knife down into
the side of their victim's head, and his
body twitched violently for a moment
before falling still. She ripped out the

blade and wiped the brain matter off of it on the corpse's shirt.

"Okay, I'll bite," she said as she stood up. "What the hell was up with the Vietnam question?"

"Well, you said if he answered your questions you'd let him go," Rufus replied with a shrug. "So I asked him something he wouldn't know. You're a lot of things, but a liar ain't one of 'em. Just wanted to, you know, protect your honor."

Sparks stared at him for a moment and then swallowed hard. "You know, for a tough old bastard you can be a big ole softy."

"Only with certain things," he replied with a wink, and leaned down to grab ammo from the fallen cops.

"We should get moving," she holstered her knife.

Rufus nodded as he pocketed the ammo. "Agreed. South part of town?"

She nodded. "Lead the way."

CHAPTER NINE

The hijacking trio crept up the road towards the exit ramp.

"I'm really worried about Sparks," Mary said quietly.

Ricky squeezed her arm gently. "Aw, baby, don't worry, she's just blowing off some steam after a rough couple of days."

"By murdering an entire town full of people?" She raised an eyebrow.

Jeff shrugged. "I mean, it's not like they don't deserve it."

"I know," Mary replied, biting her lip. "But she's just… different. I wish we could have convinced her to come with us to escape. I don't want anything to happen to her."

"Don't worry babe, she's a tough girl," her husband assured her.

Jeff nodded. "And Rufus will do anything to protect her, too," he added. "She'll be fine."

They reached the base of the exit ramp and knelt down in the bushes, peering at the two officers about sixty yards away with their backs turned.

"Alright, there they are," Jeff said.

"How you wanna do it?" Ricky asked.

The skinhead shook his head. "Terrain is too rough on the side of the road, so flanking them really isn't an option. They'd hear us coming."

"Don't think any of us is a good enough shot to hit them from here," Ricky worried. "Let alone hittin' both of 'em."

"They aren't even looking this way." Mary motioned flippantly, lips pursed. "Why don't we just walk up on them and do... do what needs to be done?"

The guys glanced at each other and shrugged.

"That's just crazy enough to work," Ricky said. "Good job, baby."

"Alrighty then," Jeff agreed. "Walk softly, guns out, and nobody fires until you're within ten feet."

Mary put up a hand. "Or they turn our way."

"That too," the skinhead agreed.

Ricky checked his handgun and stood. "Well, here goes nothin'."

They spread out across the ramp, marching in unison, stride for stride. They were careful not to stomp or drag their feet, but at the fifteen foot mark one of the officers caught a glimpse out of the corner of his eye.

"What the hell?" he blurted, but before he could even draw his weapon, bullets riddled the pair. The corpses hit the ground and the guys double checked to make sure they were really dead.

"Everybody good?" Jeff asked.

Ricky nodded. "Peachy."

"I…" Mary stammered. "I'll live."

"Baby, you okay?" Her husband furrowed his brow.

She nodded. "I'll be fine. Just not a fan of all this killing."

"I know." He rubbed her shoulder. "But this is an us or them situation."

She nodded again. "I realize that. Doesn't mean I have to like it."

"Guys," Jeff cut in, "we'll have plenty of time to talk this out, but right now we need to hide the bodies and get changed into their uniforms."

"What the fuck?" Ricky blinked at his comrade. "I ain't wearin' that."

"Gonna have to if we want to take the truck by surprise," the skinhead replied. "If they don't see two cops standing here, they'll just drive right over us."

"Babe, I shot a man in the back so we could get the truck," Mary said firmly. "You're gonna put that uniform on or you're gonna be sleeping on the couch whenever we find a place that actually has one."

Ricky sighed. "Yes, dear."

They got to work stripping the officers as she walked over to the closest cruiser. She opened the passenger side door and sat down facing the interstate.

She swallowed and blinked rapidly a few times, but couldn't stave off the sob that tore its way from her throat.

"Babe, you okay?" Ricky called.

She furiously wiped at her eyes and took a deep breath. "Yeah hon, I'm okay. Just gonna keep watch for the truck."

CHAPTER TEN

Rufus knelt to wait as a patrol car drove by. "See anything, girl?"

Sparks peered through the window of the house they were hiding behind. "Thrift store furniture and a bit of a mess," she said. "Not sure something went down in there or if they just aren't good housekeepers."

"Well, I'll feel right at home, then," he replied.

She patted his shoulder. "Oh, wait, I see a couple of deer heads on the wall," she said. "Could be some guns in the house."

"That's good, cause if there's thirty of these fuckers we're gonna need a little more firepower," Rufus said.

She took out her knife and jimmied the window open before looking down at him. "Can you give me a boost?"

"Because I'm a gentleman," he said with a grin, "I won't attempt to turn that dirty." He turned and cupped his hands together.

"Aw, don't go soft on me now, old timer," she replied and planted her foot in his hands. He lifted her up and she dove through the window, landing in a crouch, knife drawn.

She waited. When she didn't hear any movement, she walked to the back door and unlocked it to allow Rufus entry.

"Help me with the chair," she whispered as he gently closed the door behind him. They dragged the heavy recliner in the living room over as a makeshift barricade in the living room door. Once it was wedged into place, Rufus banged loudly on the doorframe.

A tall teenage zombie tore around the corner, bloody torso hitting the back of the chair and flipping her forward.

Rufus drove his blade into the back of her skull. "Well, that worked better than expected," he said.

Sparks nodded and banged on the doorframe a second time. "Just to be sure," she said. This time there was no response.

"If it's all the same." He readied his knife. "I'll do a pass through the house for any other threats."

"I'll see if there's anything left in the cupboards," she replied. They parted, and Sparks headed into the kitchen to rifle through the cabinets. She tossed a box of crackers onto the counter and found a pitcher of sweet tea in the fridge.

"House is clear," Rufus said as he entered the kitchen. "Looks like some shit went down in the back, but nothing's moving. How's it look in here?"

"How does crackers and tea sound?" she asked.

He shrugged. "Little too British for my liking, but hell, not gonna complain at this point."

"Don't worry, it's sweet iced tea," she assured him, and laughed. "Although the mental image of you with a teacup is amusing."

He wagged a finger at her. "Hey now, I can raise my pinky just as good as anybody."

"Hopefully we live long enough for me to see that," she replied.

"Speaking of which," he said, "any idea how you want to go about slaughtering this town?"

She scratched the back of her head as she picked up a sleeve of crackers. "Yeah, that's a bit of a pickle there. We have a few dozen people holed up in a fortified position, and I'm not sure we even have fifty bullets between us."

"Plus, based on the firepower that took out the bus, they ain't fucking around," Rufus added as he poured the tea into two glasses.

"Hey, when you cleared the house, did you see any weapons?" she asked.

He nodded as he lifted his glass. "Gun cabinet in the back bedroom. Looked like there were a few hunting rifles in there. Don't know how much ammo."

"Well, let's go check that out," she said as she clinked her glass against his.

They took a deep draught, and then Rufus wiped his whiskers with the back of his wrist. "You got an idea?"

"I always have an idea," she replied. "The question is whether it's a good one or not."

They each took a handful of crackers and headed back to the bedroom. The walls were covered in blood, but there were no corpses.

Sparks ignored the untold horror and crossed to the gun cabinet. "Well, that's a good sign," she said, noting the three hunting rifles with scopes.

Rufus opened the bottom door, revealing a few boxes of ammo. "And that's an even better sign."

"How good are you with one of these?" she asked, popping a cracker in her mouth.

"Hunting rifle?" He straightened his shoulders. "Pretty damn good, girl. After the war I'd go hunting several times a year with my dad. Nothing fancy, just deer and the occasional hog. Something about sitting in that deer blind just waiting for a shot was so damn calming."

She nodded. "Yeah, I've heard where it's therapeutic for some war vets. I was in the academy with a few guys who were in Iraq. They said just being up there helped them cope with their memories."

"Don't know about them boys, but for me just being camped out with a gun in my hand knowin' that there wasn't some chickenshit sniper aimin' at my forehead did the trick," he replied and shook his head.

Sparks sighed and brushed the cracker crumbs from her hands before pulling a rifle from the cabinet. "Well, guess we're both chickenshits because we're about to snipe the fuck outta these boys."

"Well, it's different now," Rufus said.

She furrowed her brow. "How so?"

"We're the ones doin' the snipin'." He pointed to his chest and then grinned. "Plus, look at us, we're fuckin' awesome."

Sparks chuckled. "That we are, old timer," she said, "that we are."

"So girl," Rufus said after finishing off his own crackers, "not tryin' to rain on your parade there, but just being snipers sounds like half a plan. Pretty sure after the first shot rings out, they gonna be divin' for cover."

"Well." She turned to face him completely. "You know how you said you wanted to blow shit up?"

His eyes lit up like a kid at Christmas.

"I'll take that as a *yeah*," she said with a laugh.

"Oh *hell* yeah, girl," he confirmed, gaze blazing. "Whatcha want?"

She shrugged. "That hillbilly dynamite seemed to do the trick last time."

"Well, not sure I'm gonna be able to find fertilizer," he admitted. "But don't despair my dear, I'm pretty sure I can find the stuff to make a redneck rattler."

Sparks cocked her head. "Think it'll be strong enough to take out a door, and something big, like a car?"

"Goddamn girl, you know how to party." Rufus' smile showed all his teeth. "Whatcha thinkin'?"

"These assholes turned a hospital full of people into zombies," she said, fire in her eyes. "I feel like those poor souls would like a word with them."

He nodded. "Give me twenty minutes, and we can go arrange a meet and greet they'll never forget."

Rufus wedged a long metal PVC pipe into the door handle of the hospital front doors. Sparks watched him from the second floor about six houses down through the scope of one of the rifles. He ran back to her, and she relaxed a little when he reached the front door.

"Grab me a drink on your way up?" she called down from her window.

He saluted up at her. "Yes, dear."

She chuckled and took stock of the hospital through her scope. Not a single window was empty. The building seemed jam packed full of zombies.

"Hope you like room temperature light beer," Rufus said as he entered the room.

Sparks shrugged. "Something something, beggars choosers…"

"My thoughts exactly." He chuckled and took a seat at the window next to her. He lifted his rifle to take a look at the hospital himself. "So, we had any action?"

"Whole lot of nothing," she replied. "How's the timer looking?"

He checked his watch. "Four, maybe five minutes on the decoy," he said. "Ten minutes on the party favor."

"So, while we have this calm," she rolled the words around in her mouth as she turned to him. "You mind if I ask you something?"

He smiled. "Hon, you can ask me whatever you want."

"Why did you want to come along on this suicide run with me?" she asked. "I mean, please don't take this the wrong way, I'm eternally grateful you're here with me. But just curious why you didn't hesitate."

"Well, when a pretty girl asks you to murder enough people to fill a dump truck, it's just plain ungentlemanly to decline," he drawled, and she couldn't help but crack a smile. He sighed. "I'll be honest girl, ever since I saw you use a cowbell to gash open Billy Ray Dudek's forehead to win the championship belt, I knew you were a special woman."

She winked. "Special is certainly one word for it."

"I'm serious," he insisted, "you are a special lady. You know, when this world went to shit I was ready to call it a day. Locked away in my shop, feet propped up and enough whiskey to drown a kindergarten class. I was good to go.

"But when you dropped in and invited me along, it gave me a reason to keep on goin'. When we were driving up to Comfort, I made the decision that no matter what you asked me to do, I was gonna be right by your side for it. The last thirty years or so may have been quiet, but by god I'm gonna go out with a bang."

She blinked and turned to gaze at him fully. "Well, for what it's worth, after the last few days I'm going to tell you something I've never told another human being, male or female." She raised her chin. "I want you to officially be my tag team partner."

"God damn girl." His voice cracked. "You gonna make an old man shed a tear."

As if on cue, a large explosion racked the block. It was the first of his rattlers wedged into a gas tank, causing a small sedan to go up in flames.

"Looks like the gods want us to cut out the sentimental stuff and get back to killing," Sparks said.

Rufus' eyes sparkled. "While we're killin', we need to be thinkin' up tag team names."

"I think that can be arranged," she replied with a grin, and they returned to their scopes.

Less than a minute went by before a truck pulled up to the hospital and six armed men jumped out to investigate the flaming car.

"How long until the party starts?" Sparks asked.

Rufus looked away from his scope to glance at his watch. "Four minutes."

"Let's give it another minute to see if our honey attracts any more flies," she said, and they watched the men form a defensive position around the truck. One of them walked up to the fiery car and pulled out a walkie talkie.

"Douchebag by the car looks like he's in charge," Rufus said quietly.

"Keep your sights on him," Sparks instructed. "If he moves back towards the truck, you drop him."

"Ten-four," he replied.

Two more trucks pulled up, and five heavily armed men jumped out of each.

"Well, would you look at that," Rufus said, excitement in his voice, "this is gonna be a big-ass party."

She nodded. "Time check?"

"Two forty-five," he replied.

The leader wandered back to the center of the trucks, pulling some of the men into a huddle.

"Looks like they're getting their marching orders," she murmured.

Her companion held up his wrist. "Two-thirty on the clock," he said.

"Shit, that's a goddamned eternity." She sighed. "Okay, as soon as they break the huddle, I want you to take out the leader. Hopefully that will keep them

405

pinned down there until the other guests arrive."

"I can just wing 'em if you want," he offered. "Tie up a couple of them boys as they drag him to safety."

"Good call," she agreed. "And once the firefight begins, focus on their trucks. We need to make sure they don't have a getaway vehicle."

The huddle let out a *whoop*, as if to signify the beginning of a hunt.

Rufus took careful aim at the leader, just off his center mass to it wouldn't be a kill shot. "Here we go." He gently pulled the trigger and a deafening crack echoed through the neighborhood. The bullet tore through the leader's left shoulder, spraying blood and bullet fragments into the men behind him. The shattered debris dropped two more men to the ground, moaning in pain.

The sudden attack send the remaining men into a panic. A few of them squeezed off a few panic rounds, shooting wild and not knowing where they were aiming for. The rest of the men grabbed their fallen comrades and dragged them behind the trucks.

"That got them riled up," Sparks said.

Rufus checked his watch. "Just gotta keep 'em agitated for ninety seconds."

"Hit the trucks," she instructed. They took aim at the tires of the trio of vehicles, popping off round after round to flatten the tires. The sustained fire gave away their position, and the small army of men began to pepper the house with bullets.

Glass shattered and drywall exploded as Sparks and Rufus hit the ground. They crawled away from the windows and into the hallway.

"Time?" Sparks asked.

Rufus flung up his wrist in the drywall dust. "Thirty seconds!"

"Let's get downstairs," she replied. "When that door blows, we're gonna have to move."

They jumped to their feet and thundered down the stairs, and Sparks took a few steps towards the back door before she realized Rufus wasn't behind her.

"Where the hell are you going?" she cried.

He held up a hand to wave her after him as he headed for the front door. "Gotta make sure these motherfuckers stay put." He shot out the bay window in the front and they fired a few rounds into the trucks.

Before their enemies could return fire, the hospital doors blew open and zombies poured out of the opening like a waterfall. The men immediately turned and opened fire, but were quickly overtaken by the horde. One of them managed to get into a truck and start it up.

Rufus took aim, but Sparks pushed his arm down. "Don't worry about him," she said. "Not worth giving our position away to the zombies."

He turned to her. "If he gets away he could warn the others."

"Let him." She shrugged. "It doesn't matter if they know we're out here or not. It's not going to change what we're going to do to them."

He slung his rifle over his shoulder, and they watched as the man drove away on rims, zombies clinging to the side of the truck.

"You know, now that I think about it," Rufus said, crossing his arms, "letting that boy go to warn his buddies about us might play to our advantage."

Sparks raised an eyebrow. "How so?"

"Well, how would you react if someone who just shit himself in terror ran up to you yellin about how he just saw a dozen of his friends get shredded by some ghosts?" He grinned.

She chuckled. "And if those militia boys are there too, sharing what we did to them…"

"Goddamn girl you are so right," he replied.

She nodded. "We are a lethal pair."

"It's a damn shame we're gonna murder all of 'em." He shook his head as they walked towards the back door. "Would be kinda nice to go down as legends in the history books."

"Well, we may just have to leave one of them alive, then," she suggested. "What kind of tag team partner would I be if I didn't let our legend spread?"

He clapped her on the back. "That's my girl."

"Come on, let's get out of here before those ghouls finish with their buffet," Sparks said, and pushed open the back door.

CHAPTER TWELVE

"Hey Mary," Jeff turned to glance at the copse of trees behind them. "You doin' okay over there?" He shifted his weight and rested his hand on the large uniform belt buckle.

"Yeah," she replied as she peeked out from the bushes. "Just wish this guy would hurry up. The sooner we get up the road, the better I'll feel."

"Don't worry baby," Ricky assured her as he adjusted his uniform cap. "We're gonna get this food and be on our way. We'll be cozying up together while Rufus burns the hell out of some canned meat before you know it."

A horn bleated loudly in the distance.

"Nice of them to give us a heads up." Jeff tensed.

Mary nodded. "Don't worry boys, I got your back," she said, and ducked back into the trees.

"Bubba, this is one terrible idea," Ricky said, voice lowered so that his wife couldn't hear him. "You know that, right?"

His companion scowled. "Well, if you had a better one, you should have spoken up earlier."

"I mean I didn't," the younger man protested, "but damn, wasn't aware this being a bad idea was contingent on me coming up with a better option."

"You just be ready to draw as soon as they start getting out of the car," Jeff said as the truck came into view. There was a cruiser escorting it, and Ricky nodded, taking a deep nervous breath.

The bald man in disguise stepped forward and waved his hands. The single cruiser crept to a stop, the truck halting right behind it.

"Hey, guys," Jeff yelled. "We got some trouble in town here. Can… can you step out so I can fill you in?" He didn't see any movement inside the car, and he turned to glance back at Ricky.

A shot rang out, shattering the windshield of the enemy car. Ricky tumbled backwards, and Jeff dove behind the closest cruiser.

"Mary!" her husband screamed, gripping his wounded shoulder as he rolled behind the other car. She emerged from the woods with a scream, emptying the entire clip of her assault rifle into the passenger side window of the enemy cruiser. What was left of the enemy officers slumped forward, car horn blaring.

She stood motionless, staring at the lives she'd just taken. Tears streamed down her face as she trembled, but the sound of the transport truck shifting into gear knocked her back into reality. She reloaded, dropping the empty mag on the ground and slapping a new one in. She darted to the passenger side of the truck and hopped up to the door, tapping the glass with her gun.

"Shut it down!" she yelled.

The middle-aged trucker quickly raised his hands as he hit the brakes.

"Slowly, and I mean *slowly*," Mary said as she aimed the gun at him, "put it into park and shut the engine off." As the driver complied, he kept one arm raised, and she tilted her head to hell to the guys. "Jeff, cover his exit!"

The skinhead popped out from behind his cruiser and ran over, gun drawn. "Got you covered!"

"Slowly get out and walk to my partner," Mary instructed.

He nodded and opened the door, dropping down to the asphalt. As soon as he was in Jeff's custody, she leapt from the truck and skidded around the car barricade to her husband.

"Baby, you okay?" she demanded, gasping at the sight of him laying on his back in a pool of blood.

"Goddamn motherfuckers shot me!" Ricky cried, holding his shoulder tightly.

"Answer me!" she screamed.

He startled, looking up at her. "Yeah, babe, I'm okay," he assured her. "It's gonna hurt like a motherfucker, but I'll live."

Mary dropped her gun and burst into tears, burying her face into his good shoulder. He wrapped her up with that arm and kissed her temple.

"It's gonna be okay, baby," he whispered in her ear, letting her sob against him.

"Please, please don't kill me," the trucker whined as Jeff walked him over.

The skinhead looked down at the couple, surveying Ricky's wound. "What do y'all wanna do about-"

"Please, I'm not with them, I don't-"

Jeff cocked the hammer on his revolver, silencing the trucker. "As I was saying. What do y'all wanna do about him?"

"We've already killed these assholes," Ricky grunted. "What's one more?"

Mary shoved away from her husband, causing him to hiss in pain.

"No!" She stood and faced the trucker, nose to nose. "Are you with them?" she demanded, and he violently shook his head. "Are you going to follow us?"

"No," he croaked, hands high in the air.

"Jeff, get the keys to that cruiser," she demanded.

The skinhead sighed. "But-"

"Just fucking do it!" she shrieked, and he tossed her the keys. She held them up and pointed the metal at the trucker's trembling chest. "You listen, and you listen good, mister trucker. There's been enough killing for today, hell, for a lifetime. I'm gonna give you the benefit of the doubt here.

"Now, you're going to help my man here into the truck, and then you are going to wait patiently while we head out. When we get a little ways up the road I'm gonna stop and drop these keys to the ground. After you watch us vanish on the horizon, you can come get them and gain your freedom.

"Only rule I have?" She held up a finger. "Don't follow us. Can you handle that?"

"Yes ma'am!" he stammered. "Yes, ma'am! Thank you so much ma'am!"

"Alright, alright, that's enough," she snapped. "Now go help my man."

"You sure about this, Mary?" Jeff asked as the trucker rushed over to lift Ricky.

"I'm done killing, Jeff," she said, screwing a fist into her tired eye. "I… I just can't do this anymore."

"It's okay, we got the food," he assured her. "You did good. We'd be dead if it wasn't for you."

"I know, and I appreciate the sentiment," she replied. "But I don't want to talk about it, okay? Let's just hurry up and get up the road."

CHAPTER THIRTEEN

"Looks like they're hold up in the two furthest buildings, which means it's gonna be a bitch and a half to get to 'em," Rufus murmured as he peered through the scope of his rifle to survey the airport.

"Yeah, that kind of eliminates the frontal assault plan," Sparks said with a sigh and moved back behind the building they were using for cover.

"Don't discount that idea too much," he said and pointed up to a set of speakers on top of the building beside them. "We do have reinforcements we can call. I mean they ain't exactly on our side, but they sure as hell ain't on theirs either."

"Might be able to split them up a bit too," she replied thoughtfully. "How do you feel about taunting?"

He grinned. "Wouldn't be much of a tag team partner if I didn't have mic skills, now would I?"

"I knew I picked you for a reason." She nodded with a grin of her own. "Alright, here's what we're gonna do."

Rufus slowly opened the door to the small building, careful not to make a sound as he drew his knife. The room was dark, with a single light source coming from the far side. He ducked down behind a desk, spotting a lone man sitting at the broadcast console with his feet propped up and a bottle of whiskey in his hand. His low baritone formed around an unrecognizable drinking song as his head lolled back and forth.

Rufus glided across the floor and lashed out in complete silence, grabbing the man's mouth with one hand and driving his knife into his head with the other. The whiskey dropped and Rufus used his foot to soften its landing, holding the man until his twitching ceased.

The interloper picked up the still half-full bottle and set it on the table beside the console. He crossed to the window and drew the curtain, peeking out to the alley below. He opened the window and then headed back over to the console, picking up the mic.

He hit the talk button, sending an echoing shriek through the airport.

"Good afternoon, murderous douchebags," he greeted. "This is your ole pal Rufus here to deliver a public service announcement. Your former friends and neighbors that you relocated to the hospital have been set free. No word on whether or not they have paid your families a visit, but it might be a good idea for you to check on 'em. Oh, and just in case you wanted to reunite with your old friends, I'm gonna let 'em know where you are at." He laughed. "Get fucked, motherfuckers." He dropped the mic and hit the button for the tornado siren.

Rufus grabbed the bottle and hopped out the window as half a dozen armed men burst through the door, guns raised. He shoved a strip of his shirt into the top of the bottle and lit it, chucking the whiskey back into the comm tower. The glass shattered and splashed napalm back on the men, and he tore down the alleyway, screams echoing after him.

Sparks watched the front door from across the street, high on the roof of a two-story building. She peered through her scope as two men stumbled outside, dropping to the asphalt in an attempt to put out the flames. She easily popped off two rounds, catching both men before they were finished rolling around.

A truck revved in the distance, and she scanned the roadways, readying her aim. A dark blue semi sped around the corner, five men piled in the back. Sparks took aim and shot twice into the windshield, shattering it. The truck swerved and smashed into the flaming building, sending bodies flying everywhere. She popped off loud cracking

rounds into any of the men that even so
much as twitched.

Rufus climbed up a ladder and crept
across the roof, careful to stay out of
sight. He peeked across the way to see his
redheaded companion doing the same thing
on a flanking building. She held up her
fist, and he returned the gesture to show
he understood to wait.

He took stock of the building across
from him. There were half a dozen guards
out front, guarding two doors. There was
movement in the second floor window, but
the bars were so close together it would
be impossible to get a shot through them.
The second building had a lone guard
standing by a single door.

Everyone was straight backed and
rubber necked, all on high alert. They
tensed even further as the tornado siren
abruptly stopped, likely having been taken
over by the fire. The silence was almost
deafening, until low moans permeated the
thick air.

A few dozen zombies sprinted down the
main road, making a beeline for the
cluster of guards. They opened fire, but
the undead didn't slow in the least. One
of the guards panicked and threw open the
door to go inside, and Rufus took him
down, dropping his body into a perfect
doorjamb.

The other guards backed up and tried
to get their fallen comrade inside, but
Rufus' fire slowed them down enough that
the zombie horde was able to overtake the
opening. He grinned and gave Sparks a
thumbs-up. She returned it and they
watched from their respective vantage
points as the zombies poured into the
building. There were screams and gunshots
from within.

As the last corpse pushed inside,
Rufus darted back to the ladder and slid
down to the ground, drawing his handgun as
he his the asphalt. He snaked around to
the front of the building, taking stock of
the bodies littering the ground. He moved
cautiously across the street, keeping his
gun trained on the open door. He peeked
in.

Zombies lined the stairs, trying to
reach the survivors on the second floor.
Rufus kicked the door jamb body inside and
slammed it shut, latching it. At Sparks'
whistle, he looked up at her, and she
signaled for him to cover her. He moved
towards the secondary building, holding up
a hand. He stood at the corner, keeping an
eye on the windows across from her as she
moved to her own ladder.

One of the windows shattered and a
rifle barrel appeared.

Without hesitation, Rufus leapt into the street and unloaded the entire clip of his handgun into the window. The gun slumped and dangled before jerking back inside. He reloaded and kept his gun aimed at that window until Sparks stepped up next to him.

"Did you get him?" she asked.

"Well I got somebody," he replied, "but there's at least one other person in there. No way that asshole was gonna be able to pull that gun back in on his own."

"What do you say, tag team partner?" She grinned. "Wanna go introduce ourselves to them?"

He nodded with a mischievous glint in his eyes. "Oh yeah, let's finish it!"

They jogged over to the door and took positions on either side. He reached over and turned the knob, flinging the door open but ducking back out to cover. A few shots rang out, but they just hit the swinging door.

Rufus peeked inside. There was a single man on the stairs struggling with his gun. "He's reloading, go!" He jumped in and fired twice, causing the man to duck down. Sparks darted in to the left, flanking the enemy as Rufus drew his attention to the right.

The man finally reloaded and started shooting at the metal shelving that the older man dove behind. Sparks knelt in the opposite corner and took aim, taking out a significant chunk of their opponent's torso with her hunting rifle.

"Rufus, you good?" she barked.

He jumped out from behind the shelving. "Yeah, that motherfucker couldn't shoot for shit!" He brushed himself off as they converged at the base of the stairs, handguns at the ready.

Sparks led the way up the stairs, gently nosing open the dark office doors open as they moved along the hallway. All the rooms were clear, until she heard a shuffle behind the door at the end.

She held up three fingers and counted down. At zero, she and Rufus burst into the room, ready to shoot. They froze at the sight of a young man cowering in the corner with his hands in the air. He was covered in blood, seemingly the blood of his friend slumped beneath the window.

Rufus kicked the kid's rifle away and gave him a pat down. "He's clean," he said to Sparks, and then stepped back. "You keep your hands where we can see 'em."

"Yes, yes sir," the kid stammered.

The older man crossed his arms. "What's your name?"

"It's…" His voice cracked into a sob. "It's Brandon."

Rufus nodded. "So, Brandon, where's the Sheriff?"

"He's next door," the kid replied.

The older man cocked his gun. "You wouldn't be lyin' to us, now would ya?"

"No, no!" Brandon cried. "He's in the building next door! I swear!" He pointed to the walkie-talkie on the table. "He-he just called a minute ago asking for help…"

Rufus glanced at the table. "Did he, now?"

The radio crackled.

"Goddammit!" the Sheriff yelled through the receiver. "Is anybody there? We need assistance!"

Sparks grabbed the radio. "Do you have family here in town?" she asked as she walked to the trembling kid.

"Y-yes," Brandon stammered.

"Respond," she instructed, and handed him the walkie-talkie. "Ask him what his situation is. And just keep in mind that if you alert him to our presence, your family will be our next visit."

He took a deep breath and nodded jerkily. "This is Brandon." He cleared his throat. "What's your situation."

"Thank fucking Christ," the Sheriff replied. "We need help, where are you?"

"You can tell him you're next door," Sparks said.

The kid nodded. "I'm right next door to you, sir."

"Have the intruders been eliminated?" came the reply, and Sparks nodded.

"Yes sir," Brandon confirmed. "I was able to take them down. But they got the others."

"Good job man," the Sheriff replied with a sigh. "I don't think I know you too well but after that I'm going to promote the hell out of you, son. Now I'm gonna need some help before I can do that, though. You think you're up to it?"

Brandon took a deep breath. "Yes sir, what can I do?"

"Well, look son," the Sheriff began, "there's a few of us trapped in the command office. There's about thirty of those things outside the door, and we can't get through the bars on the window to get out. Now, there's some trucks outside the hangar that have some tools in them. You think you can get over there and grab some crowbars or something out of the back?"

"Yeah, I can do that, sir," the kid said. "Give me just a few minutes and I'll be right over."

"That's my boy, Brandon!" At the Sheriff's triumph, Sparks grabbed the radio and tossed it to Rufus.

"You did good, kid," she said, and aimed her gun at him. "Now Brandon, this is normally when I would put a bullet in you before being on my way, but I'm not going to do that."

He immediately relaxed, tears streaming down his cheeks. "Oh thank you, thank you!"

"Quiet." Rufus put a finger to his lips. "The lady ain't done talkin' yet."

"Now, just so there's no misunderstanding," Sparks continued, "I'm not sparing you out of mercy, or because you have a family, or any of that nonsense. I'm sparing you because I need you to deliver a message. Sooner or later, Sheriff Hutch from Junction is going to make his way down here, and it's going to be your job to convince him to cut his losses and not pursue us. Do you think you can do that?"

"Yes, yes, I will tell him that!" Brandon nodded furiously.

"You're going to need to do more than simply *tell* him," she emphasized. "You are going to have to *convince* him to stand down. Because if anybody from this town or Junction come within ten miles of us, my friend and I will come back to finish what we've started. And there will be no mercy next time, no survivors to tell the tale, no more warnings. We will wipe this town and every one of its inhabitants off the face of the earth. Have I made myself clear?"

Brandon nodded so hard he looked like a bobblehead doll. "Yes ma'am, I will convince him to stand down and you'll never see any of us again."

Sparks holstered her weapon. "Good boy, Brandon. Good boy. Now, you're going to sit here and count to a thousand before leaving this room. Think you can handle that?"

He continued his frenzied nodding, and the duo turned to leave.

"More whiskey?" Rufus asked as he picked up a bottle from the table. "Man, you guys know how to party, huh?"

"Junction sent us a liquor store truck a couple days ago, so there's been plenty to go around," Brandon piped up.

The older man grinned. "Well, if that's the case, you won't mind if I take a couple bottles, huh?"

"The truck is parked outside the hangar with the utility trucks," the kid replied. "Please, help yourself."

"I believe we will," Rufus said. "You can start counting now."

Sparks led the way out of the building as Rufus stuffed a tattered rag into the mouth of the whiskey bottle.

"The hangar is this way, my dear," he said and motioned to the left.

She nodded. "Well, let's go get us a truck and get up on outta here."

"Get up on outta here?" Rufus laughed. "Am I starting to rub off on you, girl?"

She failed to stifle a smile. "Yeah, just a bit I suppose."

"Brandon," the Sheriff's voice crackled over the radio. "How's it coming there, bud? We aren't gonna be able to hold this door forever."

"Oh yeah, nearly forgot," Rufus said, and held out the molotov. "Would you care to do the honors?"

She took the bottle and bowed her head. "It would be my pleasure." She pulled her lighter and set the cloth ablaze, then chucked it up through the window of the zombie-infested building.

"Brandon!" the Sheriff cried. "What the fuck is going on? Is that smoke?"

Rufus wiggled the walkie-talkie. "Looks like we have our very own radio show to listen to on our drive," he said.

Sparks grinned. "Sounds like it's going to be interesting.

CHAPTER FOURTEEN

Ricky's snores gave soundtrack to Mary and Jeff watching the sunset, sitting on the back gate of the transport truck.

"You doing okay?" the skinhead asked, happy to be back in his own clothes as he nursed a lukewarm beer he'd found.

She sighed. "I told you, I don't want to talk about it."

"I get it, but if you need it, I have an ear for you," he assured her.

"Appreciated." She continued to stare up at the stars. "You think Sparks and Rufus are gonna make it?"

Jeff took a long draught of his beer. "I've ran in gangs and been in prison, and I've never met a harder, tougher, son of a bitch in my life. And with Rufus backing her up, they are gonna be just fine." He emptied his bottle and then tossed it in the ditch before hopping down to the asphalt. "Well, they're warm as shit, but at least they're beer. Can I grab you one?"

"I don't know if I'm in the mood for one," she replied.

"Trust me, after the day you've had, you need a beer," he said and pointed at her. "I'll be right back."

"Thanks, Jeff," she said quietly, and took a deep breath. She caught a glimpse of headlights down the road and grabbed her gun. "We have company!"

He darted back around the truck, weapon drawn, and the two of them raised their guns as the vehicle approached. The headlights flashed twice, and the pickup slowed to a stop about ten feet away.

Rufus hopped out of the passenger's side. "What's with the standoff shit? Y'all expectin' somebody else?"

Mary smiled and ran up to give Sparks a hug as the redhead jumped down from the driver's side.

"Where's Ricky?" the police officer asked, eyes wide.

"He's in the cab," Jeff replied as he patted Rufus on the back. "He took a round to the shoulder, but he'll be alright."

"Yeah, we found some meds in the truck so I got him bandaged up pretty good," Mary added. "Our biggest concern is going to be listening to him bitch about it for the next few weeks while it heals."

"How did y'all fare?" Jeff asked. "We have to worry about any retaliation?"

Rufus shook his head. "At the moment we outnumber them, so I think we should be good."

"Goddamn, y'all don't fuck around, do you?" The skinhead blinked at the duo.

"Well, she made me her tag team partner," the older man declared. "So I felt obligated to live up to the mantle."

Mary raised an eyebrow. "Tag team partner?"

"Man, that's awesome!" Jeff cried. "Y'all come up with a name yet?"

Sparks winked. "Leaving that one up to Rufus."

"You know, I've thought about it, and I think Generational Kill has a nice cold-blooded ring to it." He grinned and puffed his chest out.

She smiled and punched his arm playfully. "Generational Kill it is, then."

"So, with that out of the way," Jeff cut in. "Only other question left to answer is, where the hell do we go from here?"

"Should be another exit a few miles up," Sparks replied. "We can pull off there and drive down the back roads to see if we can find a place. Almost no population out in these parts, but with some luck we'll find a spot to call our own. Bound to be someone who wanted to live off the grid."

Jeff nodded. "Mary, you want to lead or follow?"

"Sparks, I think I speak for everyone when I say: you lead and we shall follow," Mary said, raising her hands.

The redhead nodded. "Alright then," she said. "Saddle up, and let's go find us a home."

EPILOGUE

Day Zero, 9:13 PM, EST

General Adams sat in his office at the Pentagon and rubbed his eyes. He'd been staring at his computer screen for far too long. He straightened as somebody knocked on the door.

"Enter," he said.

An officer poked his head in. "Sir, there is a John Teeter here to see you."

"Show him in," Adams replied with a wave of his hand.

A short and slight man with graying hair wandered inside and took a seat. "Adams, good to see you again," he greeted, voice soft.

"You too, John," the Joint Chiefs head replied. "How's civilian life?"

"Loving every last second of it." John smiled. "Amazing what I can get accomplished when I don't have twelve layers of bullshit bureaucracy weighing me down."

Adams sighed. "I'll cut to the chase," he said. "I could use your help."

"Did you miss the part about me enjoying life without bureaucracy?" his old friend countered.

"There's a situation in Austin," the General continued. "Eight hours ago, we got word that a bio-terrorist potentially launched an attack. In the hours since, we've lost pretty much all contact with the city, and the little bit of info we do have doesn't paint a pretty picture."

John leaned forward. "Tell me what you know."

"Around eleven AM local time, our teams raided the compound," Adams explained. "Thirty minutes later, the hostile zone protocol was activated. Shortly after that, we lost contact with the team."

"Boots on the ground?" John raised his eyebrows. "Eye in the sky? Surely you know *something*?"

"Local outlets were describing a riot that originated on the UT campus, but shortly after that they went dark too," Adams replied with a shake of his head. "We did a flyover, and it looks like something is going down in the city, but we don't know what yet."

There was a sudden commotion in the hallway, complete with lots of shouting.

"I need to speak with General Adams *immediately*!" a woman shrieked, voice muffled, and the General stood up.

"What the hell?" he muttered and crossed the office to open the door. The door guards restrained a young woman with wild eyes.

She stopped struggling upon seeing Adams. "Sir, please, I have info-"

"I told you that the General is busy," one of the guards grunted.

"What's going on?" Adams boomed, and even with his salt-and-pepper hair, he still pulled rank, and everyone stood at attention.

"I'm sorry sir, the Private attempted to get into your office," the other guard said quickly.

"Because I have vital information!" She growled.

The guard scoffed. "File it with your C.O.-"

"It's okay," Adams said. "Private, what do you have?"

"I think I know what's going on in Austin, sir," she replied.

He clenched his jaw. "John, walk with us." He waved for his companion to follow her as well, and she led them to a small communications room. She sat down at her post and plugged in a set of headphones.

"We've been searching for any trace of credible information we can on Austin, but so far we've only found scraps," she said. "At first, we thought they were only hoax videos since it looked like zombies were attacking."

"Zombies?" John blurted. "Seriously?"

"Yeah, we said the same thing, too," she replied. "It was mostly college kids posting them, so we didn't think anything of it. Until I got this." She plugged in a second pair of headphones and handed each of the men a set. "This came in on the hostile zone protocol a few minutes ago. We picked it up from a college radio station in San Marcos, which is just south of Austin. It's long, but here's the key part."

"Three days ago there was a bio-terrorism attack in Austin that sickened a lot of people," a female voice drawled through the earpieces, "and has turned them into the zombies that you have no doubt encountered. We don't know a lot about the virus, but I will share what I know. It is airborne, and it targets everyone with an A-Blood type."

Adams tore off the headphones and pointed to one of the other communication staffers. "You, get on the line to the Secret Service, tell them it's a code red. The rest of you, pack up your things right now, we're headed to the Presidential Bunker."

"It's a good call, Adams," John agreed. "An airborne virus is nothing to fuck with, even without the zombie side effects."

The General nodded. "Don't suppose I could convince you to take an impromptu contractor position?"

"We can negotiate my rate later," his friend replied, "just know that I'm not going to put up with any bureaucratic nonsense."

Adams clenched his jaw. "If this thing is as serious as it appears, I'm counting on you to cut through it."

"Alright, I'm in," John agreed.

"Good." The General clapped his old friend on the shoulder. "I can use your help, since as of right now, it looks like we might be at war."

END

Sparks and the gang will return, but the story expands in the new spinoff, Dead America. The series will explore the nationwide response to the zombie outbreak. From the Presidential War Room to the front lines in major cities, and all points in between.

Get info on new releases at www.DeadAmericaBooks.com